ORIEL'S DIARY

for

Naomi & Grace

ORIEL'S DIARY

An Archangel's Account of the Life of Jesus

Robert Harrison

ORIEL'S DIARY
Published by Scripture Union, 207–209 Queensway, Bletchley, MK2 2EB, England.

Scripture Union: We are an international Christian charity working with churches in more than 130 countries providing resources to bring the good news about Jesus Christ to children, young people and families – and to encourage them to develop spiritually through the Bible and prayer. As well as our network of volunteers, staff and associates who run holidays, church-based events and school Christian groups, we produce a wide range of publications and support those who use our resources through training programmes.

Email: info@scriptureunion.org.uk
Internet: www.scriptureunion.org.uk

First published 2002
ISBN 1 85999 684 1

British Library Cataloguing-in-Publication Data: a catalogue record for this book is available from the British Library.

Cover design and photography by David Lund Design, Milton Keynes; with grateful thanks to Donald Kidlin of Rugby for assistance with photoshoot.

Internal design and typesetting by Servis Filmsetting Ltd of Manchester.

Printed and bound in Great Britain by Creative Print and Design (Wales) Ebbw Vale.

Foreword from the author

Oriel's Diary is my own dramatised re-telling of the story of Jesus, based firmly on the Gospel of Luke. It tells Jesus' story from the perspective of an archangel and is a fictionalised presentation of events that actually took place in the Middle East, two thousand years ago.

Oriel's Diary is a story to be read. It is not an historical reconstruction, though I have tried hard to be historically accurate. It is not a theological allegory, though I have endeavoured to express the theological traditions of Christian faith. It is certainly not a thesis on the nature of angels. It is a story to be read and enjoyed just as a meal is to be eaten and savoured.

The question that I have asked myself on turning to each new episode in Luke's account is: what was really going on here? Armed with years of study and my imagination, I have coloured in the brief sketches of Luke's Gospel. I sincerely hope that *Oriel's Diary* conveys some wholesome truth about the most influential life in human history.

My portrait of angeldom is inspired by the numerous accounts of angels that are found in Jewish and Christian scriptures. The angelic figure of Oriel appears in the Jewish 'Book of Esdras'. But these brief insights leave plenty of space for imagination. I have avoided the poetic imagery of flowing white robes and glowing halos, and presented angels as hardworking spirits who serve their God loyally without always understanding what he is up to. For example, there is nothing which states that angels thoroughly dislike water, but the idea was stimulated by a curious observation in Revelation 21 that in God's perfect new creation, 'there was no longer any sea'.

Spiritual realities can never be fully expressed in human terms and it has been necessary to make do with a limited perspective on those parts of Jesus' story that are beyond human experience. Death is one such inexpressible reality. I have built my picture of 'Death' around numerous stories and metaphors that are found in the books of the Bible, but this image is inevitably incomplete.

I am enormously grateful to Dr Martin Davie at Church House,

Westminster, and to Lin Ball and John Grayston at Scripture Union, for helping me to chart a straight path through the jungle of conflicting opinions that surrounds the story of Jesus. I am even more grateful to my wife, Katharine, for all her love and support. Finally, my greatest thanks go to God for conceiving the fabulous story that I have retold.

Robert Harrison

A place beyond time

For an Archangel to sin is a deep and complicated business. To be tempted towards sin, however, is a great deal simpler. As I sit in my office, considering my situation, I feel sorely tempted to plunge into an ocean of jealousy and self-pity.

Earlier, I and the three other remaining Archangels – Lucifer having set himself up in opposition – were called for a confidential meeting with . . . . There is no word in human language that could begin to express our term for the one we ceaselessly serve. It will have to suffice to say, 'my Boss'. He gathered us in his office to unveil the crucial phase of his plan to rescue the physical Universe and revive that tarnished jewel in his crown, the human race. The details are strictly confidential and I cannot record them now, but once again Archangel Gabriel gets the best job while the rest of us are left with our usual scraps.

I did point out that all Archangels are quite capable of making themselves visible to the shadowy creatures of planet Earth. I also suggested that if the rest of us had more opportunities we would be as good at it as Gabriel. But to no avail. Gabriel gets the glory, Michael was asked to continue our fight against the Opposition. Even Raphael will get to put in an appearance on the cloudy planet. But, 'Oriel, none of the others can oversee the logistical side of things with the same thoroughness as you.'

I learned long ago that my Boss never flatters people. He was pointing his laser-like gaze at the weakness that most concerns him – in this case my tendency to marinate in self-pity.

All Angels, Michael included, are ordered to have a 'thorough rest', then we shall get started.

Why in all Heaven does he want to help the flabby little wretches anyway? I didn't ask him this to his face; one doesn't. The humans have been nothing but trouble since shortly after they emerged. It seems crazy that such a dangerous plan should be undertaken for the benefit of something as fleeting as *homo sapiens*, while the leader of the Opposition is still very much at large in the Universe, trying to wreck everything we do. All will, I have no doubt, become clear.

I can't help feeling that my Boss loves the human race more than he loves us, yet we are made of the same solid, spiritual stuff as he is. 'Oriel,' I can imagine him saying, 'Can you be loved more than completely?'

24th March 4 BC (Earth Time)

I have just sent Gabriel off on his second visit to Earth since this campaign began. (The first was to an elderly priest in the Temple at Jerusalem). I expended considerable effort trying to calm him down before he left. At his last appearance he rendered the man speechless with fear. Today's visit is to a mere teenager and Gabriel is so excited I am concerned that he will terrify the poor girl.

'Oh, Oriel,' he said, dismissively, 'Humans are much more robust when they're young.'

We did agree that our Boss was unlikely to choose a girl who would be scared witless at the sight of an Angel but I still urged him to be careful.

'These humans are fragile,' I reminded him, 'You only have to appear a fraction too strongly and their faint bodies simply burn up.'

'Oriel, why do you think the Boss gave this responsibility to me?'

The truth of his reply stung me like medicine on an open wound.

'You get on with the administration,' he suggested, 'And leave the humans to me.'

Gabriel realised how sharply his words had struck their target and paused.

'I know that you are better with humans than the rest of us,' I conceded, 'But they barely know that there is more than one Archangel. And here I am, arranging rotas for millions of other Angels whose hard work will never be acknowledged, let alone remembered.'

Gabriel spotted this – my notebook – and said, 'Are you going to write the whole thing up? What an excellent idea! You had better check it out with Michael though, in case you breach his security measures.'

To be honest, the idea of an official record had not crossed my mind. From my vantage point outside of time, it is difficult to place events in what humans would understand as 'historical order' but it is possible.

'I could do,' I replied.

'You should do.'

'I will call Michael.'

Gabriel smiled, 'I'll be off. I have a lady to frighten.'

I swallowed his bait. 'Gabriel!' I yelled.

He was gone. He should be delivering the Boss's message while I am writing this. I must consult Archangel Michael about my diary.

Later

I have spoken with Michael and our Boss and they have both encouraged me to keep a diary of the operation, on the condition that I only record what has actually happened on Earth and do not reveal our plan before it is fulfilled. I shall have to keep a careful watch on the monotonous flow of Earthly time. Never mind. If this is to be an 'official' diary, and may be read by others, then I will have to be very careful.

I must confess to feeling more than a little nervous about today's business. I know that my Boss has been searching through a great span of Earth Time for a suitable woman and the right set of circumstances, but if Gabriel's mission fails will we have to scrap the entire operation? You can be sure that our Boss will not 'just manage' on something as important as this. He will insist that we return to the beginning and start all over again.

It terrifies me to think that the future of the human race and their vacuous Universe currently rests in Gabriel's experienced, but nonetheless excited, hands.

The next day (Earth Time)

He did frighten her. I knew he would. Poor Mary fairly jumped out of her skin. Human eyes never know what to make of something as real as an Angel.

Anyway, she said 'Yes'.

Alleluia, alleluia, hooray, alleluia! I am enormously relieved.

You may wish to know that Gabriel and I have just performed a most exuberant dance around my office in celebration. We have permission to proceed!

It is an amazing thing that the greatest plan that our Boss has ever formed should so totally depend on the good will of a tiny creature an experienced Angel has to concentrate on very hard even to notice.

I must go. I have a meeting with my Boss.

Later on

I had expected that things would begin slowly, but our Boss has ordered all Angels confined to quarters immediately and until further notice. He insists on going down to Earth to handle the moment of conception himself and on his own.

Apart from the headache, for me, of assembling the entire Heavenly Host at short notice, Michael was concerned that too many parts of our work will be left undefended against the Opposition. Our Boss pointed out that the Opposition would be far too interested in his visit to Nazareth to get up to any mischief elsewhere.

With Gabriel's help, I have gathered the entire company of Angels in our headquarters. It's a strange moment. Heaven is stuffed full of Angels but the Lord of all Heaven is not here. He has gone, as a human fisherman might say, 'hook, line and sinker' – Father, Son and that mysterious part of our Boss's person we encounter only rarely and call the Director. The place feels as good as empty.

I must get on with organising the various duties that will be required as soon as my Boss has completed phase one.

Another day passed

It has happened. My Boss, in the person of his Son (that bit is complicated, I won't begin to explain) has become the minuscule speck of life that is a human embryo. Fresh in my mind, I can remember when we worked together on the moment when the

Universe exploded into being. Together we channelled its narrow stream of time and gave form to its fragile substance. And now, the One who held every atom in his grasp is no more than a clutch of watery cells in the midst of a teenage girl, in an obscure village, in a defeated nation, on one of the smaller planets that orbit an ordinary star, in an uneventful galaxy that turns on its little axis in that gassy cloud that is the Universe, which the Son himself made.

Such smallness I can barely begin to imagine. This is Love.

Next

I have been watching the Son's human development. The bundle of watery cells is beginning to look rather like a blind fish. How can he continue to sustain the existence of all his many creations?

Raphael called into my office on his way to choir practice. He took one look at me and asked, rather accusingly, 'What is it now, Oriel?'

'Do you know what a human foetus looks like?' I responded.

'No.'

'How can the Son still keep together all he has made while being . . . .'

Raphael interrupted. 'Oriel, have you noticed any change in the state of any of our Boss's creations?'

'No.'

He left.

Four weeks later

Trouble.

You may remember me noting that if Mary said 'No' our entire scheme would have to be scrapped. Well *she* hasn't said 'No' – *Joseph* has.

It is a feature of human selfishness that although you always know it is there, you can never be quite sure what form it will take. Joseph is a lovely, godly human, as humans go; a man of faith and principle. But with the news of Mary's unexpected pregnancy, his love for his bride has been overwhelmed by a need to protect his own reputation.

'But no Angel has come to speak to *me* about it,' is, I suppose, a reasonable objection for Joseph to make. We had assumed that he, in his considerable love for Mary and faith in our Boss, would accept his fiancée's word. He didn't. He has taken the news very badly and is planning to break off the engagement.

I raced to my Boss's office in full panic to find out what I should do. He was as calm as snow on a windless day.

'Oriel,' he asked, 'Do you trust me?'

I was trying very hard to. 'But we need Joseph to marry Mary,' I reminded him.

'I know.'

The gentle flakes of my Boss's confidence began to cool my burning anxiety.

'So what should I do?' I asked like a whining child.

My Boss smiled a reassuring smile. 'Sort him out.'

Gabriel is off to have a chat with Joseph. Little does the carpenter realise that meeting his demand will involve him being scared witless by my colleague.

Next instalment

There is something you will need to understand about meetings between humans and Angels. Only some Angels can assume the extreme thinness that makes them visible on Earth. Similarly, some humans cannot see or hear our Heavenly form even when it is suitably thinned.

You can probably work it out for yourself. Gabriel did his Archangel best to speak to Joseph but the man was completely unaware that he was there. Gabriel claims that he used every trick in his repertoire. He is not a happy Angel. After some moping and whinging, however, he suggested that we try a dream specialist. Some humans can be reached more easily when their conscious minds are switched off. Gabriel has gone to find Jophael who is well known for his work with Joseph, son of Jacob, and Belteshazzar (commonly known as Daniel).

Next Earth day

The dream worked! I have no idea how Jophael does it but he appeared in Joseph's dream just as he was waking this Earth morning and told him not to worry about the baby, which is our Boss's, and to marry Mary as planned. As an extra touch, he told Joseph the given name for the child. Mary had not got round to mentioning this before Joseph walked out of her house and slammed the door in her face.

Joseph has abandoned his plans for a quiet divorce and we are back on schedule. Thankfully, the Rabbi in Nazareth is one of those solid men who would never betray a confidence even when amply drunk.

I can feel a deep sigh of relief spreading out through my being. I was anxious that Mary should agree to her part in my Boss's plan but I never really doubted that she would say 'yes'. Now I realise how foolish that confidence was. This whole scheme could collapse at any moment. There are no guarantees of success. Everything is a potential danger. Even the dark warmth of Mary's uterus could become the theatre for an eternal tragedy. I must review my plans and add extra layers of protection at every turn of this road.

Three weeks later by human reckoning

In Earth terms, I have been working without a break for months but in a different stream of time. After the Joseph near-disaster I stepped up the levels of security and back-up by several degrees. Nonetheless, my Boss insists that we must not interfere, even in the slightest way, with the natural course of events around his Son. Any intervention must have his personal approval. Accepting that condition, I have deployed a squad of Angels to maintain a constant watch on Mary, Joseph and their surroundings. Every detail of their lives is relayed back to me via a watch of four Angels working in the next office. I am pleased to be able to report that this system has now settled in, and I no longer have to keep a permanent vigil myself.

Human foetal development is, I understand, something of a mystery even to humans, so I shall spare you the details of our excitement at moments like the Son's first flexing of his earthly muscles and the first rays of light to be received by his formative eye. Needless to say, Mary is sharing our repeated delight as she feels the child grow and move inside her. Equally needless to mention is Joseph's detached bewilderment at the entire process.

The one notable event since I last wrote was the hostile reaction of the good people of Nazareth to the rumour of Mary's pregnancy. They are an honest-living, God-fearing community and they could not understand why Joseph would not go through with the formal marriage procedure, now that his betrothed is pregnant. After much chattering behind closed doors – especially the doors of the synagogue – poor Joseph let slip, in a moment of exasperation, that Mary's child was not his own. Gossip rapidly turned to scandal and the scandal swept through the village like a tornado.

My team were fabulous and within an Earth hour we had formed a public relations strategy and presented it to our Boss for his approval. He refused to use it, saying – I thought rather vaguely – that he was sure Joseph would be able to deal with the situation on his own.

At first light the following day, Mary was packed off to the Judean hill-country to stay with her elderly uncle Zechariah, who was the silent victim of Gabriel's first message. Zechariah and his wife Elizabeth are expecting their first child after many years of frustration and disappointment; he, too, has a part to play in this plan. Mary is already on her way, accompanied by an unseen entourage of trusted Angels. We have conducted a thorough 'sweep' of the small guest house outside Jericho where we expect her to spend the night. She should make it up the long hill to Judea sometime tomorrow afternoon.

Next day

What a marvellous occasion! After weeks of struggling against human doubt and prejudice, something has finally gone utterly right. When Elizabeth saw Mary trudging wearily towards her house, she quickly understood the young woman's situation. The wonderful, heavily pregnant, elderly lady scrambled down from her rooftop garden as fast as her swollen ankles would carry her and threw her arms around the sick and frightened teenager on her doorstep.

Elizabeth's words of greeting to the girl brought a relieved cheer from the Angels crowded into our Operations Room. 'What an honour for me,' she said, 'that the mother of my Lord should come to stay in my house.' Little Mary dissolved into gasping tears as she sank into the ample embrace of her ageing aunt. The stresses of her hurried departure and long journey poured out in uncontrollable crying.

In that moment I caught a brief glimpse of what it is that makes my Boss care for these humans so deeply. That tender blend of love and grief touches a depth that all the celestial goodness of Angelkind could never experience. This, somehow, is what our mission is all about. With pure joy we watched the two pregnant women walk, arm in arm, into the modest courtyard, the elder saying to the younger, 'When I heard you call out to me as you arrived, my baby did the most enormous kick.' And after a few moments of rich silence, she added, 'He recognised him, you know. Isn't that wonderful!'

Two days later

Mary is now settled in and I have some ease to reflect on all this. It is an ideal solution to our problem and I have to concede that my Boss's faith in Joseph was well placed – this time. Mary can help her aunt do the daily chores without the continual pointing and whispering that accompanied her every action in Nazareth. In this tiny hillside community nobody knows who Mary is and no one has any reason to be concerned about her expectant state. Indeed, there is so much amazement here over Elizabeth's late pregnancy that my Boss could do just about anything and not an eyelid would flutter.

Most importantly, Mary and her child are as safe here as a human can be. That leaves me with the opportunity to forge ahead with some plans for the trickier times that lie ahead.

Mid October 4 BC

I have not written for some while because I have been preparing for events that lie in the Earth's future and to record them would risk the security of my Boss's plan. Down on the blue and white sphere of Earth, life has been fairly calm as far as our interests are concerned. Mary stayed with Elizabeth until shortly before the elderly mother's first child was due to be born and is now making her way back north at a gentle pace. I have put Archangel Raphael in charge of looking after Elizabeth and her unborn son, John. That leaves me free to concentrate on the main campaign.

For us a key item of Earth news has been announced today by Emperor Augustus. He wants a thorough survey of all Roman territories. In order to divide any groups of trouble-makers, the wily politician has demanded that every man must register for the census in the town of his birth. We have known about this all along, but the Opposition are limited to terrestrial time and were quite possibly ignorant of this detail. Hence my 'radio silence' of recent months.

It is now only two circuits of the moon around Earth before the Son will be born, in Bethlehem. (This fact was foreseen hundreds of Earth years ago by the prophet Micah who, to be honest, did not fully understand what he was talking about; Gabriel quietly slipped him the lines and Micah obediently included them.) Joseph was born in Bethlehem and so will have to register there for the census. Mary will have to go too, because she is legally betrothed to Joseph. The timing has been carefully planned so that the Son will be born a few days after their arrival in King David's picturesque home town.

And now it is time for me to execute what I think is the cleverest part in this section of our great plan.

Next day

This morning, less than twenty-four Earth hours after the Emperor signed his census edict in Rome, an apparently ordinary human checked into a quiet hotel on the edge of Bethlehem. Under the disguise of a Greek historian researching the descendants of King David, he is, of course, an Angel.

I came across Sephrim at a party that my Boss held to celebrate what humans rather quaintly call The Big Bang. (In truth, he has pulled off a good many greater bangs but this particular little pop remains one of his favourites.) Sephrim was doing a hilarious impersonation of Adam blaming his wife, Eve, for his own weakness.

At the time of the party I was particularly concerned about the crowds that we are expecting in Bethlehem around the time of our big event. It is vital that the notoriously dangerous process of human birth takes place in the safest environment possible. I needed to guarantee that Mary and Joseph could find suitable accommodation when they arrive in the town. While the Heavenly Host quivered with laughter at Sephrim's act, I had an idea. When the party ended, I called Sephrim to my office and commissioned him to put his human impersonations to more serious use.

For the next two months Sephrim will occupy himself by gathering useful intelligence for me. The primary purpose of his stay you will discover in due course. I am experiencing a considerable joy in this creative solution to a particularly tricky problem.

A few weeks on

Sephrim has been an inspiration. Not only is he supplying me with some fascinating detail of the paternal strengths and weaknesses within Joseph's family, he has also talked the innkeeper's wife into studying midwifery.

Meanwhile, in Nazareth, news of the forthcoming Roman census has been greeted with predictable paranoia and grumpiness. Joseph is panicking, but Mary has remained remarkably calm – I do like this young girl.

Four days later (It takes me ages to calculate these wretched Earth days.)

Oh dear! I'm in trouble with our Boss over part of my plan and have to make a number of changes to it. I need to ensure that the Son, now nearly eight months developed in his mother's uterus, is fit and ready for the long journey south. After all, it is important for numerous reasons that he is born in Bethlehem and not half way down the Jordan Valley as a result of the poor child constantly bumping up and down on Joseph's donkey. (I am pleased to say that we did manage to arrange a new donkey for him; his old one was *very* old.)

There is very little useful information available on the subject of foetal moods, even if you look across a good few centuries. Failing in my research, I called up Phermian, an Angelic expert in human children. I asked him to speak to the *unborn* Son (a spiritual conversation, not a human one) and find out how he felt about the prospect of a couple of weeks on the back on a donkey.

My Boss summoned me to his office as soon as he saw what we were doing. He claims that it is unnecessary interference, that it is not normal for a human foetus to engage in spiritual dialogue with a Heavenly being. I pointed out, in my defence, that spirituality comes 'naturally' to human children and is only later starved out of them by their adult relations. But my Boss insisted that we were overstepping the boundary of normal experience – against his directions for this particular project.

'My Son must grow up as a totally normal human being and I will not allow any compromises in the natural processes of his life on earth.'

I said, 'But . . .' and did not get any further. Moses may have argued with his God and won, but that is not within the reach of Angels, even Archangels. I did wonder whether I should raise the matter of Sephrim's mission to secure a safe room in Bethlehem, and ask if that counted as interference. But as he didn't mention it, neither did I.

The trouble is that I have spent goodness knows how much effort putting systems into place to protect the life of my Boss's Son. Now I have to review every single one of them to make sure we do not step over his invisible line. And yet this whole project has to work; and if it is to work the child has to survive at least into adulthood. I know that the Boss is an expert at bringing good out of all manner of disaster but I cannot see that he will be able to do much with a stillbirth in some gloomy back street of Jericho.

Six days later

Joseph may be a worrier but when he is under pressure he is as safe a pair of hands as you could want any son to be held in!

He and Mary set off today; their fit young donkey piled high with provisions. He has even allowed for two rest days, in Tiberias and Jericho. For a while the noble carpenter was considering the short route through Samaria, which set me panicking. However, even though he could not hear every Angel within a week's radius shouting, *'Don't you dare!'* he dropped the crazy idea.

Mary and Joseph are accompanied by an unseen entourage of five Angels: the usual guardians for mum and step-dad; Phermian, the paediatrician; Hagogue who, believe it or not, helped the Son to design the common donkey and is on hand to keep a close eye on Joseph's beast; and Maphrael. Maphrael is the team leader, a brilliant Angel who insists, unfortunately, on being called Maff. He will act as guardian for Jesus once he is born and he will report directly to me. All five are under strict instructions that they must not intervene in any situation without my permission. Archangel Michael is shadowing their movements with a small detachment of fighting Angels, just in case there is trouble from the Opposition. I am aware of Opposition eyes watching but I suspect that they are biding their time, waiting to see what my Boss is up to.

Next morning

Time for a quick note while Mary and Joseph wash and then eat breakfast. (What a nuisance this eating business must be for you humans!)

Yesterday went smoothly. They made their way down the Galilean Hills towards the lake that gives the hills their name. Mary walked a fair distance on the grassy, downhill sections and they arrived in a tiny village for supper. Today they hope to reach the lakeside town of Tiberias where they will stay and rest, as tomorrow is the Sabbath. Most travellers pass straight through these little fishing communities. The Jews, by and large, do not like the sea and are suspicious of those who make their living on it.

The first rest day

Mary and Joseph are staying in a homely lakeside inn in the centre of Tiberias. This afternoon they took a gentle walk along the shore of the lake. Mary even ventured a short distance into the water to cool her swollen feet, much to the amusement of the group of fishermen who were relaxing near their boats.

When the couple had returned to their room, Maff nipped up to see me in my office. He informed me that Mary is anxious that her labour might begin while they are miles from the nearest village. She is not the only one.

A week later

All is well. It is rest day number two and the travellers have left the cool shade of the Jordan Valley for the long ascent up into the Judean mountains. Mary has hardly left her room all day. The heat has affected her badly. Her feet are now very swollen, her back aches and her heart pounds like a bass drum every time she walks more than a few paces. This is bad news because the rest of the journey is an unrelenting climb.

Poor Joseph cannot do anything right. He is in trouble for making Mary spend an extra day in 'this waiting room for Hades'. He got into trouble for suggesting that they go for a short walk to stop their limbs from stiffening. He was curtly informed that he 'appears to care more for that wretched donkey than for his promised wife'. And Mary has just stated categorically, 'There is absolutely no way that I can even begin tomorrow's climb up into those mountains.'

'I am sure that we could make our excuses to the census people,' the harassed husband replied. 'But didn't we both agree that it is almost certainly God's will that your baby be born in Bethlehem?'

'Well, if God wants us there, God can very well get us there himself,' was Mary's strained reply.

If only our Boss would let us do a simple translocation, we could solve the whole thing perfectly safely and with no more distress. I have asked Mary and Joseph's guardians to ensure that they get a good night's sleep and to try to plant some encouraging dreams in their heads.

I am not hopeful that Mary will be fit to travel tomorrow and I have just received word from Sephrim that all the accommodation in Bethlehem is now full. The local residents have taken to sleeping under the stars so they can let out their homes for huge sums of money. There is no shortage of money, it seems, amongst King David's descendants – with the notable exception of Mary and Joseph.

Dawn next day

No joy. Mary's feet are now so swollen that she can barely walk and there is no realistic possibility of their going anywhere today.

Maff has an idea. If Joseph spends his money on the services of a doctor, we can arrange for Sephrim to give him some more when they get to Bethlehem. This is pushing at the boundary of non-interference, so I shall have to consult my Boss. To do that we will need to discuss about the whole Sephrim plan which I am afraid he may not like.

In the meantime I have Maff, Phermian and Hagogue scouring Jericho for an honest doctor who knows his trade.

Back from my Boss

We have permission to go ahead with the plan and Sephrim has plenty of money left. My Boss reaffirmed that it is important for his Son to be born in David's town. He even agreed to 'a little indirect assistance'.

Hagogue and Phermian have both found doctors that they consider to be suitable but neither Angel trusts the other's judgement. Maff suggested that we direct both physicians towards Mary and use whichever one gets there first. However, I decided that we should focus our efforts on Phermian's chosen medic. Hagogue is sinking into a sulk. (I would have gone with his choice if we had been searching for a vet, but I sensed that now was not the time to say so.) Our next task is to get Joseph to find the right doctor. Pre-arranging for two human beings to meet one another is an imprecise science.

That night

Mary is asleep. Joseph is praying (which is good for us because it will make him more sensitive to our help). The doctor cost Joseph every Roman coin he possessed. Maff had to send the morose Hagogue out into the street to find a generous passer-by to fund the prescribed herbal remedy. By our Boss's grace he quickly spotted someone who was praying – it makes humans more easily visible to Angel eyes – and they were happy to help the pregnant mother. Hagogue is now a little happier.

Phermian reports that the potion is doing the job required and Mary may be fit to travel on in the morning. We have lost a valuable day.

Next morning

Mary has had a large bowl of herbal brew and our party set off as soon as there was enough light to travel by. Now for the most dangerous part of the journey. The road from Jericho to Jerusalem is long, steep and notoriously dangerous. It has to be completed in one day.

Mid afternoon

If physical creatures could hear the voices of Angels, the inhabitants of the Universe might have been deafened by the wail of dismay that just echoed round Heaven. The donkey has gone lame!

Up to this moment, Joseph has patiently absorbed the mounting tension of his situation but a few moments ago he snapped. He yelled, swore and kicked the faltering animal – understandable but unwise. Before Hagogue could intervene, Maff and Phermian were desperately half carrying, half pushing the witless beast up the mountainside. I had to bawl for order to allow our shy animal expert to take control.

Apparently the problem is quite simple – a sharp stone caught in the soft flesh of the donkey's hoof. Joseph should be able to deal with the situation if only we can get some sense into his panic-stricken head.

After some debate it was agreed that the surest access to the carpenter's mind came when he was asleep. But he is unlikely to sleep while he is marching up and down the mountain track, angrily throwing rocks. Eventually we got to him through Mary, who said, 'Sit down Joseph and breathe deeply for a while. When you have calmed down we will talk it through together'. If he does drop off to sleep, Hagogue will instruct him, several times, how to remove the stone. With all that prayer last night, he should get the message; and that same prayer last night has left him tired enough to sleep.

Next instalment

Joseph woke from twenty minutes sleep looking brighter than he has looked for days. Mary said calmly, 'Alright, let's work through the options we have. Whatever happens, we know that God is with us.'

Joseph replied, 'Yes, we'll do that in a moment, but first I want to have a look at his hooves, just in case he has trodden on a sharp stone.'

They are already on their way again. They will not make it to Bethlehem tonight, but at least they should reach one of the Jewish villages around Jerusalem before sunset. Maff has gone ahead to arrange some accommodation for the night. It should not be too hard to find someone willing to take in a young girl who is on the verge of delivering her first baby – I hope.

That night

By sunset we had guided them to a sympathetic young family with three children and a large house, but we have discovered another snag. Tomorrow is a Jewish holy day and therefore a day of rest. The family are more than happy to entertain their guests for an extra night, and to oversee the birth if need be, but we will lose another day. Joseph is too good a man even to consider travelling on a religious festival. Mary, like us, is aware that her baby is very close to being born and that she is not yet in the right place.

I and the team must talk.

The following afternoon

Mary, Joseph and the donkey are all looking much better for a rest and some relaxed family worship. They have been royally spoilt by the motherly Mrs Matthewson. The two women have been seated in the garden discussing the gruesome details of childbirth. Joseph is having a foretaste of family life sharing an energetic and playfully violent game with Mrs Matthewson's two boys. According to Phermian, the rest has caused Mary's early contractions to slow down. This is good news for our chances of getting to Bethlehem in time.

I instructed all the Angels to rest too (our Boss's demand for his creatures to have regular rest periods applies to us as well). They took the morning off. As Mary and Joseph were finishing their lunch, another problem emerged.

Mrs Matthewson is insisting that Mary is in no state to travel any further and that she must stay and have her baby where she is while Joseph goes to Bethlehem alone. Unfortunately, Mrs Matthewson is not a lady one can easily say 'no' to and is convinced that it is her duty to force Mary to stay. Poor old Joseph is as far out of his depth as he was with his own mother when three years old. He cannot explain the real reason why they must move on and he will not tell even the smallest untruth. Mrs Matthewson has concluded that he is an idiot.

Shortly after sunset

Twice during the afternoon Joseph carried all their luggage down to the stable and started to load it on his donkey, only for Mrs M to carry it back to their room, telling Joseph, 'You are a stupid and useless man. You do not deserve such a beautiful wife.' Whenever Mary tried to intervene Mrs M would say, 'You sit down, my dear, and let me handle this.'

24

Shortly before the sun sank behind the mountains we had a lucky break; the youngest Matthewson fell and received a nasty cut to his right knee (nothing to do with us, I assure you). While Mrs M was dealing with blood, dirt and tear-filled eyes, Joseph threw their bags on the donkey and our two travellers slipped quietly back onto the Jerusalem road. They left a polite note of thanks for the bewildered and furious Mrs Matthewson.

The holiday is over, Mary and Joseph are on the move again and Joseph is determined to reach Bethlehem tonight, no matter how long it takes.

And he will need to. Phermian has just informed me that the motion of the donkey has sent Mary into labour for real and that the Son will be born tonight. This sent us into a force ten panic. I need someone to go ahead to check out Bethlehem and tell Sephrim to pack his bags, but who? Phermian must stay with the baby, I dare not take Hagogue away from the donkey and I need Maff's quick thinking in case anything else goes wrong. I have decided to go myself. The Angels in the Operations Room will manage without me. Here goes!

An hour before midnight

Sephrim and I are sitting in his room, waiting for our little entourage to arrive. Since I left my office I have not had any direct contact with Maff and his team. I am told that they are still on their way and that the baby has not yet started his final descent into the thin airs of planet Earth. The Sephrim plan is beautifully simple. He has occupied his room for weeks. When Mary and Joseph arrive at the hotel, he will leave and they can go straight into the vacant room.

Now that I am completely immersed in the narrow stream of Earth Time, I can do nothing but wait.

I must say, Sephrim's human disguise is superb. I passed over his room twice before realising that he was indeed the Angel I was looking for. We have talked over the plan so many times that Sephrim refused to do so again and snapped, 'Why don't you do something else like scribble in that old notebook of yours.' Clearly he has been affected by the rudeness of his terrestrial surroundings; we will probably have to put him in some sort of quarantine when he goes back to base. Anyway, here I am, scribbling in my diary while Sephrim anxiously watches the North Road into this sleeping town.

The wait gives me a moment to reflect on what is going to happen tonight, right here in the comfortable little room which Sephrim carefully chose. Here, the Creator of everything that is, was, or ever will be, is going to squeeze his way out of a very tight place and become just one of goodness-knows-how-many tiny creatures that are totally dependant on their tired mothers.

Ah! Sephrim has spotted a man with a donkey walking up the hill in the moonlight.

Early hours of 25th December 4 BC

Probably the best way to fill you in on the latest calamity in our catalogue of disasters is to tell you the story as it happened.

As planned, once we knew the weary traveller was Joseph, I flew down into the courtyard of the *David's Rest Hotel* and waited for him to arrive. Sephrim was to wait in his room until I called him. When Joseph appeared through the gateway he was exhausted and very tense. Mary was in the middle of a contraction and pleaded with him to stop, but he refused firmly. Maff greeted me with great relief and was about to speak when Phermian interjected, 'She's fully dilated, on the brink of stage two and we have absolutely no time to waste.' Hagogue appeared to be in some sort of a trance, watching each footfall of the donkey.

Joseph knocked frantically at the hotel door leaving Mary to slide off the donkey cautiously on her own. Hagogue removed the overworked beast to the box of hay that was propped up against one wall of the courtyard. The sleepy-eyed hotel owner opened the door and quickly asserted that all his rooms were full beyond capacity. While Joseph began to explain their situation, Mary gave a great yell and added, 'Here comes another one, Joseph.' Meanwhile, I gave a spirit-whistle to Sephrim, who appeared, bags in hand, and announced that he had to leave immediately, to be in Jerusalem by sunrise.

Joseph begged the owner for a room of some kind where Mary could deliver her child. Sephrim replied cheerfully, 'How wonderful, not only have you woken me up when I was in danger of oversleeping, but you can have my room all to yourselves. It's quite clean – I'm a bit fussy that way.' (Maff is of the opinion that Sephrim performed his part perfectly – but I think that he could have done it without lying. He will *definitely* be in quarantine when he gets home.)

Whatever the merits of Sephrim's performance, it failed. The owner of the hotel destroyed months of preparation with one sentence, 'It's already paid for by someone else.'

Joseph tried to argue his case but I could tell from the older man's cold spirit that there was no hope. With just one word of command from me, Maff, Hagogue and Phermian, along with the three guardian Angels and Sephrim (who dumped his human clothes and belongings in a drainage ditch), flew off round Bethlehem looking for somewhere suitable for the Son to be born. Maff quickly had an inspired idea and called us together to look at his discovery.

The Bethlehem Central Synagogue is a large, stone-built hall with grand columns in the Greek style. We quickly agreed that it was the ideal place for this great event. Maff suggested that it was quite possibly our Boss's original idea but that we had all been too occupied with the Sephrim plan to listen properly. I left Maff and Sephrim to prepare a suitable bed for the birth while the rest of us raced back to the *David's Rest*.

When we flew into the small courtyard we met the saddest scene of the whole disastrous campaign. Mary was lying, curled up into a tight ball, against the whitewashed wall of the hotel. She was covered in blood. Joseph was seated next to her, blank-faced, methodically tearing one of his tunics into strips of cloth; and the donkey was tied up in the farthest corner of the yard because the baby was lying, sucking his little fist, in the animals' hay box.

For a long time we stopped, watching in dumb silence. After months of careful planning for the most important event in the history of the Universe, this is all we have achieved. I shudder to think what my Boss will say.

Next morning

My gloomy meditations were interrupted by the sound of singing. Without warning, Archangel Raphael and his Angelic choir descended on the tatty yard in full song. Joseph, although still awake, was oblivious to the invasion. Mary stirred in her sleep and before I had a chance to glance in the direction of the hay box, Phermian leapt up and screamed as loud as he was able, 'Shut, the Heaven, up!' Then, when the music had stopped, he added more calmly, 'The baby is asleep.' At this, the baby in question promptly woke up and began to cry, which woke Mary. Joseph stopped his cloth-tearing to deal with the situation.

Raphael looked towards me awkwardly and mouthed, 'We've got to sing. Our Boss booked the choir himself.'

I replied rather crossly, 'Well, not here. We've quite enough to cope with as it is.'

Sephrim intervened. 'There'll be some night-watchmen out on the hillside with the sheep. Why don't you go and sing to them?'

I had completely forgotten that Sephrim was still with us and asked him to lead the choir to a more appreciative audience.

Peace again.

Briefly.

Raphael, whose joy at tonight's birth was untempered by its squalid circumstances, was so bubbling with enthusiasm for the occasion that he coerced his bewildered audience into paying us a visit. And, dutifully, they came – a shamble of shepherds. Four ill-kempt hairy heads peeped around the gateway of the inn yard just as the sky was brightening with pre-dawn light.

By and large, human beings cannot see Angels unless we make a considerable effort to become visible. One of the shepherds, however, looked straight at me and said, 'Ah, you again! Where's this baby then?'

I was so startled to be mistaken for the oh-so-smooth Raphael that I did not manage to reply before a younger specimen of the same species exclaimed, 'There it is, you dumb goat, wrapped in strips of cloth and laying in a manger, just like the fairy told us!'

On another occasion, to be mistaken for one of the frivolous spirits of idle legend would have been exceedingly upsetting, but when you have reached the ocean bed of despair you cannot sink any lower. I scowled at the intruders, but Mary and Joseph were pleased to have visitors and proudly showed off the baby, answering a string of apparently obligatory questions about Jesus' size, weight and home town. To see these rough and filthy herdsmen transformed into gentlemen by the presence of a small baby was a revelation. Perhaps the Son's life on Earth will not be quite as bleak as I had presumed.

In the end, Joseph gently reminded the men that they had sheep to care for and ushered them out into the street. As the scruffy group passed me, the oldest of the shepherds looked directly at me for the second time and asked, 'Are you lot going to come and sing to us again?' He did not wait for a reply but went on his way whistling one of Raphael's tunes.

Somehow the shepherds' visit dispelled the cloud of gloom that had hung over the inn yard all night. Since they left, Mary, Joseph and the baby have all slept. The people of Bethlehem are now waking up, oblivious to the fact that they have just missed the most remarkable event in all of my Boss's many creations.

The baby, I should probably tell you, is called Jesus (the name was chosen by his Father – my Boss, not Joseph) and weighed approximately seven pounds, I'm told.

It is now time for me to return to my office and leave Maff in charge again. I shall have to report to my Boss as soon as I get back.

That evening, as Earth Time would understand it

Once I had Sephrim safely detained as far as possible from the Universe, I spent most of the day with my Boss. I told him, in precise detail, everything that happened last night. He knew it already, of course, but he likes to hear his creatures telling their own stories. All the way through my account he restricted me to a straight telling of the facts as I saw them and it was only when I had reached the very end of the drama that he looked straight at me and asked, 'Well?'

My Boss is often frustratingly economical with words and I knew that this was an invitation to give my opinion.

'I'm sorry,' I began, reciting the short speech that I had carefully prepared for this moment.

'It was an awful mess and that was my fault. I should have used a more orthodox approach.'

I fell silent, hoping that he might say something yet dreading what he might say. He said nothing.

As always happens to me in such silences, I could not bear it for long and spoke again. 'Have I completely fouled up your plan?'

My Boss smiled. Not a frustrated smile, nor an amused one; it was a huge beaming smile of the kind that only he and his Son can give. In the light of that smile the scattered pieces of my story fell effortlessly into place. The struggle, the distress, the humiliation, the awfulness and the sheer panic of the last few days in creation's brief history all took shape in my mind. For a moment I saw the whole episode from my Boss's perspective. The human tragedy that I had just witnessed – that *was* the plan.

For some while my Boss and I cried and laughed, and laughed and cried. Then I left him alone to consider the helpless bundle of atoms and energy that his Son has become.

Galilee, AD 9, a week before Passover (allowing that there never was a year 0)

Some years ago (as your time scale would understand it) my Boss called me into his office to talk about my diary. He was adamant his Son's private life should remain private and insisted that the formative years of Jesus' time on Earth should never be published within the Universe of time and space. I begged him to allow at least one sample of Jesus' childhood to remain. Below is the episode that he chose.

I am often surprised to observe how my Boss has become increasingly like a human father during this process of his Son's growing up. I am quite sure that the unmoved Mover of the Universe has been moved by the experience. I cannot quite define what I mean, but nothing here in Heaven is quite as it was. This thought has hung, unexpressed in my mind for a long time but now the mist of uncertainty is clearing. The Son set off towards Jerusalem this morning for his bar mitzvah. He will complete his thirteenth Earth year during the winter and is about to become a man. My Boss is on the edge of his seat with excitement and – dare I say it – paternal anxiety.

Today's travelling has gone smoothly. Jesus and his friends raced ahead of their families on the downhill section of this morning's trek. There is something in the carefree antics of teenage boys that reflects the excitement of Angelic life; although

Angels do not tend to kick one another's backsides with mindless regularity. The young men are all soundly asleep now, while their parents lie heavily on makeshift beds, worrying over the innumerable details of human life.

Next day

Breakfast was the usual travellers' fare of stale bread. The boys all complained, 'It makes your jaws ache.' During their youthful protest, Mary cast an anxious glance towards Jesus. He kept quiet, mostly, although he did agree with them about the discomfort of eating the stuff. It fascinates me how he manages to blend in with his fellows without falling in with their petty selfishness.

During the day there was more running, kicking and shouting. After a midday break, the parents teamed up to protest at the lack of load-carrying by their sons. 'If you are going to become adults, you must share the work of the adults.'

'We didn't ask to be a year older,' one of them replied.

Jesus chipped in, 'If a Roman soldier can make us carry his pack for one mile, I reckon we should do at least two if our aged parents ask us; don't you think?' Jesus' suggestion carried the day and the lads carried the packs. Before long they had transformed the chore into some sort of competition and the competition kept them entertained for the rest of the day's journey. Relieved parents, exhausted boys – everyone is happy.

Day four of the journey – a Sabbath

A day of rest by the River Jordan; a day for adults to relax in the shade of the Jordan Valley's abundant vegetation and for the boys to get thoroughly wet, playing in the river. Jesus and his friends were discovered by a rabbi from Tiberias, trying to catch fish with a sharpened stick. The five of them were marched, in disgrace, to their families and subjected to a lecture on Sabbath law. After this they were each taken aside for a parental inquisition.

To an accompaniment of nearby slaps and yelps, Mary and Jesus sat quietly against the trunk of a large tree.

Mary was the first to speak. 'Well?'

'Fishing is not my work, so how can I be working on the Sabbath if I try to catch a fish? Anyway, if the rabbi's work is upholding the Law of Moses, then he is the one who has been breaking the Sabbath, not me.'

Mary was thoughtful. 'That is an interesting interpretation, but for now you must stick to the interpretations of your elders.'

'Even when they are wrong?'

'When you are a rabbi,' Mary replied, 'you can expound your own views. Until then, you must respect those of our community. I insist.'

'God gave us the Sabbath to free us from our work, not to enslave us in boredom.'

'I insist.'

It was typical of Jesus that he conceded, not with a sulk, but with a broad smile. 'Yes, Mum.'

The only other significant event of the day was the shared worship service between groups from various different Galilean villages. Jesus sat with his mother at the back for the last time. Next Sabbath he will be with the men.

Four days later – Bar Mitzvah Day

Mary and Joseph arranged a shared bar mitzvah for Jesus and his cousin, John, so they are staying at the home of Zechariah and Elizabeth in the hillside village outside Jerusalem. I am afraid to confess that I find these human rites of passage rather tedious. Mary cried, Joseph stood proudly with a lump in his throat, and Jesus sailed through the whole rigmarole.

My boredom must be an Angelic weakness. After an Earth hour of watching the procedure from the Operations Room, I decided to call in on my Boss, who has been increasingly 'human' about the whole matter over the last few days. I found a note fixed to his door:

ANGELS, PLEASE DO NOT DISTURB ME
THERE IS NOTHING IN HEAVEN OR ON EARTH
THAT CANNOT WAIT FOR THE MOMENT
TRUST ME

Next morning

I visited my Boss again to ask if there are any changes to be made in our work now that Jesus is technically a man. This time the door was open but there was no one inside. A second notice was placed over the first:

> *OFFICE TEMPORARILY MOVED*
> *TO THE TEMPLE AT JERUSALEM*
> *CONTACT ME THERE*

My Boss has not been completely present in the Jewish Temple since the year that King Uzziah died and that was only a passing visit. I quickly worked out what was happening. The Son will enter the inner courts of the Temple today for the first time in his human life. The Temple, according to Jewish tradition, is my Boss's house. Clearly, he wants to be there to welcome his Son home. Bearing in mind that today is the day of preparation for the Passover, this is an event not to be missed.

A quick glance into the Operations Room showed me that the Son is still crunching his way through his unleavened breakfast. I am nipping down to join my Boss.

Later

Passover in the Temple at Jerusalem is a bloody affair, but not without reason. Jews from across the world stream in through the gates to purchase a young lamb. The men of the family then drag the poor creature through to the inner court where it is slaughtered by priestly butchers. The blood is drained onto the floor, the innards are removed and the men then carry the carcass back to the place where they are staying, for it to be roasted for the evening meal.

I found my Boss waiting, like an anxious mother, inside the gateway that leads to the inner court. I took my position opposite him on the other side of a long queue of tired men and terrified sheep. I took one look at the scene before me and roared with laughter.

My Boss looked at me and asked. 'What's so funny?'

'Here are thousands of human beings,' I replied, 'who have all come with the express purpose of worshipping you. And here you are, in person for the first time in hundreds of their years. But every single one of them is walking straight past you without even a momentary glance in your direction. I think that's funny.'

My Boss smiled. 'Don't you just love them?'

Before I could answer, Maff appeared, having heard my laugh from the neighbouring Court of Women.

'What are you doing down here?' he asked, stopping right in front of me. Somehow he had failed to notice his Boss's presence in the building. I looked past him and nodded to indicate who was standing at the other side of the queue. Angels of Maff's rank do not often find themselves in the total presence of their Boss and he was shocked into embarrassed silence.

Our Boss noted his discomfort. 'What do you think of my house, Maff?'

I chose Maff for this job because of his creativity, not because of his tact. His reply was as quick as it was direct. 'It's a mess.'

'That's a good answer,' our Boss responded with a smile. 'You will be glad to hear that it won't be here for much longer. How is my Son?'

'Very indignant at the profit margins in the sheep market,' Maff replied.

'Good.'

'I had better go back to him,' Maff said. 'Just before Oriel boomed with laughter, Jesus was considering some radical alterations to the tables of the money changers.'

Some time later, Joseph and Jesus emerged through the great gateway of the Temple. The young Jesus looked straight towards his Dad and ran to his embrace. Joseph, thinking that Jesus' excitement was in response to the beauty of the building, called after him, 'You can have a look around, but make sure you come back before I get to the front of the queue.'

Father and Son disappeared into a quiet corner. I stayed and chatted to Maff while Joseph and his sheep moved slowly towards the front of the line. Joseph was content to be on his own in the middle of the Passover rush. The sheep seemed blissfully ignorant of its impending fate.

Jesus and my Boss returned just as Joseph reached the line of blood-sodden priests. The two of them stood very solemnly as Joseph's lamb was efficiently slain. Then, as Joseph hoisted the bloody carcass onto his shoulder, my Boss bid farewell to Jesus, saying, 'Now go and enjoy the feast. I am going to stay here in the Temple, so come back and see me whenever you have a chance.'

Jesus departed through the Temple gates and turned to give his Dad a huge smile as he did. My Boss smiled back, but behind his smile I could sense a mountain of sadness.

Late the next day

My Boss came here to be with his Son. Jesus, however has not been in the Temple all day. I rose up into the air and cast an eye around Jerusalem for Maff; where Maff is, Jesus will be also. After searching the Mount of Olives, the historic sites of King David and various other popular tourist attractions, I finally spotted Maff, Joseph and Jesus in a carpenter's workshop down one of the dark back streets of the city.

Maff greeted me with a sigh, 'We are visiting all the famous carpenters in Jerusalem,' he said.

'Our Boss is waiting for his Son in the Temple,' I informed him. (I must confess that I have still not got used to calling Jesus by his human name.)

Maff explained. 'Now that Jesus has become a man, he must work for his living and it is assumed that, being the eldest son, he will join Joseph's business. So Joseph is following up all his most valuable contacts and introducing Jesus to the latest techniques and tools of the trade.' He paused and then added, 'I am utterly bored. It's good to see you.'

'When is Jesus scheduled to visit the Temple again?' I enquired.

'Joseph is faithful man and devoted to his God,' Maff began, 'but he is not a great lover of organised religion. His schedule of trade visits is planned to last until Monday night, and they all leave for Galilee the next morning. To quote Joseph's words, "Prayer is vital to a good man, and so is work. Pray while you work and work while you pray."'

'Can't you persuade Mary to persuade Joseph to take Jesus into the Temple for the evening service?' I asked.

Maff thought for a moment. 'I'll try.'

'I'll see you then.' As I set off back to the Temple, Maff called after me.

'Maybe I could persuade Joseph to show Jesus the finer points of the woodwork in the Temple.'

Tuesday morning

It's been a grim few days waiting in the Temple for Jesus to show up. My Boss, as you will appreciate, is not one for changing his mind. Having chosen to spend the Passover week in the Temple of the Jews, that is exactly what he has done. Maff has dropped by briefly each day to give us an update of the woodworkers' tour. Apart from that, our Boss has spent his visit delighting the faithful and being driven to distraction by the attitudes of the religious leaders. Today Jesus walked in, looked around, spotted us camped in the right hand corner of the inner court and ran to join us. Father and Son immediately fell into excited conversation. Maff and I withdrew a little and watched the happy reunion.

After a while I noticed someone was missing. 'Where's Joseph?' I asked.

'I haven't a clue,' Maff answered. 'Jesus ran up into the city as soon as he woke up this morning because he didn't have to visit any more carpenters today. I came with him.'

We interrupted the divine reunion. 'Where are Mary and Joseph?' I enquired.

'Packing for the return journey,' the Son informed me, (It is strange to hear him speaking with the voice of a twelve-year-old human.) 'I imagine they will come and get me when they're ready.'

I suggested that if our Boss was looking after the boy, it would be a good opportunity for Maff and I to take a break. He said that he would call us when Jesus is collected.

It did not take us long to decide that we both needed to escape from the relentless throb of time. After briefing Michael and his troop about what was happening, we left the Universe altogether.

Three Earth days later

It is only when you get a chance to drift timelessly in free space that you realise how the pressures of life in a broken creation gradually build up. Our holiday, however, came to a sudden end. Jesus has gone missing. Joashel, Joseph's Angel guardian screamed up to us, faint with worry, saying that Joseph and Mary had spent the last three days revisiting every workshop in Jerusalem in search for the lad, but without success. They had walked the full day's journey down to Jericho before they noticed he was missing having assumed that he was haring along with the other youths as usual.

Maff broke into the panic-stricken tale. 'He's with his Dad.'

'What do you mean, he's with his Dad?' the distracted Angel replied. 'I've just spent the last seventy-two hours with his dad hunting for the boy under every lathe and workbench in the city.'

Maff and I replied in amused unison. 'His Dad. Your Boss!'

Maff added, 'Not the old man with the grey beard, you dim Cherub.'

I continued, more helpfully. 'They are in the Temple. We'll come with you.'

The three of us headed straight back to Judea. Maff and Joashel went in search of the carpenter; I made my way to Temple Mount. There I found my Boss and the Son, seated together, surrounded by the wiser and less vain members of the ruling council. The old men were questioning Jesus about his interpretations of the Law of Moses and my Boss was helping him with his answers. The lawyers and teachers were shaking their heads in astonishment at the twelve-year-old's replies. Jesus was thoroughly enjoying himself.

Before long, the party was brought to an undignified halt by Joseph bursting into the inner court while Mary stood, agitated, in the gateway.

'What on earth are you doing here?' Joseph demanded. 'Your mother and I have been worried sick.'

The leaders of the Jewish nation melted away in embarrassed silence. The Boss turned to Jesus and said, 'I think it's time for you to go home.'

He wrapped his eternal arms around the young man and they said their goodbyes. Jesus jumped up and ran to Mary with a cheery, 'Hi, Mum.'

'Where have you been, Jesus? We've been looking for you all over the city.'

'Didn't you realise I would have come to see Dad?'

Mary studied her son intently as she soaked in the significance of his words. 'You could have left us a note, or something.'

'I did. Didn't you find it? I put it under my sleeping mat.'

AD 27 (18 years later)

Jesus announced today that he is leaving the family business at the end of the financial year and moving to the small fishing community of Capernaum on the northern shore of the Sea of Galilee.

We have been waiting for this moment for many years. Our real work now begins. For security reasons we have not been able to talk or write about Jesus' future. It is only in the most secret places of Heaven that our Boss's plan has been discussed. But now the flag is up and the Opposition will most certainly have heard the news. I have called an Archangelic Council immediately and before it starts I must speak with my Boss.

Later

This was the first discussion I've had with Michael for many Earth years. Throughout Jesus' human life so far, Michael and his troops have been maintaining a 'spirit exclusion zone' around Nazareth to enable Jesus to grow up without any unusual spiritual interference. Michael arrived at the meeting in a festering grump.

'Capernaum is a ridiculous place for him to live,' he asserted. 'It is very close to the border between the Jewish and non-Jewish territories and, to add to the problem, he has chosen a waterside location which is very hard for us to defend.'

Having raised this exact issue with our Boss earlier, I was equipped to handle Michael's outburst with the same reply I had received. I calmly said, 'That's right.'

Michael was too distracted by worry to pick up the point.

'Why, for everyone's sake, does he not move to Jerusalem? Which is, after all, the obvious place for him to go.'

'He chose Capernaum,' I stated.

'Why?' Michael persisted.

'For all the reasons you just explained.'

Michael is an excellent warrior but he is rarely quick to understand the workings of his Boss's mind. There was a long silence while the Commander of the Angelic Armies struggled to comprehend what was happening.

'Are you telling me,' he said slowly, 'that the Son wants to live in a place where he is utterly open to the attacks of the Opposition at a time when they are concentrating all their resources against him?'

'Yes.'

'So what do I do?'

'Watch carefully and wait for orders,' I explained. 'But, most important of all, make sure that none of your forces interfere without authorisation from either myself or the Boss.'

Michael was quiet. Next it was Gabriel's turn and I suspected that he would not like his instructions either.

'Jesus' arrival is not going to be announced in the usual Angelic fashion,' I explained. 'Our Boss wants to leave everything in the hands of the humans he has chosen. Our role is to watch carefully but keep our hands and mouths to ourselves. Gabriel, the job you usually do will be done by Zechariah's son, John. You already know the family.'

He nodded.

'I want you to lead John out into the Judean desert and help him to proclaim the message outlined here.' I passed him the file our Boss had given me. Gabriel took it with an air of resignation.

'Remember,' I continued, 'As with Michael, you must keep out of sight and let the humans do the work.'

Gabriel pulled a dissatisfied face. He likes to be where people can see him and enjoys his earthly reputation as *the Angel of the Lord*. Several months or years spent unseen in an earthly desert, watching a human attempt at proclaiming our Boss's message, is not an assignment he would have chosen.

'The leader of the Opposition will mash him!'

Michael's sudden outburst surprised us all.

'Jesus is only a mortal man now,' he continued. 'He doesn't stand a chance.'

'He has made us a little lower than the angels.'

Raphael's calm voice added a new dimension to the tense atmosphere in my office. We all looked at him, bewildered by his apparently meaningless contribution to the proceedings.

'It is a line from a Jewish hymn,' Raphael explained. 'It points out that humans and Angels are not as different as we like to suppose.'

I rather wanted to end the meeting at that point, but there was one more item of business.

'Raphael,' I said, 'Your role is to lead the worship of Heaven, as usual. Thank you, friends.'

A few weeks later

Today I'm visiting Gabriel by the River Jordan where John (they call him the Dipper) is based. I was surprised to find my old friend in buoyant mood.

'Look at this,' he exclaimed, showing me to the place where John was busy dunking another candidate in the murky waters of the Jordan. 'I usually pass the Boss's messages to one individual at a time, but this man is telling it to hundreds of them all at once. And every day they keep coming.'

We stood and watched as Jesus' cousin answered questions from the large crowd of humans surrounding him. They were asking how they could respond to our Boss's wishes in the particular situations of their different lives. To each simple, practical question John gave a simple, practical reply. And all the while, Gabriel watched and glowed with delight.

'How are the two of you getting on?' I asked.

'Fine,' said the Great Messenger. 'Every evening, when crowds have gone home, we sit and talk in front of a fire while John brews up his locust and honey soup. The soup smells disgusting but the conversation is excellent.'

I think I will stay the night and join in.

Next morning

The conversation certainly was excellent. John's life of solitude and simplicity has helped him develop a strong spirit. Here in the desert, away from the usual selfish clamour of human life, he could hear every word we said without any fear or misunderstanding. Now I understand why Gabriel is enjoying himself so much.

Last night we talked about the Son. John already has a fair understanding of what is happening. The heart of his message is that someone greater than himself is on the way. I was eager to know if John knew that person was his cousin from Nazareth. It seems that he has a general awareness that Jesus fits into the picture somehow but the two of them have not seen each other for many years. Having both Gabriel and myself there was a great help to him and he quickly learned to recognise our different spiritual voices as they echoed in his thoughts. I am fairly sure that he will be able to recognise Jesus when he chooses to show up. (So far in this operation, we have controlled the timings but now the Son is in charge. For the eternal Son to be in command is a familiar experience for us, but the factor I find difficult to accept is that the affairs of Heaven are now in the hands of a human being.)

While John slept, Gabriel said, 'You're looking troubled, my friend.'

When I explained my concern about the Son being human he suggested that we talk to Raphael. Raphael was busy teaching his choir a new song when we arrived in Heaven. He does not like to be disturbed.

'What do you two want?' he asked.

'Oriel's worrying,' Gabriel said bluntly.

'What's new?'

'Raphael,' I began, 'The Son has become a man so now our Boss's whole plan is in the hands of a human being. Isn't that dangerous?'

'My dear Oriel,' Raphael replied, 'Jesus is the eternal Son, and therefore our Boss's plan is in the very hands that created you. Could it be safer?'

He turned back to his choir. 'We will take it from the seventy-third Alleluia.'

The same evening

Well, there was I, this morning, considering the fact that Jesus is in complete control of the timing of his work and this afternoon, guess who showed up?

John was sitting on a rock by the river's edge talking about my Boss's desire to sort out his creation, when he suddenly stopped. Everyone turned their heads to follow John's gaze, and a murmur of 'What's he looking at?' rippled through the crowd. For Gabriel and me the question was quickly answered. There at the back of John's large congregation stood Jesus. The riddle was solved for the crowd when Jesus walked right up to John. From the silence in the valley it was evident that everyone knew that something significant was happening.

Jesus spoke first. 'I would like to be dipped,' he announced.

The crowd waited quietly. This was not an unusual request. Every week hundreds of Jews have been dunked in the river by John. It was John's reply that revealed something very strange was occurring. He simply said, 'No,' and then added, 'I won't do it.'

Gabriel was fascinated and whispered a commentary to me. 'For months now, he has been dunking anyone who asked him. This is the first time he has refused.'

Jesus and John silently searched one another until each was quite sure who the other was.

'Shouldn't it be *you* who dips *me*?' John asked out loud.

'No.' Jesus was clear and confident. 'It is important that we do this.'

Again they searched each other in silence for a long while before John spoke. 'Alright.'

As the two cousins stepped down into the water, something turned this common sight into a compelling drama. Jesus knelt on the river bed with the greenish liquid reaching up to his chest. There was a pause, then John grasped the younger man by his shoulders, plunged him under the water and held him down.

For reasons that I cannot explain, Angels have a great dislike of water. So to see the Son held firmly underneath the stuff woke a hundred irrational fears in my being. I leapt up and was about to shout, 'Don't kill him, you idiot, he's my Boss's Son,' but Gabriel grabbed me from behind.

At last John raised his precious victim up into the warm air. Jesus refilled his lungs hurriedly. All of a sudden and only for the briefest moment, the spiritual fog that normally surrounds the Earth cleared away and our Boss could be seen, bathed in the light of Heaven, above the Jordan Valley. He had about him that slightly tearful pride that human parents feel when their children pass the milestones of growing up. Jesus immediately looked upwards and his Dad said, 'Well done my Son.' His voice was full of pleasure and parental pain.

As I watched, I saw that most mysterious aspect of my Boss's nature, the Director, gliding down through the atmosphere like a bird to land on the Son's head. The whole episode had only taken a few Earth seconds but for those few seconds, Heaven and Earth had been united.

Gabriel whispered to me, 'Look, they all saw.' He directed my attention to the four hundred or so humans who had been seated on the grass, listening to John preach. They were all looking up to the same place in the sky. They had all, just for a moment, seen something of their God.

Two days later

Having been in the right place at the right time to see my Master and very good friend embrace the task that lies before him, and having seen my Boss affirm that commitment, I slipped quietly back to my office. From the Operations Room (it would now be better named the Observation Room) I watched Jesus walk off into the desert, leaving behind the fuss and chatter of human society. As he went he was accompanied by Maff, as always, and also by Michael leading a small troop of his most trusted assistants. Michael was still wearing the look of disapproving resignation that he has had since our recent meeting.

That was two days ago. This morning (Earth Time) the great Warrior-Angel stormed into my office and launched directly into a detailed demand.

'I need authorisation for all-out war – immediately,' he insisted.

When he noticed that I was not responding to the urgency of his request he continued, 'Jesus is about to be totally surrounded by several battalions of Opposition forces . . . led by Lucifer himself.'

Still I waited. Michael fired off another round. 'A short while ago, Jesus entered Opposition-controlled territory. There is nothing I can do there with a small troop. I will need all our full-time forces if we are to have any chance of Jesus coming out of there alive.'

I could tell that my silence was irritating Michael and had just resolved to speak when he started again. 'For Heaven's sake, Oriel, sign the wretched declaration. We do not have any time to spend on logistical niceties.'

'Michael,' I said firmly. 'Do you think Jesus knows that the desert is a stronghold of the Opposition?'

'Of course he does,' he replied impatiently.

'And am I right in thinking that he walked into the desert of his own free will and headed directly for their headquarters?'

'Yes.'

'Considering that he is your Boss's Son and that you are only an Archangel, which of the two of you do you think is most likely to understand exactly what is happening here?'

'But if I am not supposed to help him in a face-to-face confrontation with the leader of the Opposition, what good is it my following him around at all?'

'If it is a face-to-face confrontation,' I replied calmly, 'I have no doubt whatsoever that the Son is quite safe. Your job is to watch his back and that back is currently unprotected because you are too busy panicking.' And then I added more firmly, 'Now get down there and do the work that your Boss has given you.'

He left.

It is a long time since the leader of the Opposition had a face-to-face meeting with his Creator. He will, I'm sure, try hard to exploit the inherent weaknesses of Jesus' human nature, and human nature, as we know, can be terrifyingly weak. My position of *no doubt* is rapidly changing. The more I think about it, the more I find myself agreeing with Michael. This is a very dangerous venture.

Next day

The atmosphere here is very tense. There is none of the usual storytelling and song singing of Heaven. Everyone knows that our Boss's campaign has reached crisis point. There have been so many Angels happening to drop into my office saying 'I just thought I'd say hello', and then straying next door into the Operations Room, that I have installed a large monitor in the great Gathering Place of Heaven. Apart from essential tasks the whole of Angeldom are watching and waiting for the Opposition to make its move. So far, nothing has happened.

Some Earth days later

Still nothing has happened, as far as we can see. Jesus is on his own in the middle of the desert, surrounded by Opposition forces. Every day at sunrise and sunset he walks two or three miles across the sand and rock to a small water spring, has a long drink and then returns to the cave where he has been sheltering from the desert winds. Every day a detachment of Opposition spirits follow him. The leader, however, stays outside the Son's temporary shelter.

I expect something is happening that we cannot see from Heaven, something utterly earthly; they are in the leader of the Opposition's home territory. Tomorrow I shall visit Michael and Maff to find out what they can tell me.

Late the next day

Michael is much happier than last time I spoke with him. He has settled into the bizarre routine of this silent stand-off. He posted his small force at strategic points so that he knows exactly what the enemy are doing at any time. He has also insisted on providing Maff with a personal security squad.

Maff, apart from being irritated by the constant attention of his Angelic minders, has been watching Jesus intently. He explained to me that the leader of the Opposition is concentrating entirely on Jesus' physical appetites and fears. That is why we, in Heaven, have been completely incapable of seeing what is happening. He said something about stimulating certain areas of the brain so that Jesus can see things in his mind that do not actually exist.

With Michael's permission, I pushed through the ring of rebel Angels that were escorting Jesus towards his evening drink and walked along beside him. We said nothing. He is physically weak from not eating but I was more concerned to discover that he is spiritually weak from the unrelenting bombardment of terrors and passions that the leader of the Opposition has subjected him to. I expect that the enemy's plan is to wait until his resolve is broken down and then attack. I wish I could be sure that such a plan would fail.

Day 39

I received a message from Maff today, delivered by one of Michael's toughies. *Jesus is very weak indeed. Expect the enemy to make his move.*

I sent a message back to Michael, 'Remember, do *nothing* unless I tell you.'

Day 40

Maff was right. Jesus did not emerge from his cave this morning and did not walk to the spring for a drink. Noticing this, the leader of the Opposition entered the rocky hole. The most rebellious of all Angels stooped down and picked up a stone from the cave floor. Michael tensed and moved a hand to his weapon, anticipating that the enemy would throw the stone at Jesus. He did not. His tone was gentle – his target was Jesus' mind, not his body – and he focussed on his most immediate physical need. 'If you are the Creator's Son,' he said smoothly, 'tell this stone to turn into bread.'

Jesus looked longingly at the lump of rock that was held out to him. I believe that in his mind the enemy was conjuring the smells and flavours of freshly baked bread. Among the Archangels we have tended to underestimate the powers of our former colleague who has taken over the globe of Earth. This was a very clever attack. I didn't doubt that the Son would see through it. The question was whether he would be able to resist it.

After a long pause Jesus replied, 'It is written, *Man does not live by bread alone.*'

A few moments later, Lucifer emerged from the cave, followed by Jesus. Slowly, and for Jesus painfully, they climbed to the top of the rocky outcrop into which the winds of centuries had carved Jesus' cave. At times *the Prince of the Earth*, as he likes to call himself, even helped Jesus' fragile body up the rocks. From the vantage point at the top they could see to their north the Judean mountains in which Jerusalem is situated. To the south and east lay the deep valley of the Sea of Death and beyond that the territories of Israel's former enemies, now also conquered by Rome.

'I will give you all of this,' the leader of the Opposition asserted, 'It is mine, after all – if you will kneel down and worship me.'

Jesus did not stop to reply, but turned to climb back down to his cave. As he went, he said to himself, 'It is written, *Worship the Lord your God and serve him only.*'

The Enemy had preyed on Jesus' physical needs and now he had leant on the human lust for power and authority. While Jesus clambered slowly downwards, his opponent remained on the hilltop considering what other weakness he might exploit.

All of a sudden the dark Angel flew at Jesus and scooped him into the air. Followed by Michael, Maff and other assorted Angelic spirits they headed straight for Jerusalem and came to rest on the roof of the great Temple. Clearly the leader of the Opposition had been rattled by Jesus' resilience; his tone was no longer conciliatory. His target this time was the insecurity that is a fundamental feature of all human minds.

'If you *are* the Creator's Son,' he shouted, 'throw yourself down from here. For it is written, *He will command his Angels concerning you to guard you carefully; they will lift you up in their hands, so that you will not hurt your foot against a stone.*'

There was silence as Jesus floundered in a whirlpool of self-doubt. The question nagged in the folds of his brain: 'Am I the Son of God? Am I really? Is that possible? Wouldn't it be good to be sure, once and for all?' As I watched from the safety of my office I became aware that someone else was in the room, standing behind me. I turned round to see my Boss stooping over my shoulder, his attention fixed on the roof of the Temple.

Jesus walked to the edge of the roof and looked down at the stone pavement far below. As he did, I looked to see if Michael or Maff were moving. They were as still as Death, waiting for a command from me. I, in turn, looked to my Boss.

Without removing his gaze from his Son, my Boss spoke quietly. 'Whatever happens, do nothing.'

I repeated the instruction to Michael and Maff, then waited for

Jesus to choose between faith and certainty. Did he understand, I wondered, that if he attempted to grasp certainty, he would lose everything?

The leader of the Opposition was motionless, no less anxious than we were. This was his best shot. His plan was poised on the brink of failure as much as ours.

Jesus straightened himself and turned to face his tempter. There was a strength in his posture that I had not seen for many days. 'It is written,' he said, *'Do not put the Lord your God to the test.'*

Without a word, the leader of the Opposition flew off, defeated. His cronies followed. My Boss spoke to me urgently. 'Get Jesus out of there and get some food into him.' With that he left the room.

I sent an order down to the Temple roof. 'Well done, team. Maff, fly Jesus out of there to a secure place and nurse him back to health – Boss's orders. Michael, take a few day's rest.'

I am still shaking from the tension of that encounter. Our enemy has become an expert at manipulating the thoughts of humans. We must be careful never to underestimate that ability.

Some days later

Today Jesus embarked on his new career. Maff looked after him at one of the safe houses we maintain for people needing a break from the struggles of divine service. He has recovered from the spiritual and physical ravages of recent weeks. At the first village he entered on his journey home, he was immediately recognised by someone who had seen him being dunked by John. The rumour spread rapidly and soon half the village had gathered at their well to see the man about whom John had foretold so much.

'We have heard John's teaching,' their rabbi said, 'What is *your* message for us?'

Jesus was quite startled by the suddenness of the request and could not recall any one of the ideas that had filled his mind during his long years of chopping up bits of dead tree in his step-father's workshop. The only thing he could think to say was to repeat what John had been saying on the afternoon that he was dipped.

'It's time to make a new start,' Jesus told them. 'God is making a new start and you need to . . . to . . . you need to . . .'

'Give the poor lad a chance,' an elderly woman called out. 'He's come to our well for a drink, not to give a sermon. Sermons are for the synagogue on the Sabbath. Let him tell us then. In the meantime, will someone please give him a drink?'

Maff, who had been as unprepared as Jesus for an impromptu sermon, gave the woman a great hug, which she felt as a warm tingle running down her spine. The rabbi took control.

'He can stay with me until Saturday; in the meantime you all go back to your work.'

As the villagers dispersed, he placed an arm around Jesus and guided him towards his house.

'There's been great excitement here over John's preaching,' he told Jesus. 'Would you like some wine? Our local brew is really rather good.'

Jesus now has less than two days to compose his first ever sermon. He spent the rest of the day on his own in the synagogue, sipping wine, studying the scrolls of the scriptures and talking – non-stop – to his Dad.

Two days on – the Sabbath

Jesus has often sat in synagogues, thinking about what makes a good sermon; today he must deliver one. His mind is buzzing with nervous energy. I am not worried, though. The Son has given innumerable stirring addresses to gatherings of Angels. I'm sure he can manage a small synagogue of humans.

Later

They loved him! He talked to them about wine – a subject close to their hearts. He reminded them what a waste it would be to put a new vintage into second-hand wineskins. The local wine makers were shocked at the very idea.

'God is doing something *new*,' Jesus told them, 'So he needs new people to work with.'

The rabbi, a devoted fan of the local produce, did not seem bothered by the implication that he was an old wineskin; he was too interested in the prospect of God's new wine.

Within minutes of the end of the service, Jesus was surrounded by people offering their services to my Boss's new vintage. He was also invited to speak at various neighbouring synagogues as he travels north. He is a busy man already.

A few weeks on – another Sabbath

After a few weeks of preaching in the villages of Jordan and Galilee, Jesus travelled home to Nazareth yesterday to visit his family and transfer some of his belongings to his new home in Capernaum. I hoped I might catch up on my writing at last. No chance. Within an hour of Jesus' arrival, the Nazarenes tried to kill him. These humans are more stupid than I had imagined!

Having been delayed on the road yesterday afternoon, Jesus slept in a field last night and went straight to the synagogue this morning. Being already a renowned preacher, he was invited to address the congregation and began his sermon by reading from the prophet Isaiah. Not long into the sermon itself, the mood of the people changed from 'Hey, this is our Jesus. Hasn't he done well?' to 'Who does he think he is, coming here and telling us what to do?' The next thing I knew, they were half pushing, half carrying their former carpenter out of the synagogue and down the road to where the hillside has fallen away and there is a sheer drop into the valley below.

There they held Jesus, just inches from certain death, while they argued about what to do next. There was a confusion of opinions from the straightforward, 'Kill the carpenter!' to 'They're all mad in Capernaum' and pleas of 'You can't kill a prophet just because you don't like him'. The commotion continued until one of the men shouted, 'We can't do this to Joseph's son.' To which someone replied, 'But is he Joseph's son?' This stimulated a chant of 'Bastard, bastard, bastard. Push him, push him, push him.' I could see Archangel Michael growing more and more tense and hoped he wouldn't do anything stupid.

Above the rising chants one of the women shouted, 'Some people say he is the Son of God.' This was the last straw. They took that to be blasphemy, and blasphemy, for Jews, is the ultimate crime, deserving immediate death. In the microsecond that followed, I simply prayed. Michael acted. He swooped down into the mob and blasted a path straight through the middle of them. While the people were standing, wondering why they had all stepped aside, Maff took the opportunity provided and guided Jesus to safety.

The result was that the crowd stood dumbfounded as Jesus walked calmly through the middle of them and away from his home village. Jesus may be safe, but I expect that his Father will consider Michael's action to be undue interference. I have asked Michael to report to my office immediately.

Later

As soon as Michael stepped through the doorway, we were both called in to see our Boss. The meeting was brief.

'Michael, did I instruct you to interfere with events in Nazareth? Or did Oriel?'

'No, Lord.'

'Did I give you clear instructions to do nothing unless you were given a specific order?'

'Yes, Lord. I'm sorry. I was afraid for Jesus.'

'Michael, do you trust my Son?'

'Yes. Of course, I do.'

Wanting to take some pressure off Michael, I interrupted with a question.

'Lord, what would have happened if Michael had not acted as he did?'

My Boss looked straight at me, noting my fervent wish that I had not asked such a stupid question. Gradually his face brightened to a forgiving smile.

'Oriel,' he said with twinkling eyes, 'we will never know.'

A week after

Synagogues seem to be dangerous places for God nowadays. After a quiet week visiting the villages around Capernaum, Jesus went to his local synagogue this morning and was invited to preach, as has become usual. This time, just before the end of the sermon, an Opposition spirit charged in, riding on the spirit of a particularly troubled member of the congregation. They were followed by a forlorn-looking Angel guardian. Using the poor man as a mouthpiece, to ensure that all the humans could hear, the Opposition spirit shouted out, 'What have you come here for, Jesus of Nazareth? Have you come to destroy us all? I know who you are. You are the Son of . . .'

'Be quiet!' Jesus ordered, in a voice that demanded compliance. 'And leave that man alone.'

The rebel spirit threw its hostage to the floor like a broken toy and fled the building twice as fast as it had entered, helped by a hefty shove from the man's guardian Angel.

The wiser members of the synagogue looked at Jesus with a new respect. They may not have understood what the Opposition spirit was trying to tell them, but they certainly appreciated the fact that Jesus had confronted a rebel spirit and won with a knockout in the first round. One of them was the head of the local fishing fleet, a man called Simon. He invited Jesus to join his family for lunch.

I must remember to congratulate Michael for doing nothing.

That evening

The Sabbath is supposed to be a day of rest, but Jesus must be exhausted. Lunch at Simon's turned out to be much more than either a good meal or a relaxing one. Simon's wife is away and his mother-in-law was ill. The lunch, prepared in a hurry by Simon himself before the Sabbath began, was a mixture of under-cooked and overcooked dishes (he may be expert at catching fish, but he certainly can't cook them). Jesus' first action was to visit the mother-in-law, who was sleeping in the corner of the house, and heal her. After that, the meal began to look more hopeful.

Word that Simon's mother-in-law had been miraculously cured by the preacher quickly spread around the village. At sunset as the Sabbath ended just about everyone, especially anyone who was sick in any way, made their way to Simon's house by the waters' edge. As Jesus healed one person after another a carnival atmosphere began to develop. This came to a sudden end when a handful of Opposition spirits gate-crashed the party, again riding the bodies and spirits of local people.

Once again I saw how skilled the Opposition have become at using human beings. They seem to latch onto people who have, in some human way, rebelled against my Boss. Their plan today was clearly to uncover the facts of Jesus' full identity but Jesus spotted them immediately and sent them packing before they could finish what they had to say.

Again Michael excelled himself by doing nothing.

While the party atmosphere gradually returned to Simon's swollen household, Jesus slipped away for an early night. He has an appointment with his Father and me early in the morning.

Shortly after dawn

My Boss called me into his office during the Earth night and explained the agenda for our meeting with his Son (most of which I am not permitted to write here). When Maff nudged Jesus out of his slumbers, the Boss and I transferred ourselves to the top of the grassy hill behind Capernaum and waited for Jesus to join us.

Looking over Lake Galilee and watching the changes in the light as this part of the world spun into the rays of its yellow star, I caught a brief insight into the lives of the men and women of planet Earth. Before long we saw the shadowy figure of Jesus climbing slowly up towards us. He sat down, breathing heavily from the effort of his early morning walk.

Prayer cannot be properly reported by the simple conventions of human conversation and I will not attempt to do so. But my appreciation of human life has grown rapidly today. After sharing insights into the Son's work so far, we turned our attention to the next phase of his mission. We had only just begun considering the relative strengths and weaknesses of Jesus' new friends when a deputation of local villagers, led by the ever-enthusiastic Simon, interrupted us.

As they puffed their way, red-faced, towards what they saw as the lone figure of Jesus, Simon's brother Andrew said, 'We've been looking for you everywhere.' (Human speech can be laughably inaccurate!)

They urged Jesus to return to their village and pick up where he had left off last night: teaching them and healing their sick.

'I must travel through other towns and villages,' Jesus replied. 'They need to hear about my Father's love as well.' His announcement was met with a disappointed, 'Oh!' No one quite knew what to do or say next. Jesus broke the silence.

'I need some breakfast,' he said. 'Who wants to join me?' Immediately he jumped up and set off down the hillside leading the band of crestfallen fishermen.

Three weeks later

Something about the quirky little fishing village of Capernaum has captivated me. With a desire to deepen my understanding of this place the Son has made his home and to get better acquainted with the local people, I have spent a considerable amount of time here recently. They are an honest people, who have a deep respect for my Boss, but they wouldn't notice an Angel in their midst even if I were to dance on the table while they ate their dinner.

Jesus' departure left the whole community feeling flat. There had been much chatter about being specially chosen by my Boss. As news filtered back to them about Jesus doing the same things in other villages that he had done in Capernaum, jealousy began to grow. Repeatedly I've heard the sentiment, 'I never could understand what he was talking about, anyway' or 'They're all a bit odd up there in Nazareth.' Again I find myself wondering, 'Why does my Boss trouble himself with these tiresomely selfish creatures?'

It took less than two weeks for most of the people to stop talking about Jesus altogether. Simon and Andrew, on the other hand, have hardly talked of anything else. Andrew spent most of the off season listening to John the Dipper down in Judea. He met Jesus there on one occasion and has a faint glimmer of understanding concerning who he might be.

Yesterday I joined the two brothers and their partners, James and John Zebedee, as they sat mending their fishing nets on the beach. The conversation was about whether they could afford to take a few days off to track Jesus down and listen to him again.

They won't need to.

Next day

Midmorning, the scruffy group of tired fishermen were again seated in a circle, stitching over the holes in their nets, when the youngest, John, leapt off his stool shouting, 'He's back, he's back.'

John ran towards the Tiberias road while his elder brother shouted at him, 'Don't do that with my new net, you great donkey.' James returned to his work, muttering into his beard until he heard John's footsteps return to the shingle beach followed by somebody else's. The men turned to see Jesus approaching their circle. Each one rose and offered him their stool. Jesus thanked them and sat on the ground between John and Simon.

Word soon spread that Jesus had returned, and complaints about his teaching and home town were quickly forgotten as Capernaum stopped work and gathered on the small beach. Before long there was no space left and Jesus had to stand up in order to be heard. When the rabbi arrived with his school class, Jesus called them over to the place where he had been standing and then climbed into Simon's fishing boat.

Simon and his colleagues had quietly resumed their net repairs while Jesus taught the crowd. When they heard the boat timbers creak, it was Simon's turn to drop his work and leap to his feet. His natural reaction was to yell, 'What do you think you're doing?' But before his mouth could form the words, his anger was disarmed by Jesus' smile.

'Simon,' he enquired calmly, 'Could you push me out a little from the shore? It would make more room for the children.' Simon left his net where it had fallen, beckoned his brother Andrew to join him and walked over to the boat. With a single shove the two men launched the small wooden vessel onto the water and leapt into it. After three strokes of Simon's paddle, the boat was stationary with Jesus facing his audience on the shore. Andrew dropped the anchor stone and joined his brother in the stern where they sat side by side, as proud as two peacocks.

When the sun reached its highest point above their heads, Jesus brought his succession of stories to a close and encouraged the villagers to return to their work. As the last feet stepped from the noisy shingle to the silent grass, Jesus turned to the two men seated on the stern bench. 'Let's go fishing,' he said. There was silence. The brothers looked at each other, not knowing what to say.

In the last few weeks I have learned a good deal about the craft of fishing. They do it at night because the fish swim closer to the surface when it is dark. To go fishing with a throw net at the height of the day would be a waste of time.

Then Simon spoke. 'We were out all night and didn't catch a thing.'

Jesus said nothing and waited for Simon to continue. He is just like his Dad!

Andrew kicked Simon gently and Simon went on, 'Alright then, if you say so.'

Simon can be a surly character, but deep in his spirit I saw a trusting openness to Jesus' suggestion. Without a word he climbed out of his boat, waded ashore, picked up Andrew's net and threw it to him. Giving the boat another heave, he vaulted effortlessly into the bow and waited for the boat to stop moving. When it did, he nodded to his brother who threw him the net. With expert hand, Simon placed the rope between his teeth and spun the net across the surface of the water. It splashed into the lake making an almost perfect circle. When the net had sunk sufficiently, Simon closed it with a sweeping pull on the rope with his right hand. At the end of that routine movement, he froze. His net was stuffed full of teeming fish!

What followed was a panic of activity. As soon as Andrew had also taken a pull at the taut rope, James and John were summoned to launch their boat and help. While Jesus sat and watched in silence, the four fishermen shouted and signalled and manoevered their boats so that the bulging net was between them. Ever so carefully, they eased the net above the waterline and brought the boats together beneath it. This was accompanied by repeated shouts of, 'It'll rip any moment now,' and 'It's going, it's going!'

The two boats tipped towards each other so dramatically under the weight of fish that they began to fill with water. Simon Peter released the rope and a writhing cascade of fin and scale poured into the floundering craft. Jesus sat unmoved by the flipping mass of suffocating fish that reached almost to his knees.

Simon yelled, 'Let's get ashore before we sink completely.' Four men splashed into the water and dragged their valuable boats up onto the shingle then collapsed exhausted beside them. Jesus still did not speak, but stood in the midst of the slithering cargo. Simon rose to his feet and helped Jesus to disembark. Jesus looked into his eyes, a steady smile forming in the fragile medium of his human face. Simon, still holding both Jesus' hands, sank to his knees.

'Go away from me, my Lord,' he said, tears welling up in his eyes. 'I'm just a stupid, selfish man.'

Since the days of Moses, the Jews have held the belief that anyone who sees their God face to face, as it were, will die. (This is not without reason, considering the delicate nature of the human form.) Watching Simon's spirit I could see a holy fear. Far below the level of his mind, he knew that he was in the presence of his God. He expected to be burnt up by pure goodness like a dry leaf in a fire.

'You don't need to be afraid,' Jesus assured him. 'From now on, you will be fishing for men and women.' He looked around at the four wet and out-of-breath men and said, 'Come with me.'

Simon, Andrew, James and John hauled their two boats right up out of the water and ran after Jesus. Their bewildered employees were left to deal with the mountain of fish.

Ten days on

For the last few days, I have been in my office processing various administrative details. Jesus has carried on with his new routine of visiting Galilean villages and urging the people to get themselves ready to meet his Father. The only difference from his previous tour has been the presence of the four fishermen, which has caused considerable amusement up here in the Heavenly realm. Today I need to speak with Jesus about his choice of friends.

Earlier, the five new friends were just leaving Meroth when they heard a cheap bell clanking ahead of them round a bend in the road. Jesus was walking on his own, slightly ahead of the others, followed by Simon and Andrew. James and John were in the rear, arguing. But they would all have heard that bell even if they had been singing to the tops of their voices. It was the bell of a man with leprosy, warning people of his advance. The four fishermen stopped on the track. Jesus continued.

Simon shouted after Jesus urgently, 'Teacher, stop! We'll climb onto this bank and wait 'til it is out the way.'

'I'm going to have a chat with this man,' Jesus replied. 'Then I'll come and join you.' He walked on.

A man dressed in old sacking limped into view. His face was scarred and bleeding. One hand was engulfed in a crude bandage.

At the sight, Simon turned pale and struggled not to be sick, but he stood his ground, as did the others behind him. 'Come on,' he instructed his companions, 'We're going with Jesus.' Simon walked stiffly, holding his breath. The others followed. When Jesus held out his hands to the disfigured man, the four companions watched, transfixed. All that they had been taught from childhood about the terrible dangers of leprosy was being confounded by Jesus. They drew closer to hear him instructing the man to be sure to get a certificate of healing from the priests in Jerusalem. Finally he looked directly at the man who, quite clearly, was utterly cured and restored, and said, 'Don't tell anyone how this happened.'

The man walked away, free of his limp, his head and hand uncovered. Simon joined Jesus, saying, 'No chance of that!'

'No chance of what?' Jesus asked.

'Of him not telling anyone.'

Later

Through this whole Jesus business, I have become quite accustomed to being totally ignored by humans. Occasionally one appears to be vaguely aware of my presence, but most of the time they behave as if I did not even exist. Hence I was caught out this afternoon when Jesus, having taken his leave from the four fishermen, looked straight into my eyes and said, 'Well, Oriel, what is it?'

'Why do you bother healing them?' I asked, 'They are going to die anyway.'

'Why do you think?' he replied – a characteristic question.

'Well, you love them, obviously,' I said. 'But surely you haven't decided to turn back the great tide of human illness and disease?'

'Illness and disease aren't the real problem, as you know, Oriel,' my Master replied. 'But I have come to put humanity right and these healings are signs that point the way ahead.'

I considered his words. 'Now, why have you come to see me?' he asked.

'A message from your Father,' I explained. Jesus sat down and I continued. 'He asked me to tell you that it is time you started picking some suitable men and women to take over from you when ... I mean ... later on.'

'I've already made a start,' Jesus informed me.

'Oh, excellent! Who did you have in mind?'

Jesus looked towards the fishermen who were entertaining themselves by plucking blades of grass in a pointless attempt to be the one with the longest blade. I laughed, assuming that Jesus was joking. He asked, 'Which do you think should be the leader, Simon or John?'

I was shocked. 'I had in mind someone more, er, educated,' I said. (The truth is that the current theory in Angeldom is that Jesus was keeping these four buffoons rather as some people keep pets, for relaxation and general entertainment.)

There was no doubt that Jesus was utterly serious but I was too taken aback to be able to answer his question. 'Your Father suggests that you select twelve,' I said, changing tack. 'Maybe we should take a trip to Jerusalem to check out the university?'

'No need for that,' he said confidently. 'I know exactly who to ask next. Why don't you join us tomorrow?'

He had a certain twinkle in his eye which I recognised from of old. I am quite sure that I am in for an even bigger shock.

The following morning

I have just been chatting with Raphael and asked him if he had any ideas as to who Jesus is going to choose next. He echoed my suggestion about the university. When I put to him the 'Simon or John?' question, he replied, 'If those two men were the only humans left in the physical Universe, I would choose Andrew.'

It is time for me to join up with Jesus and his little shoal of fishermen.

Late afternoon

Jesus acknowledged my arrival and led us to the West Galilee Tax Office, outside of which stood a long queue of extremely grumpy people. They were all waiting to pay their monthly revenue contribution. Every one of them was complaining, saying how the cost of living was going up but incomes were going down and taxes were getting steeper. To be honest I could understand very little of their talk but the general mood was unmissable – Matthew, the Revenue Officer, is universally despised.

We stood in the queue for ages surrounded by this self-obsessed misery until Jesus' turn finally came and we entered the ornately furnished office of Matthew the tax collector. The whole concept of money is utterly beyond me but I had assumed that Jesus was there to pay his own contribution before we moved on. I was as bewildered as Simon, Andrew, James and John when Jesus simply said, 'Matthew, come and join me.'

Without a moment's hesitation, the thin-faced Jew wearing Roman clothes left his desk, his money and his life's work and followed the Son. Jesus, with a broad smile on his face, opened the door and ushered out four pale fishermen and a beaming ex-tax collector. As I passed, I whispered in Jesus' ear, 'You've either gone completely mad or this is a stroke of outrageous genius.'

When Jesus and I were alone, he replied, 'Neither. It's simply that Earth is a dangerous place and you can achieve nothing without taking some carefully considered risks.'

He walked out into the sunshine leaving me to ponder this new dimension to our mission. I know we are taking risks and have already had some close calls, but the stakes have just been raised. As I was deep in thought, Jesus returned to the tax office and said, 'Oriel, I don't suppose you have ever experienced a human party.' He was right. 'Meet me at Matthew's house tonight.' He added casually, 'You might even enjoy yourself.'

I couldn't help feeling that the Son is getting a little too involved in human existence. A small cloud of jealousy drifted across my mind. I had always thought of humans as pathetic, tragic figures and it had never entered my mind that it might be fun to be one.

When I stepped out of the small office, I encountered an astounding scene. The queue was still there and was longer than ever. The grim misery had blown into raging fury. The very people who had earlier been moaning that they had to pay taxes were now furious that there was no one on hand to relieve them of their hard-earned income.

'I've been queuing here for over an hour and I'm not moving a step until someone comes to see me,' one said. And another, 'It's not as if I hadn't a thousand other things I could be doing.'

I will never understand humans!

Early in the morning

In order to continue my study of human beings, and so that I might help Jesus in his choice of leader, I decided to stay in Earth Time and follow young John. As he washed himself meticulously, he was both excited and scared about the forthcoming party. Watching the thoughts that darted back and forth across his soft brain was exhausting. John had never met such a rich man before and anticipated foods and wines that he had barely imagined. On the other hand, Matthew kept 'bad' company and John was frightened by the prospect of being at a party with such people, people he had been brought up to avoid. 'What would my mother say,' he asked himself, 'if she knew where I'm going? People say Matthew's parties end up as orgies. Does Jesus know this? What should I do if . . . ?' John's body thrilled with excitement and then descended into an anxious sweat.

In this confused state he stepped out into the night, dressed in his smartest clothes to meet Jesus. His heart skipped down the road ahead of him.

You may remember me explaining that to an Angel's eye, humans are not at all easy to see. It is also the case that those who are closest to our Boss in love and faith shine with Heavenly life, whereas those who have abandoned any concern for our Boss can become almost invisible. In Matthew's house the whole spectrum was represented, from Jesus himself – who is as bright as the Angels of Heaven – to one or two of Matthew's friends who are little more than faint shadows. Matthew was glowing and as I watched him in conversation with the four fishermen I could see why Jesus has chosen him. My own attention was attracted to one of a group of scantily dressed women who, to my eye, stood out from her companions. When she joined Jesus' little band of followers, John's blushes identified her to me as one of those women whose company his mother would not approve. Matthew introduced the girl to Jesus as Mary from Magdala. When Jesus gave her a great hug, the whole room crashed into silence. Jesus, undeterred, continued to talk with Mary and Matthew, and the other guests returned to their conversations. My attention, however, was fixed on young Mary. Jesus' embrace had a remarkable affect on her. She was growing in Heavenly brightness with every turn of her discussion with him, so much so that she soon became the brightest human in the room – apart from the Son himself.

My observations were interrupted by Archangel Michael who arrived to warn me that trouble was on its way. Shortly afterwards there came a loud banging on the door. A delegation had been sent from the local synagogue to enquire what the young rabbi was doing in such unsuitable company. Jesus walked out into the courtyard and spoke to the synagogue leaders while curious partygoers peeked round the curtains. I was amazed to see that whereas Jesus' brightness (so to speak) had illuminated the lives of Matthew and Mary and others at the party, it seemed to cast a shadow on the faces of the synagogue leaders. After an intense but fruitless debate, they left. As Jesus crossed the courtyard to return to the party, he stopped beside me and said, 'Do you now understand why there is no value in visiting the rabbinical university?'

He was sad as he stepped back into the house and was confronted by silence; everyone was anxious about what he might do or say next. 'Matthew,' he called out in a clear voice, 'I would like to taste some of that Roman wine you were telling me about.' Everyone relaxed.

The feast is now finished and I've returned to the office, still tingling with the excitement of my first human party. I expect that Jesus and the others will be asleep for a long time yet, which will give me time to catch up with my staff.

Later that day

Jesus emerged from his bed early in the afternoon. As always, he started his day in conversation with his Father. I joined in to brief him on some things I had learnt during the morning.

One of Michael's 'listeners' was present at the emergency meeting in the synagogue the evening before and at a second meeting this morning while Matthew's guests were sleeping off the party. Jesus, according to the synagogue leaders, is falling scandalously short of our Boss's guidelines – as given through Moses. I was furious at the suggestion, especially considering that it was the Son and I who had worked the whole lot out for Moses in the first place. In the minds of the religious officials Jesus is a common lawbreaker, and all because of that wonderful party.

Jesus was quiet as I explained it all to him. I could see that he was hurt. After the triumph at Matthew's house, where people who had not given his Father a moment's thought for years began to grow in faith, this was a grim blow. Jesus' silence was as deep as the pain he was feeling.

Several days later

Michael and Maff requested a special meeting with me to discuss developments down in Galilee. Michael is becoming increasingly anxious about the religious leaders and he brought with him Harpheth, the overseeing Angel for the synagogue in Capernaum.

In brief, Harpheth is worried because his synagogue is in danger of splitting. Some of the people think that Jesus is wonderful and wish that all rabbis were as much fun as he is. The synagogue leaders, on the other hand, are extremely cross with him for drawing away their congregation. They are planning to lay traps for Jesus so they can have him formally silenced.

Michael is agitated because the Opposition are forming up their lines of attack behind the religious leaders. 'If it comes to battle,' he informed us, 'we could end up destroying two thousand Earth years of hard work in order to protect the next phase of our plan.'

Maff has obviously been talking with Michael. He said, 'Jesus is being manoeuvred into destroying the very thing he's gone there to restore and I'm not sure that he can see the danger.'

I told them their concerns had been registered and they should carry on as before unless they received specific instructions to the contrary. I finished by reminding them, 'Angels do not trust humans, they never have. But our Boss has chosen to trust them and we trust him, don't we?'

No more was said.

The following Sabbath

Of all the things the synagogue leaders *could* get upset about they have latched onto the most petty matter imaginable!

Last Sabbath one of them was walking home from the service on the same path as Jesus and his friends. The man was scandalised to observe that some of Jesus' followers were chewing wheat they had picked from the fields as they passed.

I had better explain. The problem is not that they were *stealing* the grain – there is a beautiful line in Moses' laws that insists on such small-scale generosity from farmers. The problem is not that they were *eating* the wheat without cooking it – although the man did point out that they were eating this 'meal' without performing a ritual hand washing first. The problem is that Jesus' companions were rubbing the ears of wheat between their fingers to extract the grain – and that counts as *work* (even for fishermen!), which is not allowed on the Sabbath day.

In response to this 'deeply criminal act' a group of Jewish hotheads have decided to hide themselves in a hedge in order to catch Jesus and his band of outlaws in the act. Even as I write, there are five of them, boldly suffering scratches, bites and stings from the local flora and fauna in their quest for righteousness. Their passion for legal purity was set well and truly alight during this morning's synagogue service when Jesus was asked to heal a crippled man shortly after the 'Prayers for the Sick'.

'Are there not six other days in the week for doing these things?' the rabbi muttered to his assistant.

Jesus retorted, 'If your donkey fell in a ditch on the Sabbath, would you leave it there until the next day before you rescued it?'

'Don't be stupid,' I noticed the rabbi thinking, although he said nothing.

Whether or not Jesus heard him, he could see the message in the old man's eyes. Jesus replied, 'Then why should this man, descendant of Abraham that he is, have to wait until tomorrow for his arm to be restored?' With that, Jesus asked the crippled man to stretch out his twisted arm and it was completely restored.

The legalistic ambush party stomped out of the synagogue immediately and in their present mood they would sit on an adder's nest if they thought they had a chance of shutting Jesus up. Harpheth, the synagogue Angel, went after them with a look of depressed resignation on his face.

Jesus stayed for the rest of the service and is now heading towards them, chatting to his chums while they chew carelessly on freshly-picked, hand-rubbed wheat grain. Michael and Maff are with them, but I insisted that Michael leave his Angelic militia down by the lakeside. I am tempted to whisper into Jesus' ear, warning him about the welcoming party that is crouching in the bushes, but I mustn't. Instead I have perched my Angelic form on top of the hedge next to Harpheth, immediately above the synagogue subcommittee, who are far too caught up in their own fear and hatred to notice a couple of Angels.

Later

It was all something of an anticlimax in the end. When Jesus and his companions walked past the hedge-sitters, he was in the middle of explaining a new story that he is working on and did not notice the spies. Once he had passed, the synagogue leaders crawled uncomfortably out of hiding and followed him. They called after Jesus and pointed out that his followers were in breach of the official rabbinical application of the fourth commandment.

Jesus explained patiently, 'The Sabbath law, like all God's laws, is given to help and protect people, to encourage them to rest and lead a balanced life. People were not created in order to keep the law.'

The synagogue leaders had no reply to this and turned back towards Capernaum, scratching their sore bottoms. They did not hear Jesus saying, quietly, 'Don't you realise, it was me who invented the Sabbath?'

Jesus returned to his friends and continued working on his story, but I could see in his heart a shadow of sadness at the reminder that the spiritual leaders of his people are so short-sighted. I offered Harpheth a transfer to some more optimistic task but he turned it down. 'Irritating though they are,' he told me, 'I am learning to love them.'

The following month

Over the last few weeks, Jesus' life has settled into something of a pattern. The mornings he usually spends studying the scriptures and praying. After that he gathers together some of his friends and they walk together to one of the Galilean villages. As soon as word gets around that Jesus is on his way, the villagers come to meet him, bringing anyone who is sick or disabled. Jesus talks to these people, heals them in his Father's name and then settles down to tell stories until supper time. When supper is finished, Jesus and his companions walk back to their homes and families.

In all this there are three continuing frustrations. Firstly, the religious leaders – who still see Jesus as a threat to their positions and who carefully note his every word for their private discussions. Secondly, the people – who get greatly excited at the healings and laugh wholeheartedly at the stories but do not seem to understand what Jesus is *really* saying. And the third frustration is that Jesus can only travel a limited distance in one day but cannot travel any further because most of his companions have families and jobs to get back to.

Next day

Jesus climbed up the hill to meet his Father and me after all the people of Capernaum had closed their doors for the night. It was strange to watch the Son, who I could see shining brightly with the light of my Boss's love, fumbling his way towards us because he could not see the path in front of him on this rather cloudy night. He informed us that it is time for him to select the twelve of his many friends and companions who would be able to travel with him further afield and whom he could train up to share his work.

We spent the night working down his list, one name at a time. The Director, who has been Jesus' frequent companion, filled in his understanding of their occasional strengths and numerous weaknesses. We gradually narrowed the list from well over fifty to less than twenty. Then, while I was contrasting and comparing the relative situations of two men called Justus and Matthias, I was suddenly aware that the Son had fallen asleep. As he lay there with has head resting on his arm it reminded me of when he was a little boy. I was about to give him a gentle kick when his Father told me to leave him for a few hours. These humans are fragile creatures!

I was all for finishing the job off and giving the Son a list of twelve names when he woke up. 'I am not entirely happy about this,' I explained to my Boss. 'You saw him stumbling blindly up this hill because he couldn't see in the dark. There are many things that he can't see now that he is human. His insight into people's souls is limited. He may be right about big-mouthed Simon having a heart that's as steady as a rock but aren't you worried that Jesus still hasn't spotted Judas' ambition and double values?'

My Boss said nothing while time drifted past us and Jesus slept. He watched his Son intently and although an Archangel can never fully understand the Creator's thoughts, I could see hope and pain rising in his mind like restless waves against a beach. As sunlight slowly invaded the Galilean darkness, my Boss looked at me. 'Oriel, there are many things that you see and he does not, but there are many more things that he sees which you never will. Now let us go.'

I returned to my office leaving the Son sleeping on the hilltop. When he woke he returned to the village and called together Simon, Andrew, James, John, Philip, Bartholomew, Matthew, Thomas, James son of Alphaeus, Simon the Zealot, and both Judases, and asked them to go with him. (Simon is very much their leader and in acknowledgement of this Jesus has started calling him 'the Rock', which in their language is 'Peter'.)

I am trying hard to hold onto my Boss's unshakeable trust in his Son. I cannot record all of my thoughts here, other than to state that if it were left to me, I would have chosen differently.

Several days on

Jesus has been back at his house in Capernaum for the last few days, teaching the local people to understand their lives from his Father's perspective. He is always more relaxed when he returns there. These simple lakeside folk have a wonderful openness to my Boss and the Son. In their relative poverty, their minds are uncluttered with the preoccupations of their wealthier fellow countrymen. However, open though they are, they still share the tunnel vision that seems to afflict all humans.

Most days Maff joins Jesus for his early morning prayers. Today, he has asked me to join them. He is concerned.

An hour later

Jesus was intense and serious. 'As you travel above the Earth,' he told us, 'the walls and fences that people build are not a problem to you. To you they are no more than lines on the ground that mark the end of one field and the beginning of another.'

This was an unusual opening and I had no idea what he might be about to say. 'But to us humans,' Jesus continued, 'these walls are impassable barriers. A woman can live her entire life without ever knowing what lies just the other side of the wall at the bottom of her garden. Sometimes she might imagine a cool glade with a thousand flowers, at other times she might dream of wild monsters. What you can so easily see to be neat rows of vegetables is, to her, a matter of horrors and fantasies. Do you understand?'

Maff and I replied with Angelic honesty. 'No.'

'Judgement,' Jesus resumed. 'Every day you see human spirits crawl, some barely alive, from the bodies of people who have died. You watch the Opposition spirits grab them and take them away to Death. You know what my Father planned for them but the humans see nothing of that. All they see is an end beyond which there is nothing other than nightmare and fable.'

None of this was exactly new to me and I was not surprised to gather more evidence of the pathetic weakness of humanity. But I could not understand why this should so preoccupy the Son, who has known these things for thousands of human years.

'Isn't that what he's come to sort out?' Maff whispered to me.

Jesus continued, 'There is a Roman official in the village who is a wonderful, bright man. He abandoned the feeble gods of his upbringing many years ago and now worships his Maker. We often talk together. One of his servants is very ill: a young woman who was born into his household. She is close to dying and he is terrified for her. In the usual carelessness of youth she has given little thought to matters beyond her immediate needs. She isn't ready to face my Father's justice.'

Jesus was quiet, caught up in the intense struggles of the people he loves. I quietly sent Maff to speak to the centurion's Angel protector, and also to the girl's. His report was encouraging. The man had always prayed for the members of his household and since this servant fell ill he has been quietly fasting for her.

I spoke to the Son as he struggled with the pain of human suffering. 'There is a wealth of prayer that has been given on behalf of this girl. What is it that you have in mind to do for her?'

'I want these people to see that my Father's love reaches beyond fear and Death and I want them to appreciate the great value of their faith in him.'

'Good,' I said.

Jesus was still struggling. As I watched him, I began to realise that he too is afraid to scale the wall of Death that stands around his humanity. He too is caught up in the fear of Death and judgement that touches all mortal creatures.

I tried not to sound as though I were addressing a fresh-faced Cherub. 'You love this man,' I said, 'and have prayed for him. He loves his servant and has prayed for her. Faith and love together are your Father's gift and power in this broken world. Use them.'

The Son looked at me intently. 'Thank you,' he said. With that he stood up and trudged slowly back to his home, leaving me more than a little shaken. Since when has it been the task of a mere Angel to give advice to the One who is before all things?

That evening

Maff has just reported to me the events that followed this morning's conversation. Jesus' centurion friend sent a messenger to him, asking him to heal his servant. Jesus gathered up all the love that had been lavished on the sick girl, combined it with his Father's love for her and she was completely restored. I expect that there will be a few glasses of good Roman wine drunk in that household tonight. I am rather tempted to look in.

A few days later

Maff came to see me during the Earth night. He is still concerned for Jesus. 'He seems to be struggling with doubt,' the brightest of our guardian Angels informed me. 'I understood he is down there to guide humans into faith – but there he is, tossing and turning in his bed every night, worrying about Death and judgement. Surely the Son can't be doubting his own existence? It doesn't make sense.'

I have to admit that I am inclined to agree with Maff. In the silence that followed I considered taking up the matter with our Boss but I already knew what he would say and that is what I said to Maff.

'Is Jesus our Boss's Son?' I asked the confused Angel opposite me.

'Of course he is,' came Maff's impatient reply.

'Then trust him.'

Maff returned to Capernaum to watch over Jesus in his fitful sleep. I stayed in my office asking myself the question that Maff had raised: 'Is Jesus allowed to have doubt?'

Next morning

I decided to join Maff for Jesus' morning prayers. As always when at home, he climbed the small hill behind the village and sat on a smooth rock, looking over the lake where his fishermen friends were scratching their, now occasional, living.

'Someone who is rich can never really understand what it is to be poor,' Jesus began. 'He may try to imagine it but his imagination will always fall far short of the truth of poverty.' Jesus was in the same preoccupied mood as before. I indicated to Maff to say nothing.

'One who has knowledge,' he continued, 'cannot appreciate what it is to be ignorant; and one who has faith cannot comprehend doubt.'

Jesus watched the small wooden boats moving across the surface of the water below.

'What's all that about?' Maff asked me.

I studied the shapes and patterns of Jesus' thoughts until I began to understand where they were leading. 'I think he is saying,' I replied to Maff, 'that is not wrong to be poor; poverty is a gap that can lead to wealth, given the chance. What's wrong is to deny someone that chance. Similarly, ignorance is not wrong if it leads to knowledge. So it is with doubt; doubt is the space into which faith can grow.'

My question was answered but I could see from Jesus' heavy heart that he had one of his own, and that question lay at the centre of his doubt. He continued to stare across the constantly moving water of the lake. I began to sense a certain depth in the silence around us that informed me that my Boss was close by.

Not until the fishermen had hauled their boats up onto the rattling shingle did Jesus' question come.

'Death and judgement,' he said suddenly. 'Can any human survive them? Can it be true that there is real life beyond it? Or is that just a human fantasy?'

Maff nearly burst out with five times as many answers as there had been questions but I just managed to silence him before he uttered a word. Otherwise he would certainly have taken us over the line into inappropriate intervention. While Maff struggled to maintain his silence, there came a gentle voice from Heaven, the same still, small voice that once calmed Elijah's storm of doubt.

'There are three things that last for ever,' my Boss said, 'and the greatest of them is love.'

With his Father's words echoing round his mind, Jesus stood up and returned to the lakeside to join his friends. Maff stayed with me, full to bursting with the things he had wanted to say.

'Maff,' I said sternly, holding back the flood. 'Do not speak a word until you have focussed your mind on our Boss and away from your own concerns.'

I waited while Maff wrenched his mind away from his own ideas and directed it on the pure love of his Boss. Eventually Maff's Angelic mind turned to me, now calmer, and he asked, 'Does the Boss ever give a straight answer to a simple question?'

That evening

Before I begin to describe to you all that happened today, I need to explain some more about Angels. You humans, so far as I can understand, see people according to the dimensions of the physical Universe, that is according to their height, their width and their depth. So if someone is particularly wide or particularly high then you can see them more easily. Well, with Angels it is rather similar except that we can hardly see physical things at all. What we see are the spiritual dimensions of faith, hope and, especially, love. To our eyes, those who love little are little, while our Boss, for example, who loves all his creatures, is – well – unmissable.

Earlier today, after I had returned to my office, Jesus set off again on his travels, up into the hill country near Nazareth where he was brought up. His friends had spent the last few days busily fishing (watching Matthew, the tax collector, trying to handle a boat is entertaining) in order to provide for their families before this next trip. Jesus, as you know, has spent that time agonising about Death and judgement but he also got round to repairing the roof of his house which had been all but demolished by four faithful but clumsy friends of a man who was completely paralysed – until he met Jesus.

Jesus and his friends were just entering a town called Nain when they encountered the funeral procession for a local man who had died leaving his poor mother an unsupported, penniless widow. Now, whatever this woman's human predicament, she was huge in her love for her dead son. To my eyes she stood out from the crowd like a whale in a goldfish bowl. Just as Jesus spotted this woman – he could hardly miss her – I heard the fragmented concerns in his mind smashing together into gloriously united understanding. Jesus stepped up to the dead man's coffin and, combining his own renewed faith with the astonishing love of the bereaved mother, he called after the man's spirit which was tangled in the web of his own human selfishness.

'Young man,' Jesus said, 'Come back!'

The Opposition spirit that was carrying the man away to Death stopped instantly, throwing away its captive as if it had been stung. The Director of my Boss's work gently guided the discarded spirit back to his empty body. Immediately the dead man sat up. Jesus helped him out of his grave clothes and presented him to his astounded mother. A great cheer went up from the crowd of mourners. Jesus and the woman stood facing each other, each wearing smiles that might have split their fragile faces. Then I turned and saw one more smile that was even broader and deeper than theirs. Standing in my office doorway was my Boss.

Wednesday 15th November

Over many months Jesus has been travelling with the Twelve – his chosen group of human apprentices – teaching in synagogues and village squares. He also spent times at home in Capernaum, thinking and praying and preparing for future journeys while his companions fished, mended their nets, and then fished again.

All this while Jesus' fame spread, mostly for all the people he healed or freed from Opposition influence. Against the near hysteria caused by these acts of kindness, Jesus has struggled to focus people's minds on his Father's plan and on the challenge to be ready for that life which lies beyond human death.

Today began much as any day. Jesus and his entourage left the town of Asochis and headed off for the next place on their itinerary, Sepphoris, up in the Galilean hills. While they were travelling, there was a knock on my door from a flustered Angel, one Sharriel who, I have to admit, I hardly recognised.

'Yes, Angel?' I enquired of the timid spirit on my threshold.

'Can I come in a moment?'

'Of course you can.'

It is all too easy to forget that whereas I have Angels at my door several times a day, for some of those Angels it is a once-in-an-aeon trauma to visit an Archangel. Sharriel looked furtively up and down the corridor before hopping into my office and shutting the door silently. I smiled at the frightened spirit and invited him to sit down. At the same time I glanced through my files to find out who this agitated individual was. By moving at the steady pace that Angels expect from their seniors I managed to locate the relevant file, and calmly asked, 'What is it that brings you so far from Nazareth, Sharriel?'

'You probably won't remember me,' he began. 'But I have been appointed as guardian to James Josephson, the brother of . . .' At this point he leaned across the desk towards me and spoke in hushed tones. 'I shut the door because Archangel Michael warned us that we were not to mention a word of this to anyone but I assumed that it is alright for me to tell you and I didn't want to bother our Boss in case there was nothing really to it all.'

Usually I can read the thoughts of lower Angels before they speak but this poor spirit was in such a dither that his thought patterns were a total jumble. I was also annoyed to hear that Michael had been giving instructions without informing me.

Putting my irritation to one side for the moment I told Sharriel, 'You are wise to be cautious but I do not think that you need to worry about Opposition ears here.'

'"You can never be too sure," Archangel Michael told us. "Even the leader of the Opposition sometimes disguises himself as an Angel of Light."'

'It may be so,' I replied reassuringly. 'But I promise you that I am not he dressed up as me.'

The Angel looked momentarily worried and I managed to catch his thoughts as he wondered if he had been over-hasty in knocking at my door. Then he considered what he might have done to check out my identity. I interrupted. 'You were telling me, Sharriel, who it is that you look after. James the brother of . . . ?'

The Angel said nothing but pointed towards the office where the Son used to work before taking up residence on Earth.

'Sharriel,' I said. 'If you have any important information relating to Jesus of Nazareth, then you were quite right to come to me.'

'I tried to tell Michael but . . .'

'You were quite right to come to me.'

'The thing is,' said the Angel, beginning to relax. 'The thing is that James left Nazareth this morning along with his mother and his younger brothers and they are headed for Sepphoris to stop . . . to stop, er . . . you, er . . .'

'To stop Jesus?' I completed his floundering sentence.

'Yes. The whole thing has been brewing for a few weeks now, with James gathering stories of Jesus' activities. He thinks he's gone too far. That is, James thinks Jesus has gone too far, if you understand me.' I nodded.

'"This is too much, too much," he keeps saying. And now he plans to stop Jesus altogether and take him home to Nazareth.'

A sudden darkness clouded my spirit. We had expected resistance and confrontation but it had never entered my mind that such activities might come from Jesus' own earthly family. I know he had a bumpy ride in Nazareth last year, but this was a shock and Michael, for all his scaremongering, had overlooked the danger just as easily as I had.

I stood up, gathering my paperwork. 'Sharriel, you have done very well. Let's go and catch up with James before he catches up with Jesus.'

Plunging back into the restless currents of time, Sharriel led me to his human charge. James is not in any way a headstrong character. He is a gentle and cautious man who is always sensitive to the concerns of the people around him. (When he and Jesus played together as children, Jesus was always the adventurous and outspoken one. James would reprimand him saying, 'You can't go around saying things like that. Someone might misunderstand you.')

It was in the same anxious mood that we found James and his family that morning on the hilly road to Sepphoris. All the family were worried about Jesus. They had tried to stop him from packing up his tools and leaving Nazareth in the first place. Now they were nervous of his mushrooming fame and terrified by rumours that the authorities in Jerusalem were taking a keen interest in every aspect of his career.

As Sharriel and I followed along behind Jesus' relations I tried to make out what Mary's part was in this family uprising. Surely she would understand the nature of her son's calling? Why was she part of this posse? Did she really plan to bring an end to Jesus' work?

Like Sharriel, her thoughts were too distracted for me to be able to read, but her guardian helped me out and I was astounded to discover the level to which Mary really understands Jesus. Is it usual for earthly mothers to be quite so perceptive about their children? I was suddenly humbled to discover that this peasant woman has a clearer understanding of some aspects of Jesus' mission than I have. I made a mental note to arrange a higher level of security around her – if the Opposition picked up half of what was flowing though her mind we could be in serious trouble.

We proceeded in silence and I considered whether I should alert Michael about the security threat posed by Mary but I was still cross with him for his interference with the routine work of my Angels. Also, I was not confident that he could restrain himself should events in Sepphoris get ugly. Instead I sent Michael a message asking him to meet me in my office during the Earth night. I do not know what subtle pressures human mothers and brothers can exert on their sons and siblings but Jesus will have to handle these familial forces on his own.

When we arrived at Sepphoris, Jesus was already packed into a modest-sized home, talking about lamps and lamp stands. (I learned long ago that it was fruitless to try to understand the creative twists and turns of the mind that managed to create both giraffes and mice out of the same set of bones.) A message was passed to Jesus that his mother and brothers were waiting outside and would like to see him immediately. A hum of anticipation buzzed around the crowded room. People were eager to meet the close relatives of a man who had such remarkable powers. Perhaps they too could heal sick people and raise the dead.

Jesus looked carefully at the faces of the simple village folk who had left their daily tasks to learn about his Father's love. Their attention quickly returned to him, meanwhile James quietly squeezed his head around the door frame, noticing the letters J.J. carved neatly into the corner of the frame – a craftsman's signature which informed him that Jesus himself had built this house. Jesus noticed his brother and addressed the crowd, 'Who is my mother and who are my brothers?' The question caused a surprised murmur in the room. 'Could it be that the Teacher from Capernaum did not know his own family?' Such a situation would be unthinkable for a Jew.

Jesus looked into James' eyes as he waited for quiet. It was a look that I have seen many times before and it means 'I know that you cannot understand what I am about to do (or say); please trust me.' When the people were still, he stretched out his arms to encompass everyone present and smiled broadly at the few children sitting on the floor at his feet.

'Here are my mother and my brothers,' he said. They looked at him, enchanted by the idea that they might consider themselves so close to one so famous. 'Whoever does God's will,' Jesus continued, 'is my brother and sister and mother.'

James looked intently at the one with whom he had played as a child, the one who had given him the family business. He felt a pain of loss in his heart as he tried to share his remarkable brother with everyone else who serves God. A hand grasped his. The cool, firm hand of his mother.

'Come on, James, my love,' she said. 'We'll go home. He's fine. Let's go.'

James held on to Jesus' gaze as he retreated from the house, his body a battleground of conflicting emotions. As he set off towards Nazareth I returned here to my office to wait for Michael.

Late that night

Waiting is not easy for Angels because we are not often so tightly constrained within time. Michael was late. The longer I waited for him, the closer I came to feeling what humans would call anger. When he finally stepped into my office I greeted him coolly. 'Are you aware that there was a serious attempt made this afternoon to bring an end to the Son's mission?'

Michael's reply had the same flavour of cool irritation. 'Are you aware that the Opposition are planning a major offensive against us?'

I wasn't.

Michael continued. 'I sent Sharriel to you because I was too busy to help him. I trust that you managed to diminish the heated anxieties of young James?'

'There is nothing heated about James,' I replied. 'He's the calm one, remember?'

I was concerned by the hostile nature of our conversation. Such behaviour is very rare among Angels and is a clear sign that the Opposition are gaining ground. Just then, our Boss appeared in the doorway. 'Are you two alright?' he enquired. Instantly we both relaxed and our fears melted. 'Call me if you need me,' he smiled, and left us.

I turned from my Boss's reassuring smile to the grim concern that shouted from every part of Michael's Archangelic being. Clearly, in my own preoccupations, I had misjudged the situation regarding Michael. I allowed him to speak first.

'As you are aware,' he said, 'the Opposition have been amassing their forces around the shores of Lake Galilee while the Son has been travelling through the hill country to the west. You are not aware that the leader of the Opposition has been up to the most abominable tricks, twisting and manipulating the spirits who serve him.'

I interrupted. 'Michael, I'm sorry to change the subject, but we need to increase security around Mary. She has grasped the basic principles of our entire plan and if Lucifer looks into her thoughts, like I did today, we will lose almost all the advantage we hold.'

'In which case,' my shrewd partner replied, 'it is equally important that we do not draw his attention to her.'

'I wondered if I should ask Gabriel to take over as her guardian. He knows her.'

'You might as well mark a big black X on the map saying, "Look here!" The Opposition would head straight for her. Not even Moses was guarded by an Archangel.'

We sat in silence, considering our options. It seemed that we were agreed on the idea of a more experienced guardian for Mary. The only question in our minds was, 'Who should that be?'

'I suggest that you redeploy Maff,' Michael said at last. 'Now that Jesus is being left to fight his own battles, Maff is wasted. Put him onto Mary and it doesn't really matter who you give to Jesus, seeing that they aren't allowed to do anything anyway. Just make sure they're the same rank as Maff so his move doesn't look suspicious.'

'There is more to the work of guardian Angels than fighting spiritual battles,' I reminded the commander of Heaven's armies. 'And your Creator and Master has many other struggles beyond the feeble plots of the Opposition.'

'Those plots have moved on from feeble.' Michael steered our conversation back to his concern.

While we glared at each other in moody silence, the door opened again revealing our Boss.

'Oriel,' he said gently.

'Yes, Sir?'

'I would like *you* to take over the day-to-day care of my Son.'

My whole being thrilled at the prospect of being set free from my office to enjoy the company of the Son. 'Yes, Sir,' I replied. 'I would be honoured to serve him. But who would look after the office?'

'You can run operations from the ground.'

Suddenly the security of my office, safe from the constantly deteriorating Universe, seemed very attractive. The idea of being stuck in time and space became less attractive. Although it is useless to argue with my Boss I felt a need to put up at least a token resistance.

'Operating from within planet Earth will cause numerous logistical difficulties.'

'I could ask Raphael to mind your office for you,' he suggested with a playful smile. (Raphael, may I note, is to administration what the leader of the Opposition is to honesty, as my Boss knows very well.)

'That's an interesting idea!' I replied in the jesting spirit of the suggestion. 'I'm sure I'll manage.'

The door closed. Our Boss's hand, in any matter, always brings with it a sense of goodness and rightness; it changes one's outlook and attitude. It had certainly changed Michael's. 'Good!' he said. 'It will be a great comfort to have you around.'

It was time to address the issue that Michael had brought to our meeting.

'Tell me about the latest abominations of our former colleague, Lucifer,' I asked.

'He has gathered a large force around Galilee . . .'

'We knew that.'

'Indeed you did. But do you know what he and his battalions have been up to since Jesus headed into the hills?'

'No, I don't.'

'He's been driving them out onto the water.'

I was confused. For reasons that I do not understand and certainly could not explain, spiritual beings and water do not mix. I remembered Michael's unease when Jesus chose to live at the water's edge. But what could Lucifer hope to achieve by forcing his own troops onto the hated soup that fills the lake?

'What's he up to?' I asked.

'I can only assume that he is planning to attack the Son in the one place where we won't be able to defend him.'

Without doubt the leader of the Opposition's self-imposed exile on Earth has caused him to think like Earth people. I have never known of something as human as an ambush being used by spiritual creatures.

Michael broke into my thoughts. 'I need volunteers for emergency training in marine warfare.'

'We have a few aquatic specialists who look after the great creatures of the oceans,' I offered limply.

'I need fighters, not biologists,' he replied. 'This might well be the greatest of all the spiritual battles in our war. It could even be the last battle.'

The gravity of our position became clear to me. We have a plan to bring about the ultimate victory of love against selfishness. In all the ups and downs of the past years I had never seriously considered that our Boss might actually lose. Now it seems to be a real possibility.

'Jesus travels back to Capernaum tomorrow,' I informed Michael. 'There is no time to train your Angels even if that were wise.'

The great Archangel rose above me. 'I can't stand by and watch all that we have worked for dissolve into the water. I can't do nothing while damned Lucifer destroys the last hope for men and women on the Earth.'

I have seen Michael in similar moods before but today I snatched a glimpse of Archangel Michael as his enemies must see him: vast, uncompromising and unconquerable. There could be no gain from rising to the contest – I would not win.

'Michael!' I snapped, summoning all the authority and command entrusted to me. It checked his furious advance. 'If you strike a single blow against the enemy, you will, with that one act, demolish our entire plan. And that you know.'

He sat down.

I continued, 'I will inform Jesus of the situation and you will stay by my side until this episode is past, for good or for evil. Neither you nor I know the fullness of our Boss's strategy and neither you nor I will raise a finger without his clear command.'

Michael was silent.

I began to tidy my desk. 'I have to close up this office and prepare for life on Earth. You can help me.'

Those arrangements are all now in place. Michael sat, grim faced, in the corner of my office while I have spent some of the Earth night writing this journal. Both of us are weighed down with the same question: 'What if Jesus, the Son of God, should die?'

Next day

I met up with Jesus and Maff at their morning meeting. Maff has left for Nazareth to look after Mary, and the Son graciously accepted me as his new guardian Angel. He received the news of the Opposition's manoeuvres without comment. I spent the rest of the day following him and his ragtag bunch of followers towards the enemy-occupied lake. How slowly you humans move!

We arrived at Jesus' house in Capernaum some while after sunset.

The following morning

I am waiting at the usual spot while Jesus climbs the hill for his pre-breakfast briefing with my Boss and myself. Michael is beside me, carefully studying the Lake of Galilee and its shores with his tactical eye. There are literally thousands of Opposition spirits slithering and sliding on the surface of the water. Some appear to be enjoying themselves, most are simply far more terrified of their leader than they are of the thin liquid below them.

I know that Michael is trying to work out a strategy for defeating this awful army should it come to a straight fight. What he does not know is the conversation that I overheard this morning as I left Jesus' house.

Jesus was picking his way over a row of sleeping disciples when Simon Peter, barely awake, raised his head and enquired, 'What are we doing today, Boss?'

'Let's go over to the other side of the lake.'

To which Peter responded, 'I'll walk round to Bethsaida and get a boat ready.'

A short while later

Jesus had very little to say. With something like the skill of a poker player he did not give away either his thoughts or his feelings. Michael could not restrain himself and pointed out the horde of Opposition spirits below us.

'What do you intend to do?' he asked.

'There is a man in the region of the Gerasenes who is suffering enormous torment at the hands of the Opposition,' Jesus informed us. 'He needs me.'

'You will be walking there, I assume,' Michael added pointedly.

Jesus replied, 'Peter offered to take us in his boat.'

I could feel a volcanic eruption building up inside my colleague.

Jesus was calm. 'I can see Peter's boat now, so I had better go.'

Mid morning

I checked in with my Boss to see if he had any special instructions for me. He said, 'Oriel, you only have one task today and that is to restrain Michael.'

Once I had discovered that there was no alternative but to row into Lucifer's trap I found myself caught in an unexpected dilemma. I couldn't help wondering which frightened me most: the prospect of Jesus being killed by our vile enemy, or the idea of travelling in a boat.

My Boss resolved the uncertainty. 'Oriel, you don't have to row across the lake if you would rather not.'

I did not have to be told twice. Michael and I have taken up position at a safe altitude directly above the lake. Jesus, Simon Peter and a few others are just climbing aboard their wobbly wooden craft.

Here goes!

Later

There is an eerie strangeness below us. Simon Peter, Andrew, John and James are slowly pulling the small boat across a lake that is crowded with Opposition spirits but the Opposition are putting up no resistance whatsoever. As the tiny ship approaches them they move quietly aside to let it through. The four disciples are entirely unaware that they are rowing through a dark forest of evil. To them it is a calm and sunny day.

Michael is gaping in silent disbelief.

It seems to me that the tension of this stand-off is winding tighter and tighter with every stroke of those silly wooden oars. I can only imagine that when they reach the centre of the lake, all hell will be quite literally let loose.

As for Jesus, for whom this demonic welcoming party has been gathered – he is fast asleep.

Still later

The boat is almost in the middle of the lake and heading straight towards the leader of the Opposition, who is rapt in concentration.

Michael, to my utter amazement, has turned away because he can't bear to watch any longer. He asked if he could sit in my office until it is all over but I insisted that he stay where I could see him. We might yet be caught up in an almighty battle and if that happens we will need Michael's strength and skill. Jesus, meanwhile, is still asleep.

Later still

As soon as the disciples had reached the centre of the lake, the leader of the Opposition gave a silent signal. The Opposition spirits all began to jump on the thin water, each in their own chaotic rhythm, whipping up ever-growing waves and stirring vicious currents all across the lake. Above us, thick storm clouds were rolled out, depositing cascades of cold rain. While the spirits disturbed the water with their lower halves, their upper parts blew the damp air round and around the circle of the lake.

So this was the devilish plan. Nothing so simple as a battle of rival spirits, but simply to drown the son of Mary and, in so doing, to destroy the Son of God.

Ignoring the dangers of the sea I swooped down to watch the boat and its precious cargo more closely. I have come to learn something of these strange fisherfolk and their great skill on the water. I saw at once that this evil storm was far beyond their knowledge and strength. The timbers of their fishing boat creaked under the blast of successive waves and were approaching the point when they would crack and then break apart. The only thought in the minds of the four fishermen was Death. And still Jesus was asleep.

Peter grabbed him, pulling him upwards, shaking him awake. 'Master! Master!' he shouted in that final terror that precedes the quietness of Death. 'Don't you care if we all drown?'

Jesus looked at the lethal dance that raged all around him like a storm. Then he spoke. I had heard that voice when he brought the Universe into being. It was neither the great song imagined by poets nor the big bang of scientific reason. It was a clear command of such authority that nothingness had no alternative but to become something. In comparison with that day his voice was as calm as a man asking his wife to pass the salt. But it was, nonetheless, the voice of the Creator.

First he spoke to the air, 'Be quiet!' Then he spoke to the water, 'Be still.'

Once again, creation had no option but to obey the voice that brought it into being. The air was now unmoved by the limbs of the frantic spirits and the sea set like smooth concrete beneath their pounding feet. The only movement in the entire sea was the gentle rocking of the boat as it settled into stillness.

Jesus looked at his four wind-whipped companions and calmly asked, 'Could you not trust me?'

He then looked up at me, above his head, and said, 'Oriel, there is no need to fear someone who can only destroy the human body.' Then he added, 'Couldn't you trust me either?'

That question is still echoing around my mind as the fishing boat pulls its way towards the far shore and a myriad despondent spirits slide back onto the safety of dry land.

Why could I not trust him?

Evening

The sun has set. Jesus and his friends have returned to their homes, trying to understand the dramas of the day. The stilling of the storm was not the last confrontation. On landing in the Gerasenes they encountered the man for whom Jesus had set out on his dangerous journey.

The leader of the Opposition had punished those spirits who refused to go on the lake by imprisoning them all in the body of one man. On talking to the bewildered guardian of this man I discovered that he had first fallen foul of the Opposition some years earlier when tampering with spiritual matters which he did not understand. The spirit whose fancy he had unwittingly tickled had leapt aboard and used the man as a plaything ever since, driving him to excesses of violence and rage. As a consequence the man was thrown out of his village and lived alone by the shore, which was the wrong place to be when the leader of the Opposition wanted to punish hundreds of deserting spirits. When we arrived, the man was crammed beyond capacity with every kind of selfish fury.

Once the spirits saw the Son walking in their direction they knew that their judgement had come. Clumsily they united their attentions and pleaded for a stay of execution. One desperate creature spotted a herd of pigs rooting in the undergrowth on a nearby headland and asked permission to live a little longer in the body of a sow. A moment later, the whole sorry crowd were begging for the same dispensation.

Jesus agreed and they hurtled up the infertile scrubland, squabbling about who would have which animal. The unwitting pigs were caught up into the fight and were used by their parasitic visitors to barge and shove and bite one another. In a matter of minutes the whole herd had stampeded over the cliff and drowned, taking their tormentors with them.

The man was left – empty, exhausted and naked – sitting on a rock beside Jesus.

The owner of the pigs informed the local residents and they sent representatives, who asked Jesus to leave. Whoever he was, he was clearly bad for the local economy. The five Jews climbed back into their boat and rowed home across the now deserted lake.

The day's work did not end there. News of Jesus' return spread quickly and as the disciples eased their boat up onto the beach they were met by a crowd of familiar faces; all those who considered themselves to be Jesus supporters.

Before their hero had even had a chance to greet his admirers, Jesus was approached by a man who was certainly not a Jesus supporter. The excitement of the mob cooled rapidly when they saw the chairman of the synagogue committee march swiftly up to Jesus. Jairus was well known to Michael due to the fact that he has been a leading voice in the campaign to get Jesus silenced by the authorities in Jerusalem. He is not in league with the Opposition, but is an old-fashioned traditionalist who finds Jesus' style of teaching offensive. The people of Bethsaida and Capernaum knew all this very well and looked on anxiously.

Jairus knelt on the shingle in front of Jesus and the people wondered what kind of ploy this might be. Michael tensed beside me.

'My little daughter is dying,' the man said. 'Please come and put your hands on her so that she will be healed and live.'

'It's bound to be a trap,' Michael muttered, eager to warn Jesus of the danger.

'Look at the man,' I urged Michael. 'Can't you see the panic in his soul? He's desperate.'

The local people were outraged. They knew well enough that Jairus' daughter was seriously ill, but how dare the man who had repeatedly criticised Jesus for his actions now come and ask for his help. 'Hypocrite!' was the thought in every mind. Jesus looked into the man's eyes with the piercing gaze he shares with his Father and said quietly, 'Well, let's go.'

Everyone was surprised to watch Jesus walking side by side with his chief critic, carefully enquiring after the details of his daughter's health. The crowd moved as one with these unlikely partners along the shore road that led to Jairus' impressive villa.

As the impromptu procession left Bethsaida, the road narrowed causing the mass of some three hundred bodies to be squashed together.

'I wish he wouldn't get drawn into these situations,' Michael observed. 'Anyone could stick him with a knife and there would be nothing that we could do.'

At that precise moment, Jesus stopped abruptly and asked, 'Who touched me?'

The obvious answer to the question was, 'half the crowd', and as all those within range of Jesus stood rather embarrassed at his unexpected question, Simon Peter spoke for them all. 'Master, the people are crowding and pressing against you.'

But Jesus said, 'Someone touched me.' And he stood, intently studying the faces that surrounded him.

I quickly searched through the mist of humanity around Jesus for someone whose faith made them stand out. It didn't take a moment to locate a middle-aged woman sitting a little apart from the crowd, praising my Boss because the flow of blood from which she had suffered for the past twelve years had been instantly healed. I joined her and gently guided her through the crowd to the object of her worship.

Through her prayers she told me that she had thought, 'If I can even touch the hem of his coat, I know I will be healed.' And she had been right.

Jesus greeted her with a warm smile and while they talked together quietly I found myself next to the wealthy cynic with a dying daughter, Jairus. His thoughts were ablaze with a conflict to match the ones that he had caused around Jesus: 'Come on, you stupid man, or we'll be too late' was his first thought, followed by, 'Well, at least he seems to be on good form.' The image of his emaciated daughter haunted Jairus' mind and he longed to grab Jesus by the shoulder and interrupt his patient conversation with the woman.

Then a hand grabbed Jairus' shoulder. It was the synagogue secretary – a man of words who, on this occasion, spoke remarkably few of them. 'Your daughter is dead,' he announced with the tact of a supernova. 'Why bother the Teacher any more?'

Jairus froze. It seemed as if the blood had simply fallen out of his body. And there, as all his fight and fury deserted him, I saw a deep love both for his family and for my Boss.

Jesus turned towards him and said, 'Don't be afraid; just trust me.' And Jairus did.

Jesus spoke to the crowd who had gathered to meet him. He asked them to allow Jairus some privacy, promising that he would meet them on the Bethsaidan beach the following day. When only his four friends and the two synagogue officials were left, he suggested that Andrew go home to prepare some supper. Then with Peter, John and James he followed Jairus.

As we approached the chairman of the synagogue's grand home, we were met by the defeated spirit of the little girl who was being led away by an Opposition spirit to the place of the dead. She was tightly bound by the common petty selfishness that is typical of all human children. Haphradin, her guardian Angel, stopped as soon as he saw the Son, Michael and myself coming in his direction. He was depressed at the loss of his charge to the emptiness of Death and terror of judgement.

'What's going on?' he asked me.

I smiled at the terrified spirit of the girl and said to Haphradin, 'Don't let it take her away, bring her back into the house with us.'

'There's no point,' Haphradin replied. 'Her body's wrecked.'

'I don't believe that will be a problem in the present company,' I assured him, directing his gaze to the Son.

He joined our party, wrestling the girl free from her Opposition captor, and as we crossed the large courtyard Jesus spoke, through his prayers, with the spirit of the girl. They talked about the enormous love that Jairus had for his twelve-year-old daughter. The house was packed with family and friends, all loudly grieving at the death of the girl. They were surprised to see Jesus entering behind the father of the household. When Jesus insisted that they all leave because the girl was only asleep, not dead, they left the building laughing at him, reassured that Jesus was indeed an idiot, as Jairus had always claimed.

Jesus and the girl's spirit waited patiently while the house emptied, each person imparting their condolences to the bereaved parents. When there were only six humans, three Angels and the spirit of the dead girl remaining, we were led through to a room where the young corpse was laid out. We all stood looking at the human wreckage on the bed and Jesus whispered to the girl's spirit, 'Don't worry, trust me. She'll be as good as new.'

Jesus then said aloud, 'Get up, little girl.'

Her spirit slid effortlessly into the corpse and it was as if a lamp had been lit inside. The girl stood up. The mother screamed. The father nearly fainted. Jesus laughed with delight. He brought the astounded parents to their senses by saying, 'I think she could do with something to eat.'

Mother scurried out to the kitchen followed by her only child, who was skipping. Jesus turned to the father. 'Jairus,' he said, with serious intensity. 'You must *never* tell anyone what has happened here today. Do you understand?'

The man nodded, thinking to himself, 'They would never believe me if I did.'

Mother and daughter returned and invited Jesus to join them for dinner. He declined, saying, 'Thank you, but tonight Andrew is incinerating some fish for us – a joy that should not be missed.'

What a day! I'm exhausted. If that is possible for an Archangel.

Three weeks later

Since my last entry, life for Jesus and his followers has returned to something like normal. Peter (a.k.a. Simon), Andrew, John and James have been busy working, to provide for their families. Matthew and Judas have taken over the financial side of their fishing business. This has caused some bewildering conversations, especially concerning the ethics of paying or not paying Roman taxes. In short: Matthew knows every tax scam in the book, Judas would like to try out every tax scam in the book and

Peter insists on unswerving integrity in all his financial affairs. A typical conversation:

Judas: 'Didn't Jesus say that the measure we use will be measured to us?'

All present (except Thomas): 'Yes.'

Thomas: 'I never did understand what he meant by that.'

Judas: 'Well, the Romans have cheated us and stolen from us with their taxes, so we should use the same measure back to them as a sign of God's judgement on the injustices of their rule.'

Thomas: 'Oh, is that what Jesus meant?'

Peter, in an uncompromising tone: 'No.'

John: 'What Jesus said, was that if we do not treat the Romans with loving respect, God will not treat us with loving respect.'

Simon the Zealot (a former terrorist): 'But the Romans are violent and corrupt . . .'

John: 'Simon, are you telling me that you are not?'

Simon the Zealot: 'Well, if God knows my every thought and motive, I suppose . . .'

John: 'Exactly.'

Thomas: 'Look, I still don't understand . . .'

Everyone: 'Shut up, Thomas!'

Peter: 'Matthew and Judas, let me put it like this. For every half truth and white lie that you include in my tax return, I will insist that you do a night's fishing.'

Matthew, hurriedly: 'There will be none!'

Judas, bitterly: 'You can be as unfair as the Romans.'

Thomas: 'I don't . . .'

All, exasperated: 'Thomas!'

In these past weeks, Jesus has been keeping to himself, reading the Scriptures, praying, thinking, and doing minor repairs for local people who cannot afford to employ the village carpenter. During these jobs, he has been spending time alone with each of the twelve men who he invited to follow him. He either asks them to help him with a job or offers to do some work on their houses or boats. In between, 'Pass me that mallet, will you?' and 'Can you hold this as firmly as possible?' he has been searching out the level of their commitment to, and understanding of, his mission.

Thomas was first. Jesus asked him to help put up an ornament shelf for Peter's wife. The following morning Jesus re-employed him for the task of overhauling Peter's entire fishing fleet. It seems that Jesus also finds Thomas' mind to be rather slow.

Jesus has asked me to join him for a walk around the lake tomorrow. He must have something on his mind.

The following evening

It was wonderful to spend today with the Son, walking through his creation and seeing it from his particular perspective as a human. Every few minutes Jesus would interrupt our conversation and crouch down to marvel at some tiny creature. I have to confess that such unspiritual beings are almost invisible to my eye, despite Jesus' attempts to teach me how to see them. Mostly I had to rely on his energetic descriptions, but – for reasons I cannot begin to understand – I managed to see a dung beetle in all its six-legged glory.

The main item on our agenda was the Son's plans to move his work into a new phase. I am becoming quite used to surprises now and when he informed me that he intends to send his twelve argumentative friends into the villages to preach and do everything that he has been doing, I managed to keep calm and quiet – for a while.

Being a methodical spirit, I took one issue at a time. 'About them preaching,' I enquired gently, 'Do you realise how confused they all are by your teaching?'

'Of course I do,' he replied plainly. 'That's why I'm sending them out to teach.'

'Maybe you could explain?' I asked, reminding myself that I was talking with the True and Only Divine Being and not any young, irrational human.

'Think of a ship,' he suggested.

'I'm not very good with things to do with the sea,' I replied weakly.

'Well, you've seen enough of them in the last week. You know the rudder – that pear-shaped piece of wood that swings on a hinge at the back of the boat?'

'Yes,' I said, cautiously, trying to remember which was the back and which was the front.

'The rudder is used for *steering* the vessel,' Jesus explained. 'But if the boat is stationary in the water, it's useless.'

'Oh!'

'You can only steer a boat with its rudder if the boat is moving. And the faster it is moving, the easier it is to steer.'

'And so?' I invited him to connect this image with the painful picture of Simon the Zealot proclaiming the depths of divine love.

'They will never *understand* my work until they are *doing* my work,' he told me.

'I see. Would that work with Angels too?' I asked.

'I don't see why not.'

I paused to consider the possibilities of an entirely new approach to Angelic training and then returned to the matter before us. 'And are they going to heal sick people and raise dead ones too?'

'Of course.'

'How?'

'The same way that I do,' the Son replied casually.

'If you don't mind me asking,' I said, 'How do you do it?'

'Oriel,' he said with surprise, 'Surely you know that?'

'No, I don't.'

'But you were with me at creation; you must remember. I said, "Let there be light" and there was light. In just the same way, if I say to a lame man, "Walk", he can.'

'Or to the sea, "Be still", and it is,' I said, picking up a recent theme. 'But you are what they call God and they are feeble little humans.'

'I am going to give them my *authority*,' the Son explained. 'Think, Oriel. When you give some minor Cherub a message that is an order to another Angel and they say, "Do this" to that Angel, they do so not with their own authority but with *yours*. And that Angel obeys the command as if you were telling them yourself.'

'That is mostly true,' I observed.

'That is how it will be with the Twelve. They will say, "Be healed" on my authority and the sick body will obey, just as if I were standing there myself. It is exactly the same.'

'So could I heal sick humans?' I asked with interest.

'No, you couldn't,' he replied. 'This authority is not being given to Angels.'

'But it is being given to humans?'

'From tomorrow, yes.'

I have to confess that I found this conversation quite shocking. We Angels have been serving our Boss since before the Universe was ever called into being. You humans, on the other hand, only recently arrived on the scene and have been there for a tiny fraction of the time that we spent tending those great ugly brutes, the dinosaurs. Today I discovered that my Boss is entrusting a responsibility to you that he has never given to even the most senior of his Angels.

I am sure that the Son noticed my disappointment, but we had other matters to discuss so I pressed on.

'I assume,' I said with growing doubt, 'that your fishermen friends will not be giving orders to Opposition spirits in the same way that you do.'

'You assume wrong, Oriel,' the Son informed me. 'From tomorrow, these twelve men will be doing *everything* that I have been doing. I have been given my Father's authority because I am his Son. I am now giving that authority to those who have loved me and trusted me.'

Disturbed and astounded, I blurted out, 'Are these humans going to become children of your Father, as well?'

'I must get home,' Jesus replied. 'I need to get ready for tomorrow.'

With that he turned and strode off towards Capernaum. I stayed, a thousand questions flooding my mind. 'If my Boss is leaving the battle against the Opposition to humans, what will be left for Angels to do?'

Here I sit still – a timeless spirit drifting in the powerful currents of time – and now it looks as though my time has come.

Next morning

I waited in a sober mood today as Jesus came up the hill for his morning prayers. I had resolved to offer my resignation. It is clear that my Boss has a new design which does not require the ministrations of Angels and Archangels. The Son does not need me any longer.

'Master,' I said. 'I am going back home. We have done some wonderful things together and now you are taking to yourself new helpers and companions. From the beginning of this project we Angels have been instructed to do nothing that would interfere. I believe that it would be easier for everyone concerned if we were to keep away altogether.'

The Son said nothing. In silence he looked deep into my spirit at the hurt and disappointment that were festering there.

'Oriel,' he said at last, 'You are my friend and I love you. It was a great delight to have your company at the beginning of the worlds and it is just as much a delight to have you here with me today. It is true I do not need you. If you must talk in terms of need, I have never needed you. But I have always longed for you and hoped for you. Oriel, no one in all the creations has ever seen things the way that you see them, or understood life the way that you understand it. Without you by my side I would be much poorer. Please stay.'

I did not need to speak. There are those who have refused that invitation – my former colleague, Lucifer, is one of them – but I cannot resist my Boss's love.

At last the Son spoke again. 'I may not need you, my friend, but there are twelve soon-to-be-terrified men at the bottom of this hill who most certainly do need you. Follow me.'

That evening

The Son gathered his band of apprentices soon after breakfast, gave them their instructions and, by mid morning, all twelve were on the road in pairs. Unable to be with everyone, I opted for the nightmare partnership of the former Zionist freedom fighter, Simon the Zealot, and the man of a thousand questions but no answers, Thomas Didymus. I experienced a sudden rush of terror when these two chose one another's company. Jesus simply smiled. He smiled again when he caught a glimpse of my concern.

I have spent today in the company of these two lesser specimens of humanity. Simon is serious, intense and slightly paranoid. As a Zealot he pledged his life to the cause of overthrowing the Roman Empire. Jesus persuaded him to surrender his sword and join a revolution far more powerful than guerrilla warfare. Simon is impatient to be issued with this new super-weapon but, in the meantime, he is fascinated by his new commander.

Thomas is rather like a pet dog. He has next to no understanding of why his Master says and does what he says and does but he is utterly devoted and unerringly faithful. 'All spirit but no sense,' was Raphael's assessment of this rather shy young man.

Simon and Thomas walked due north, over the prayer hill and into a region that is completely new to both of them. Equipped with nothing but their trust in the Son they stopped for lunch but had no lunch. (Jesus had asked them to take neither food nor money with them, knowing that they would only manage in this mission if they were totally dependant on his Father.) With no opportunity for eating until they reached the next village, the mismatched missionaries settled for some water from a small spring. Thomas then went to sleep, leaving Simon trying to hit the trunk of a tree with an armoury of pebbles. I have absolutely no idea why a human might do such a thing but he did appear to be rather good at it.

When Simon became bored of this activity he selected a new target – Thomas' head. At the fall of Simon's first stone, Thomas woke up and the two companions resumed their journey. Towards the end of the afternoon they arrived at a village called Gischala and stood in the village square, wondering what to do next. They didn't have to wonder for long.

From the far end of the village came the noise of a woman shrieking, followed by the anxious shouts of several villagers. The commotion soon filled the empty square. A large man was dragging his wife by her ankle, shouting aggressively, 'I'll kill yer this time, I will.'

She was repeatedly screaming, 'Stop him, stop him, please, someone.'

Around the man hovered three Opposition spirits, who were taunting him and coaxing him to more violence. 'Go on, then,' they urged. 'Do it, we know you can.'

'Hit her again,' said another. 'Then she'll know who's the boss.'

It was obvious to me that the man could hear their voices but had no idea where the voices came from.

Close behind this group came an assortment of villagers who wanted to rescue the woman but were clearly terrified of her husband.

'If you come any closer,' he boomed, 'I'll do it. I will. Then you'll know who's boss.'

'That's it,' encouraged a particularly odious spirit. 'Do it now, before they try to stop you.'

I don't think the man had seen the two strangers standing at the edge of the square. Simon, noticing this, put his paramilitary training to good use. He charged at the husband, crashing his head into the big man's belly. A crude but effective tactic. The man let go of his wife, who quickly escaped into the safety of her mother's arms. Then he hit the dirt with such a crunch that he lay there, dazed for some time, which gave the villagers courage to come closer. The three spirits, robbed of their sport, looked around and were startled to see me. They would have fled immediately, but when Simon barked out the order, 'Stay right where you are and don't move a hair,' they responded as if he were addressing them. He was, in truth, addressing the man and had no idea that the spirits were even there, but they stayed nonetheless. Simon's order came with the Son's authority and the Opposition spirits were compelled to obey.

'He'll be alright now,' said an even bigger man (a blacksmith), who stepped forward to take his concussed neighbour back home. Speaking to Simon, the blacksmith added, 'He hears voices sometimes and they tell him to hit and bite. He'll be alright for a few weeks now.'

The three spirits shifted uneasily, annoyed at the reminder of their relative impotence. The wife, bleeding, bruised and scarred, slipped forward and embraced her husband, crying. For a while she knelt, whispering words of forgiveness into her husband's ear. She then looked up at Simon and said, 'He's a lovely man really. It's just that when the voices taunt him, he can't control himself.'

Simon listened, hardly believing her. Thomas stood, wondering what Jesus would do in the same situation. He concluded that Jesus would simply tell the voices to leave the man and that they would obey. I gave Thomas a kick (a 'spiritual' kick, that is) and he responded as he had to Simon's pebbles earlier in the day. He blinked and then whispered to his colleague, 'Jesus told us we were to sort out things like this.' And then after a while he nudged Simon and said, 'Go on, then.'

Simon spoke to the wife and the blacksmith. 'We have a friend, called Jesus – you might have heard of him – who sorts out things like this and he has showed us how to do it, sort of. Would you like us to have a try?'

The woman, still in shock, simply nodded. The blacksmith asked, 'How much will it cost?'

'Nothing,' said Simon, quite startled by the question; people never asked Jesus how much he charged. Simon gathered his thoughts, said to himself, 'Here goes' and then spoke out.

'You er . . . you voices, who are troubling this man. I want you to leave him alone. Right?'

The three spirits exploded into laughter and asked me, 'Are

these two little pets of yours, Oriel? They're not very well trained, are they?'

Before I could reply, the husband began to echo the same demonic laugh, at which his wife quickly retreated to the safety of the gathering crowd.

'It's happening again,' she warned and everybody became tense.

Then the spirits called to their victim, 'Joel, Joel! Time for action! Get the two strangers, quickly, before they get you. They've come to destroy you. Get them, Joel. Now!'

The man began to haul his stunned body to its feet. I gave Thomas another, more urgent, kick. He thought the situation through, muttering his thoughts as he went. 'Jesus just tells the spirits what to do. He has given me the authority to do the same. Oh, God, please help me here because I'm not going to be able to do this without you.' He then stepped forward and looked straight into the man's eyes.

'Jesus of Nazareth has given me authority over you and I'm telling you, leave this man and never speak to him again.'

The laughter of the Opposition spirits faded rapidly. They looked at me for a second opinion – I nodded. They turned and moved away, but slowly, until Simon spoke up.

'Go,' he ordered with an authority that I had not seen in him before. 'Get out of this village and never, ever come back.' The spirits fled like startled sparrows, up into the sky and away.

Their victim, meanwhile, sat down and rubbed his ears. 'It's stopped,' he announced. 'The ringing in my ears has stopped.' His wife returned to his side, obviously aware of the significance of this information. She embraced the man who had whipped her and beaten her for over fifteen years.

'My head feels so clear,' he said. 'Like someone's really washed it out.'

The woman looked up at Thomas and Simon. 'How can I thank you?' she asked.

Thomas was too shocked to reply and stood, shaking his head. Simon spoke for the two of them. 'We're very hungry,' he said.

The woman's mother spoke up. 'You can all come and have supper with me and after a good meal we will open a skin of wine and you can tell us about this man from Nazareth. What did you say his name was?'

The family made their way home, followed by the population of Gischala, who were taking it in turns to invite themselves round for the evening, promising to bring a skin or two of wine with them.

I sense a party coming on!

Night time

The party was wonderful. Somehow, even though he was not there, I could sense that same air of excitement among the villagers which follows the Son around. Thomas, it turns out, is not a bad storyteller and, helped by repeated cups of wine, he entertained the villagers with his own versions of Jesus' stories. Towards the end of the evening Thomas' tales became somewhat over-coloured by the contents of his cup, which was never allowed to remain empty. I'm not sure that 'The Sower' is likely to have sown his seed quite so liberally, but according to Thomas, 'Some seed fell on the path and was trampled on; some fell on the rocks, and the plants withered because they didn't have a thing to drink.' At this he drained his cup and held it out for refilling. 'Other seed fell among thorns, which grew up and strangled the little beggers. Some seed fell in the sea and grew into seaweed which is useless for making bread.' Pause for another drink. 'Some seed fell in the sower's pocket, which he ate on his way home; and still other seed fell into his baby's nappy, which his wife was changing when he got home; and the last lot of seed fell into his bed and gave him little scratches all over his back that night when . . .' Fortunately, at this point, Thomas tipped gently over onto a pile of dirty washing where he is still sleeping soundly.

Simon spent his evening swapping conspiracy theories with the young men of the village, but at about the same time that Thomas had folded over into the heap of dirty clothes, he began to draw together the scattered threads of their conversation. 'It's the poor who will be most blessed in God's new kingdom, not the rich. The weak will be the strongest, the sick will be the fittest, the bereaved will be the happiest and the lame will be the fastest. So arm yourselves with prayer, protect yourselves with faith, and exercise your body with fasting.' Before the young men left the house they arranged to meet Simon in a week's time so that they could hear Jesus for themselves.

All in all, I have to admit, the evening was a great success. For a couple of no-hopers, Simon and Thomas did very well indeed.

The following day

Thomas was the first to be woken, because the women of the house took the washing with them when they went to collect water shortly before dawn. Thomas crawled his way, groaning, to a half-full water jar, drank deeply, then collapsed on the floor and slept soundly.

Before the women returned, all the men were awake and the two disciples were invited to join in a generous breakfast of bread, cheese and eggs. Thomas was asked to complete the story of 'The Sower' which he had left unfinished. He asked how far he had got before being interrupted, and when they repeated his version of Jesus' carefully composed parable, he blushed radiantly and said very little for the rest of the meal.

After breakfast, as the family set about their daily tasks, Simon and Thomas bid their farewells, accepted a packed lunch each and returned to the road. At the moment, once again, they are resting through the hottest part of the day and expect to be in Cadasa by supper time.

Later on

Just a mile or so before Cadasa we were joined by a donkey. I say 'we' rather than 'they' deliberately because it was me and not Jesus' friends who attracted the shabby creature. It is not the first time in the history of the world that an Angel has been recognised by a donkey. These notoriously stubborn beasts must have some redeeming features when it comes to spiritual matters. Simon and Thomas were trudging their way up a hill when there was a great hee-hawing from their right and the donkey galloped across two fields to join us. It had obviously been ill-treated and bore numerous scars as well as a few open and infected wounds. The animal came to a sudden halt right beside me, but not before both men had dived into a hedge in fright.

Thomas and Simon inspected the creature and looked around to see if they could locate its owner. There was no one in sight. They then locked minds in an argument about whether or not Jesus had given them authority to heal sick animals. Thomas was in favour of trying but was not sure that it would work; Simon thought that it *would* work but insisted that they had a responsibility to use their gift wisely and that it didn't stretch to neglected donkeys. The dispute was brought to a conclusion by the donkey, who began to lick her own wounds. Simon then declared (not without a little help from me) that all the creature needed was some clean water and some olive oil, both of which they had. The former labourer and the ex-terrorist then set to the task of cleaning and anointing the cuts and grazes on the animal's hide.

All this took some time and by the end of the process the donkey had been given a name –'Scarbutt'. Simon and Thomas then needed to hurry up to Cadasa in order to have any chance of a meal that evening. They tried very hard to stop Scarbutt from following them but failed. Not that she was, in fact, following *them* at all. She was following me. Whether I went ahead of the companions or behind them, Scarbutt stayed right by my side. Eventually they abandoned any hope of leaving the beast behind and I opted to keep my distance, following a hundred paces or so behind, with my long-eared companion.

As we rounded a spur in the hillside, ahead of us on the road was a man with a long stick who was walking slowly and with particular care. Eager to make contact with the people of Cadasa, Simon and Thomas ran up to join him and engaged him in conversation.

The man was a blind storyteller called Matthias who worked his way from village to village telling stories in return for food and lodging. He had heard news of the storyteller, Jesus, and was fascinated to meet with two of his apprentices. Much of the conversation revolved around Jesus' technique for telling stories. Matthias was surprised to discover that such a famous teacher should use such short stories. He explained that he liked to make his own stories last for most of the evening and for many cups of wine. At this point Simon informed the man, 'I think you'll find Tom, here, to be more your kind.'

'I was in Nazareth once, just a few days after your Jesus had visited,' Matthias said, sensing the need for a change in their conversation. 'The town was divided and far too distracted to listen to my stories. Your Jesus had said that he was the one sent by the Lord to "bring good news to the poor; to proclaim liberty to the captives and recovery of sight to the blind". Is he?'

Simon and Thomas were caught out by the unexpected question and were silent. Simon had been in Nazareth on that day when the townspeople nearly threw their former carpenter to his death. Simon and his Zealot friends had been the first to take offence at Jesus' message of peace and forgiveness. Now a swell of excuses and half-baked explanations rose up through his body and paralysed him with indecision. Eventually he managed to fix his attention on one small patch of clarity in his thoughts and answered the blind storyteller's question.

'Yes, he is.'

'Well, I must visit this Jesus,' the man said.

'Why?' asked Thomas, expecting to learn of some mysterious brotherhood of storytellers.

'So he can make me see,' the man replied plainly. 'Isn't that why the Lord has sent him?'

When Thomas had caught up with the twists and turns of the conversation he stopped in the road and said, 'Oh, *we* can do that,' as if he were talking about nothing more than washing down an infected wound.

Matthias said nothing. Thomas was on a roll.

'Jesus told us to say and do all the things that he has been saying and doing. We have seen him give sight to a number of blind people.'

'What do I have to do?' the man asked, the unsteadiness of his voice betraying a certain level of excitement.

'Just trust God and stand there,' Thomas instructed.

The two disciples stepped back a few paces together. 'What do you intend to do?' Simon asked anxiously.

'Heal him,' said Thomas.

'How?'

'Oh, goodness!' Thomas was suddenly clouded with doubt. 'I hadn't thought of that. What do you think? Should we do the hands on the eyes thing, or the spitting one? Or maybe we should use mud like Jesus did in the Temple that day? Do you think it matters? I mean, do you think it won't work if we use the wrong method?'

'Is there a problem?' Matthias asked, moving in the direction of their voices.

'No,' said Thomas, like a guilty school boy. 'It's just that . . . it's just that Jesus has rather a lot of ways of healing blindness and we're not sure which we should use.'

'Does it matter?'

Simon answered, 'That's what we were wondering.'

'It doesn't matter if I sit or stand to tell a story,' Matthias observed, 'as long as the story itself is told truly.'

'You're right,' said Thomas decisively. 'Just stand there and I will be with you in a moment.'

He walked up the road a few paces to where there was a puddle caused by water splashing from a small stream. He put his hand into the middle of the puddle and scooped out a fistful of mud, which he carried, dripping, back to his patient.

'Don't worry,' he said. 'I'm just going to smear some mud onto your eyes. I'm not sure what difference it makes but it's what Jesus did.'

That done, he stepped back and commanded, 'With the authority given to me by Jesus of Nazareth, I say to you, *see*.'

There was a pause and he added in a more matter of fact way, 'Now go and wash your eyes in the stream.'

Matthias walked slowly towards the little stream, feeling his mud-smeared face. Simon and Thomas watched, growing steadily more doubtful about the whole episode.

All the while, Scarbutt and I had been working our way up the hill and the donkey, hearing the sound of water, climbed up onto the grass in search of a drink. Matthias, his ears close to the cascading water, did not hear the approaching hooves on the soft grass. While he was kneeling on one side of the stream, washing his face, the donkey came up directly opposite him and stooped down to refresh herself. And so it was that as the man looked up with seeing eyes, for the first time in his whole life, his first sight – only inches from his renewed eyes – was the bruised and swollen face of Scarbutt the donkey. He screamed loudly and ran as fast as he was able, up the hilly road towards Cadasa, yelling and howling as he went.

Simon and Thomas chased after the storyteller; I followed them and, of course, Scarbutt followed me. Whenever Matthias glanced backwards with his new-found sight, it looked as though all three of them were being chased by a grotesque monster.

That was how they arrived in Cadasa. First came the terrified Matthias, shouting, 'Help! help!' The villagers ran to his aid.

Seeing two strangers in pursuit and knowing the donkey to be harmless they converged on Simon and Thomas, pushed them to the ground and restrained them roughly.

Matthias forgot his fears as he stared in wonder at his first sight of the village. He stood enchanted as he blended the lines and colours that filled his sight with the smells and sounds of his memories. Meanwhile, Jesus' two disciples struggled with their captors, who were furious that two bandits should attack someone so highly respected as the blind storyteller. The donkey calmly helped herself from a manger of hay on a nearby wall.

After a while Matthias recognised the pained cries of his two new friends and asked the villagers innocently, 'What are you doing to them?'

'They were chasing you!' a voice replied.

'No, they weren't,' Matthias said. 'They've just given me sight for the first time in my life. It was that thing over there which was chasing me.' He pointed to Scarbutt.

'The donkey!'

'Oh!' said Matthias. 'Of course, that's what it is.'

There was an awkward pause.

'What do you want us to do with these two?' asked the man who was sitting on top of Thomas.

'Let them go, for goodness sake. They're fellow storytellers.'

Simon and Thomas were released and introduced to the people of Cadasa, and Matthias explained how his eyes had been healed in the name of Jesus of Nazareth.

Another party tonight, I suspect.

The next day

My two charges have been invited to stay in Cadasa for a couple of nights. The Sabbath begins this evening and the rabbi wants them to give the sermon at the synagogue in the morning. He is one of those unassuming country clerics who does very little outwardly, but inwardly is for ever in conversation with my Boss. He may never get offered a well-paid job in Jerusalem, but he has certainly transformed the day-to-day lives of the people of Cadasa.

Simon and Thomas tossed a coin to decide who would do the talking. Sensing the potential danger of Thomas trying to preach,

I carefully controlled the coin's turns as it fell to the ground to ensure that the task fell to Simon. Thomas has gone into the vineyards to help with the grape harvest. Simon is sitting in the synagogue feeling sick with nervousness. The rabbi keeps bringing him food and saying, 'You'll be fine, you'll be fine.' Both the bread and the encouragement have flown out of the window. I think my help might be required.

Early evening

The Sabbath meal has not long finished and both my charges are soundly asleep. Thomas, after a day's manual work and a full cup or three of wine, nearly collapsed into his supper. Simon's sleep is a little gift from me – gracious, he *is* a worrier!

Earlier I led Simon's thoughts to his favourite of Jesus' stories and prompted him to think about, simply, why it means so much to him. At that point the rabbi returned with some date and raisin loaf and reminded Simon that he must choose a passage from the scriptures for Thomas to read. Simon spent the next two hours reading methodically through the Books of the Law, while I danced, shouted, jumped, screamed and finally howled at him that he wanted the scroll of the prophet Isaiah. He ignored me. When he had worked his way through all five Books of the Law, he turned round to face the cupboard where the scrolls are stored and I pushed Isaiah down from the top shelf. Fortunately, he caught it. It was a further blessing that when he got to The Song of the Vineyard in chapter five, he thought, 'Oh, blow it, this will do. It is the grape harvest after all.' Otherwise we would still be in the synagogue waiting for him to make it as far as chapter sixty one.

Sabbath lunch with the rabbi

The sermon was a triumph! The rabbi is full of warm encouragement and underneath he is genuinely excited at the possibility that the promised Messiah might have come. Matthias, the now clear-sighted storyteller, is busy explaining to Simon how he might improve his delivery and voice projection, which is not exactly what is required at this juncture, but in his clumsy way he is also trying to say, 'Well done.'

'After lunch, you must all have a good rest,' the rabbi has insisted. No one is arguing, least of all Simon. The man is quite exhausted.

Monday, midday

The two missionary marvels are on their way home. The Son asked them to rejoin him on Tuesday morning and, at walking speed, they have a full day's travelling to do. (You humans are a remarkably slow species for your size. You would, in my opinion, have been much faster if you had four legs, but I didn't have a say in the matter.)

Very early Tuesday morning

Simon and Thomas did not get back to Capernaum until well after dark, owing to the fact that their route took them close to a compound reserved for people with leprosy. On their way they met a young woman whose face was horribly disfigured by that dreaded disease. She was returning from a visit to her home town where she had stood at a distance and watched her own children at play. The woman broke into uncontrollable tears when she told the two disciples how one of the other children had spotted her and pointed her out and how a group of boys had then set upon her son, mocking him for the hideous state of his mother. She explained how she had watched helplessly as her son and daughter were taunted and poked. Finally she described, in between barely controllable sobs, how her ten-year-old daughter had walked over to her and shouted, 'I hate you. Why did you have to come back and make things even worse? It's all your fault.'

Simon was uncomfortable in the presence of such deep emotion, but Thomas put his arm around the woman and listened attentively. When the deluge of tears finally stopped, he said quietly, 'In the name of Jesus of Nazareth, be healed.' He waited for a few silent moments and then added, 'Now you can go back to your family. Which village do you come from?'

'From a place called Cadasa. You've probably never . . .'

'I know it well.' Thomas interrupted. 'When you get to the village, go straight to the rabbi, and tell him that Thomas sent you. He will certify that you no longer have leprosy and then you can go back to your family.'

'But what about Sharon, my daughter?' the woman asked, unsure what to make of these two strangers. 'She doesn't want a mother with only half a face.'

Simon joined the conversation.

'When you get round the side of this hill here,' he pointed up the road to Cadasa, 'You will pass a small pool by a stream. Stop there and look at your reflection in the water. When our friend Jesus does something, he never leaves it half done.'

Tentatively stroking her cheek, the woman said her farewells and headed for home, hardly daring to believe that her whole body had been completely restored.

How these two men have grown in the past few days! I should never again doubt the Son's wisdom.

Midday Tuesday

The Twelve returned from their adventures; all excited, all exhausted, all amazed at the things they have been doing!

Jesus announced that today was a day off for everyone – but his hopes for a rest were soon sunk. Surprisingly early the little village of Capernaum began to fill up with Galileans so impressed with the work of Jesus' disciples that they wanted to see him for themselves. Jesus, concerned for the welfare of his co-workers, suggested that they cross to the other side of the lake for some peace and quiet. Anxious about sudden storms, Matthew and Bartholomew petitioned for a walk up in the hills, but the fishing majority were keen to get back in their boats and swung the vote.

I asked how many votes an Archangel could cast in this referendum, observing, 'The hills do look lovely at the moment.' I was rewarded with a knowing smile from the Son.

It is good to be back with him.

The fishermen have been rowing at a gentle rate, while everyone shared their stories of healings achieved, sermons delivered and battles won. The little group are currently enjoying their lunch on the lake, listening to the tale of how Peter got into an argument with a particularly stubborn Opposition spirit who refused to believe that Jesus would be so foolish as to share his authority with such an arrogant chauvinist.

From my elevated position in the sky above them I can see that if they continue with their plan to put ashore near Hippos, they will not find the restful scene they hope for. Literally thousands of Galileans are making their way around the side of the lake, watching the progress of the two boats. The news that even Jesus' companions have power to heal has caused a great wave of interest in the carpenter from Nazareth.

Tuesday afternoon

I have just counted the crowd. The arithmetic of the material Universe is rather cumbersome to an Angelic mind, but I know you humans are fascinated by such details. There are 5,763 people packed around Jesus, all caught up in a whirl of enthusiasm and all quietly hoping that they too will be entrusted with the authority to heal sick people and raise dead ones.

When Jesus spotted the crowd that was waiting for him as the boat came in to shore, I felt his spirit sink like a rock into soft mud. Any other man or woman would have turned their boat back out onto the lake and pretended that they had not seen the assembled masses. Not Jesus. With the unquenchable love that he shares with his Father, he was filled with sadness that they should be so confused about their lives. The image that formed in his mind was of a vast flock of sheep wandering across a barren wilderness because they had no shepherd. He immediately chose to feed them with stories of his Father's love – all with a strong sheep theme. We have had 'The Lost Sheep', 'The Good Shepherd', 'The Sheep and the Goats', among others. It is remarkable what meaning he can find in such stupid creatures.

Late Tuesday afternoon

As the afternoon progressed, Jesus has worked his way round this huge assembly, telling the same stories to different sections of the crowd. As the hours have passed, nobody has set back home. Indeed, more have arrived – notably a posse of rabbis and synagogue leaders from various villages. (The total is now 5,824 including children and babies.)

A few moments ago, Jesus was joined by Andrew and Philip, who tapped him on the shoulder and said, 'None of these people have eaten since breakfast. Don't you think it's time you sent them off into the villages so they can buy themselves some food?'

'You give them something to eat,' was Jesus' unexpected reply.

'We couldn't afford that, even if we had brought all our money with us.'

'Go and see how much bread you do have,' Jesus said, with a twinkle in his eye.

The two men returned to their friends with the message. First they all panicked; then they attempted to calculate the size of the crowd; then Judas added up the total value of their available cash. Then they panicked again.

'What on earth shall we do?' Thomas asked, with characteristic gloom.

'At least we should do what Jesus told us to do,' Andrew replied.

'And what was that?' demanded his brother.

'Find out how much food the people have between them.'

The Twelve spread out among the people, calling out, 'Has anyone got any food they could share around?'

Most replied, 'We never brought any, because we didn't expect you to drag us all the way here.'

Those who had been better prepared said, 'It's all long gone, sorry.'

In the entire multitude there was only one positive reply. A young boy approached Andrew with five small barley loaves and two even smaller fish, wrapped up in a cloth.

'Come with me,' Andrew said.

Of all Jesus' crew, Andrew is the most relaxed when dealing with people. He chatted easily with the child as they walked up to Jesus. Jesus noticed them approaching and held out his arms to the boy. With a big smile he said, 'This is just what we all need. I would like to share it with all the other people. Is that alright?' The lad, overawed to be face to face with Jesus, silently nodded his head and handed over the goods.

Jesus held the bread above his head in prayer, and without uttering a sound that the people could hear, said, 'Oriel, could you help me, please?'

'That's what I'm here for,' I replied, wondering what Jesus planned to do.

'You were with me when we created the Universe,' he said. 'I need you to make bread and fish for five thousand.'

'Actually there's five thousand . . . never mind that. But the Universe took us ages.'

'Well you got plenty of practice, didn't you?' Jesus replied. 'My people are hungry and I must feed them. Here's some bread and fish to work on – copy this.'

And with that he broke the little boy's supper into pieces and started to distribute them to his followers. I grabbed a couple of crumbs that had fallen to the ground and began to knit together the necessary atoms and molecules to match the recipe. It's a process that is relatively straightforward but there was no way that I could work fast enough. A more drastic solution was needed.

Every human – man, woman and child – has an Angel allotted to them to look after them and defend them from spiritual harm. These Angels work extremely hard for their charges and it is the usual practice for Angels like myself, on special assignments, to leave them to get on with their task. Today was an exception. I gave a great shout and called the whole lot to me, all 5,824 of them. In a matter of Earth seconds I had a series of production lines in action. Some were gathering the necessary atoms, others were stitching them together, still others were delivering the newly manufactured bread and fish into the hands of Jesus' trusty helpers. It was utter chaos, but somehow we managed to match our supply to the disciples' demand. Within about an hour we had fed the entire crowd and, group by group, they returned to their homes taking their guardian Angels with them.

I have to admit that when the disciples gathered up twelve fish-baskets full of leftovers, some of the abandoned fish and bread was completely inedible. Bartholemew found a small loaf that was constructed entirely out of fish flesh, with a crust made of scales. He called his companions over to witness the monstrosity but as soon as his head was turned, I rolled it down the hillside into the lake. Just after it had safely plopped into the water, the Son called me.

'Oriel, my friend, you did an excellent job.'

'You didn't see what Bartholemew just found,' I replied.

'Everyone ate, and everyone was satisfied,' Jesus said. 'Thank you.'

'Why did you do it? If you don't mind me asking?'

'There is an influential group among the people who want to proclaim me as a Warrior King and ride with me into Jerusalem to overthrow the Roman army. I needed to turn their minds away from spears and battles, so I gave them a foretaste of the great party that my Dad has planned for them.'

He suddenly switched from his prayer voice to his speaking voice.

'Peter! John! You take the others back home in the boats. I am going to stay here tonight and pray. You all need a rest and I need some peace to think. I will join you soon.'

Then turning to me he said, 'Come on, Oriel. Let's go for a walk.'

'It will be a pleasure,' I said, gladly turning my back on the water.

Some weeks later

The main theme of our conversation that night was that Jesus' massive popularity among the Jewish crowds is not helping his main task down here on Earth.

'There is a deep and strong desire in us humans,' he explained, 'to be liked by as many people as possible. But the lessons of our history show that the thing a crowd wants is not always what the people in it really need.'

Since then, Jesus and his disciples have been keeping away from the Jewish territories as much as possible, travelling in places where they are not known, where they can talk in peace. At one stage they returned to Bethsaida so that Peter and some others could catch up with their families. Within minutes of their arrival in the village, a blind man was brought to them, whose friends begged Jesus to heal him.

Jesus was keen to avoid attracting the vast crowds of last month and took the man away from the village. He restored the man's sight and instructed him not to return to Bethsaida but instead to return home across the hills. The following day, Jesus and the Twelve headed north again, away from the Jewish villages. It was time for some serious talking.

That was four days ago. Last night I joined the Son and my Boss for several hours of discussion. Jesus' 'Miracle Worker' reputation has become a significant problem. Rather than floating on the fathomless depths of divine love, people are simply splashing around in the puddles of their selfish dreams.

That's not the only hitch either. I am not convinced that the Twelve are ready for us to move into the next phase of our plan. My Boss, whose faith in humanity has always outweighed my own, declared, 'If any one of them has grasped the truth about my Son, then we shall proceed. Do you understand, Oriel? However, if none of them have a clue, then we shall wait.'

Tomorrow is examination day. Which, if any, of these twelve assorted males has understood who their leader really is? No doubt there are numerous animated conversations about this up in Heaven. From my lonely isolation down here on Earth, my bid goes on young John. He is the most intelligent of the Twelve.

The following afternoon

After breakfast, we set off in the direction of Caeserea Philippi in the northern valley of the River Jordan. As often happens, Jesus walked ahead, thoughtful and alone, while his followers chatted along behind him. After two or three silent miles, opening his spirit to his Father and listening to every nuance of eternal love, Jesus slipped a quick comment in my direction – 'Here goes!' And then he stopped and waited for the others to join him.

'I have a question for you all,' he announced as they approached.

The Twelve are always more comfortable with Jesus' conversation than they are with his contemplation. They were pleased to gather round him as they walked on, eager to be the one who could give the right answer to his question. It was not a difficult one.

'Who are people saying that I am?' Jesus asked.

A lively conversation followed, to which everyone made a contribution: a new prophet, an old prophet, the executed John the Dipper raised to life, Moses, Elijah. Philip reminded them all of the opinion of the Jewish leaders when he added, 'a pain in the backside!'

'What about you?' Jesus asked, as the laughter died down. 'Who do you think I am?'

Silence.

This has been the subject of many late night debates among the Twelve when Jesus was safely out of earshot, up a hillside praying. Jesus knew that. He also knew that it was time for them to make up their minds. It was not John, the thinker, who broke the silence but Peter, the group's quickest and loudest mouth. What he said was something that he had never mentioned in all the hours of their discussions on the subject. My attention was drawn to him a moment before he spoke; it was as if a small but piercing light had been switched on in the depths of his spirit.

'You are the Messiah,' he declared. 'You are the Son of Almighty God.'

The rest of the Twelve were astounded. According to Jewish law, what Peter had just said would be judged as blasphemy, and he could be stoned to death on the spot for saying it, but somehow they each knew that it was true. The same light began to shine in each one of them and they were united in a momentary euphoria. Smiles broke out on the faces of the twelve friends. They knew that they had passed Jesus' test. They looked at each other, grinning and nodding.

Jesus looked around the group, his face stern. When he spoke, his voice had a strength of purpose they had not heard before. 'Do not, *do not* tell this to anyone,' he commanded. The Twelve could not fail to hear the gravity in their Master's voice and their brief ecstasy of faith led directly into impending gloom as Jesus revealed, for the first time, the true nature of his mission on Earth.

'I must suffer many things,' he told his dumbfounded companions. 'The religious leaders will reject me and they will kill me and two days later I will be raised to life.'

As Jesus spoke, Michael appeared silently beside me. He knew that when Jesus' words were uttered with human breath, the Opposition would soon hear of them. Now they will know where our plan is heading. The chase is afoot. Michael looked around, searching the spiritual realm to see where the news of our Boss's plan would first be picked up. I searched the spirits and minds of Jesus' chosen companions.

Jesus' words tore through their hopes and dreams like arrows through soft flesh. It was as if I could hear the sound of twelve spirits imploding around me.

Peter, once again the first to speak up, exploded with anger, 'Don't be so stupid!' he exclaimed. 'We will never let that happen to you.'

The others nodded and murmured their support for the leader of the fishing fleet.

Jesus had been expecting a swift counter attack from the Opposition but he had not expected one to come from his closest friends.

'Out of my sight, Satan!' he ordered.

The disciples recoiled in shock, bewildered by the sudden change in their Master. Jesus saw the fear in their faces and controlled his feelings. 'You do not see this the way that God sees it,' he reassured them. 'You can only see it from a human perspective.'

The Twelve had passed their test – but only just. They have indeed grasped exactly who their Teacher and leader is, but that is all they have grasped. For a moment it looked to me as though Jesus was an adult human setting off on a dangerous expedition with a group of babies who had only just learned to walk. 'Was it wise,' I wondered, 'for humanity's destiny to be left in the hands of these men?' But then, Jesus' words to his disciples echoed in my spirit. I do not see this the way that my Boss sees it. I can only see it from an Angel's perspective.

Jesus started walking again, his followers huddled close around him. As they walked he tried to open up to them his Father's perspective, but they, faint with fear, took little of it in. Michael and I stayed where we were and watched the ragged little band disappearing down the stony track.

Michael spoke.

'They may not understand him, but they are still following him. That is all a commanding officer needs.'

I could not share either his optimism or his military insight. My mind went back to Jesus' own struggle with the nature and fear of Death some months ago. I could not see Jesus as a canny and confident strategist but only as a weak and vulnerable man. And now we are no longer protected by the secrecy of our plan; the

Opposition know where we are headed. We have lost our strategic advantage.

A week later

For the last seven days, Jesus has kept well away from the distractions of other people. He and his companions have been sleeping in the open and only visiting villages to buy food. Their time has been spent in long discussions about the true nature of life and Death. The mood of the whole group has been confused and depressed. Early each morning, the Son has joined me to talk through his intentions for the day ahead. Always the question has been, 'How can I help them to understand?' After a week of stories, illustrations, activities and conversations there has been little progress. Peter, and the brothers James and John, have made some headway, but the other nine have consistently failed to grasp Jesus' message.

This morning we opted for a different approach. We decided to focus our attention on the three fishermen who *have* understood something of the ways of Heaven. Our plan is to build on their fragile faith and allow them a small glimpse of Heaven. This is a dangerous enterprise. If a human sees more of Heaven than their faith can handle, it will destroy them. The Son has left it to me to judge exactly how much of his Father's glory these three men have the faith to manage. I shall have to slip out of Earth's time and return to my office to work on this plan.

That night, Earth Time

Some weeks ago, Jesus explained to me what a wonderful thing it is, after a long day on the dusty roads, to take his shoes off and dip his feet into a bowl of warm water. I watched while he underwent this profoundly physical experience. Well, I think that I have just felt something similar: to slip out of the constraints of time and float in ageless timelessness is sheer relief. I would not complain if I never had to return to the Universe of time and space again, but I do have to. I fear that if I dive too deeply in the oceans of eternity, I might lose touch with the day to day realities that my friend and Lord is experiencing on planet Earth. I have resolved to get on with my task as efficiently as I can and then return.

My brief is to give Peter, John and James enough of a glimpse of the Son's spiritual reality to inspire them, but not so much that it might damage the fragile creatures. I have an idea. There have been three humans in all the history of the species who were spared the long and empty wait of Death; these three exceptional men were taken directly from Earth to my Boss's home: Enoch, Moses and Elijah.

Enoch is a lovely, gentle man who lived in the very early stages of humanity, back in the days of flint arrows and cave dwellings. He listened to the voice of his Maker as it whispered through the complex patterns of creation and he learned to love in a way that no other human ever had, or has. So my Boss decided to rescue Enoch from the countless pains and frustrations that beset selfish humanity. However, Enoch is of no use to me in my present need. He takes little interest in the affairs of his own kind. He basks quietly in the loving presence of his God and is content.

Moses I must find. He is the founder of Jewish culture: a multi-lingual, richly educated citizen of three nations – and a murderer. A man who was in equal parts an ideal choice and a disastrous one to lead Abraham's descendants out of slavery in Egypt and mould them into a nation in their own right. He is temperamental; he is unpredictable; he is not an easy man to work with and I have no idea where I might find him.

The third, Elijah, was a manic-depressive loner who developed a faith in my Boss, the strength of which was outstanding, even by Angelic standards. He is a man of few words – very few. But when he said, 'It won't rain,' it didn't – for three years. And on the day he said, 'It will rain,' it did. Elijah struggled to stay loyal to my Boss at a time when almost everyone else could not be bothered. For that loyalty he was saved from Death and now lives face to face with the one whose 'still, small voice' once kept him from destroying his own life.

My plan is to locate these two heroes of faith and allow Peter, John and James to meet them. All three men have an unusual existence in Heaven. In the same way that on Earth an onion immersed in vinegar is preserved and takes on the flavour of its preservative, so these three have been preserved from Death and have become imbued with spiritual life, yet they remain human.

They are easier to see and hear than an average human but they are a great deal harder to find than any Angel. The quickest way to find them will be to speak to my Boss.

Next entry

I have found Moses. He has been watching events in Galilee with great interest and is delighted to have a part in it all. Elijah, I'm told, is in a depressive phase and has taken himself off on his own.

Next

Found him. I have explained to both Moses and Elijah – in full – the plan that our Boss has been working on since the time of Cain and Abel. Although I cannot yet risk explaining it here, I can nonetheless tell you that the news brought a broad smile to Elijah's weathered face. Moses simply exclaimed, 'I had no idea!'

The next challenge is to transport these two men back down to their home planet for the first time in hundreds of their years. It is something that we have never tried before. I have a team of Angels working on how to safely reintroduce two human bodies into the material Universe (not my speciality!).

Then

We are ready. My Boss has passed directions and instructions on to his Son. All we have to do now is to deliver Moses and Elijah to the right place and time and in one piece. Moses just raised a last minute problem.

'When I was down there,' he began, 'and our Boss showed me a glimpse of his Heavenly nature, it left me with a glowing face which frightened the wits out of the Israelite people for weeks. Have you considered that Peter, James and John might have the same problem?'

'We have taken that into our calculations,' I assured him.

'You misunderstand me,' Moses continued. 'I am not concerned that they may get shining faces, I am concerned that they might be frightened out of their wits.'

I replied, 'Gabriel is the expert in that field.'

The day – in Earth Time – after I was last in time

Jesus and his three closest human friends were already at the top of Mount Tabor when we arrived. He was praying, waiting to hear from me; and they were chatting, trying to work out why they had climbed to the top of such a high mountain. As we approached the Son with our large contingent of Angels, the light of Heaven was reflected by all the love, faith and hope that make up Jesus. The fishermen were quickly distracted from their conversation when their leader appeared to glow, brilliant white, before them. Once Moses and Elijah were safely standing on their old planet, we left the three Heavenly humans to talk together. I am not exactly sure how much of their discussion the fishermen were able to hear, but I did ask Moses and Elijah to talk in the Hebrew language so the disciples would have a chance of overhearing our plans as they were discussed. (Michael, incidentally, chose the mountaintop location so that he could cordon it off from Opposition ears. This is a conversation we do not want them to hear.)

Moses and Elijah were both overwhelmed to be back in such a familiar landscape and they were pleased to talk for hours, so many hours, in fact, that Peter, John and James slept through most of it. They stirred as Moses and Elijah were preparing to leave. Peter, in his dopey state, blurted out, 'Teacher, it's good that we're here. We can build three simple shelters, one for each of you, because there is a mountain fog on its way and it could get very . . .'

He was interrupted by a voice that he had never heard before, nor imagined hearing.

'This is my Son, who I love dearly. Listen to what he says to you.'

It was my Boss. He hadn't told me that he planned to join the party in person.

Peter was quite right about the fog, but it wasn't of the Earthly mountain variety. It was a spiritual covering to protect the men from the danger of actually seeing their God. When the Heavenly mist had cleared, Jesus was alone again with the three fishermen.

The next day

I stayed with Jesus and his astounded friends as they climbed a short way down the mountain, looking for a cave that Elijah had recommended to them. I find the concept of place almost as confusing as that of time and it is a miracle to me that Elijah should remember the location of a particular hole in the rock when so many years of time have passed by in his absence. But then, he is a remarkable man. When they found it, James lit a fire to keep them warm through the night. Peter tried to catch something for them to eat, but had the success you would expect from a fisherman out of water. The disciples slept well despite their empty stomachs. Jesus lay, thinking through all that he had discussed with Moses and Elijah. In one sense he has always known the real nature of his task, but now that it has been expressed in human words, the details lie heavily on his mind and spirit.

This morning, after refreshing themselves in a mountain stream, the group descended to the plain below. They walked in silence, Peter and John still numb from the indescribable sights of yesterday. On their return to the villages at the foot of the mountain, they stepped into the middle of chaos.

The remaining nine disciples had taken it upon themselves to do what has become routine for them over recent weeks; they spent their days in the Exaloth village square, announcing the dawn of my Boss's new work, illustrating their message by healing people with handicaps and illnesses. If they had understood anything of all that Jesus has been telling them for the last week, they might have realised that now was not the time for such activities. And so it was that Jesus' silent and thoughtful descent from the high point of yesterday's encounter ended in a scrummage of excited villagers, all anxious to hear the famous preacher from Nazareth.

Casting my eye across the mob that met us, I immediately spotted a man in particular distress. I pointed him out to the Son, but my guidance was unnecessary. A moment later the man shouted, 'Teacher, I beg you to come and see my son. He is only

117

young and he is beset with a spirit which grabs him and throws him to the ground. It happens every day. Your disciples said that they would be able to sort it out, but he is no better.'

That was just one voice among nearly a hundred, all clamouring for the Son's attention, all wanting their own needs to be met and their own problems to be solved. Jesus, preoccupied by the painful detail of his Father's plan, struggled to take in the continuing frenzy for attention which has dominated his life for the last two years. He quickly mastered his frustrations and called out to the worried father, 'Bring your son over here.'

The man and his son pushed their way forward through the crowd. As they did, Jesus asked his disciples to try to disperse the villagers because he had to leave immediately. The boy was brought to Jesus. His father was holding his right hand and on the boy's other side was a big, bullying Opposition spirit. I have seen the type before – a dull, dispirited creature – who had probably taken advantage of some minor lie or rebellion of the lad's, and latched onto him, pushing and shoving him for pointless sport. As soon as the spirit saw my Boss's Son, he knew that his game was over. Jesus, eager to get on the road, was brief. He banished the spirit from the planet, healed the boy's numerous injuries and handed him to his dad.

While the villagers stood marvelling at what they had witnessed, Jesus walked away with his disciples. The people of Exaloth never did get to hear his stories.

As soon as they were out of sight from the crowd, still walking at a fair pace, Jesus called his followers to gather around him.

'Now listen carefully to what I am about to tell you,' he said with urgency and intensity. 'I am going to be betrayed into the hands of the authorities. They will kill me and after two days I will rise again.'

No one replied. Many of them wanted to take Jesus to task about his gloomy prediction but they did not dare. They remembered what had happened to Peter a few days earlier. At last the silence was ended by Thomas.

'Where are we going, Master?'

I was pleased by his question because I was as keen as him to know the answer.

'Today we are heading home, to Capernaum. Then, as soon as everything is ready, we will go Jerusalem. We must be there for the Passover Festival.'

Jesus strode ahead purposefully and I joined him. Behind us the disciples chattered. Their chattering became a debate and in time that grew into a full-blown argument. Jesus responded by walking even faster to escape their squabbling. In his mind he was rehearsing again and again the events that awaited him in Jerusalem. Each time, the story he imagined was subtly different. All the while, I could see in him a new mood, that grew stronger and was soon influencing his every thought. To my amazement, this highly charged emotion began to affect me, filling me with a sensation which I have never experienced before. Jesus is deeply troubled by the road ahead and I was being caught up in this most human experience.

That night

The Son and I reached his modest home some while before the others. He busied himself opening up the house, filling water jars, lighting a fire and baking some bread. The Twelve arrived to find the house warm and welcoming; bread, cheese and salted fish were laid on the table for supper and bowls of warm water in the doorway for them to wash their feet. This was not all Jesus' work. There is a loyal group of local women who are always willing to give him a hand in the practical matters of life.

The travellers cleaned up and turned their attention to the food. While they filled their faces, Jesus casually asked, 'What were you arguing about on the road?'

The response was an embarrassed silence. (They had been arguing about which of them is the best disciple.)

Jesus sat on a small stool by the door, beside the bowls of dirty water.

'Whichever of you desires to be the best must become the servant of you all,' he said.

With that he picked up two bowls and took them outside to empty them. He returned with a young girl, the daughter of Salome, one of Jesus' helpers. He led the girl into the middle of the room and crouched down next to her, surrounded by the twelve grown men.

'If you welcome this little girl in my name then you welcome me,' he said. 'And if you welcome me, you welcome the one who sent me.'

Jesus and the girl gathered up the uneaten food and cleared the table. No one dared speak. The girl skipped off, smiling, and Jesus picked up the remaining water bowl. Standing in the doorway he said, 'Whichever of you is the least of all, he is the greatest.'

With that he left the house, saying to me, 'Let's go for a walk.'

A few days on

The past week has been spent packing and preparing for the journey to Jerusalem. Peter and the others have been busy fishing, to raise money for their families and the inevitable expenses of a visit to the capital. Jesus has been quietly organising his house, tidying his belongings and passing on anything that might be useful to someone else.

I am still experiencing his emotions; I cannot understand this. How can I, a spirit, be subject to the subtle alterations in the chemistry of a human brain? Whether I feel these things with the same intensity as my eternal Master is impossible to tell but every day I know how he is feeling before I go anywhere near him, because the same emotions are besetting me. What raw and powerful things these emotions are!

Today I have a sense of immovable pressure that has been building up within my mind since Mount Tabor. It is like a dull heaviness and makes me feel cut off from everything around me, especially people. This morning some children were playing in front of Jesus' house, with a reed hoop which flew in through an open window, smashing the jug of wine that he had placed on his lunch table. Instantly an explosion of anger and resentment occurred in Jesus' mind. His impulse was to tear the toy to shreds and scream at the children for their stupidity. With great effort, however, he controlled himself and then, with the slow determination of a sick man, he returned the hoop to the embarrassed boy at his door. Jesus walked inside, picked up the largest piece of his broken jug and briefly considered hurling it at the wall. Again he mastered himself and looked out at the game resuming in the street. Eventually the infectious joy of the boys and girls dispelled his rage, he smiled weakly and mopped his floor for the second time this morning.

I felt it all: the fury, the lust for revenge, the resentment of another's happiness, then the deep and familiar love that my Boss has for all his creatures and, finally, exhaustion.

Another factor I have noticed is that the steady stream of time seems to have slowed to a mere trickle. Each day creeps along with the imperceptible progress of a glacier. One question is ever present, 'How much longer will it be?'

Next day

Overnight I spoke with Michael and Gabriel. Michael wanted us to meet in the security of my office but I am too deeply immersed into the river of time to leave now. I took them up Jesus' 'prayer mountain' – a place which has received too many visits from our Boss in the last three years for any Opposition spirit to dare approach. We started to draw up detailed plans for the days ahead – plans that I may not even hint at here but which will unfold as each day crawls slowly towards our main event.

Michael is unhappy about the general orders which we have received from our Boss and I have asked Gabriel to 'assist' him. We are about to step into territories no creature, physical or spiritual, has ever ventured into, nor indeed the Creator himself. I cannot risk Angels – let alone Archangels – taking matters into their own hands.

Shortly after Michael and Gabriel departed, the Son climbed up for his morning prayer time. His feeling of heaviness and fore-boding has grown overnight to the point where it is difficult for him to focus his prayers. He stared down at the familiar scene of fishing boats returning from a night's work and yesterday's question repeated itself again and again: 'How much longer will it be?' What was once a clear encounter of love and purpose between Father and Son now feels as impotent as sending smoke signals in thick fog.

Jesus is eager to get to Jerusalem as soon as possible but the fes-tival of Passover is approaching and most Galileans are preparing for the annual trek south. The complex requirements of the local community mean that we have no real option but to leave when everyone else leaves. Our only hope of arriving ahead of the crowd is to travel through the hostile territories of Samaria. Jesus has taken that route before, but not at this time of the year when nationalist fervour is very high. The prospect of the Son being caught up in an act of petty sectarian violence will not please Michael, I'm sure.

24 hours later

The people of Capernaum and Bethsaida have agreed with the rabbis at Tiberius and Taricheae a date when they will set off together down the Jordan Valley for the Passover celebrations in Jerusalem. We will leave with them.

Michael and Gabriel have gone to see our Boss to debate the security arrangements for the journey. I say 'debate' because Michael is not in a mood to discuss anything.

Jesus is calmer now that his immediate future has some shape. He has fixed his mind on departure day and is careful not to think about what lies beyond that. His human mind (especially being the male version) has a remarkable ability to focus on one matter to the exclusion of almost everything else.

Departure day

Today the holidays begin. As we looked down on the village from the prayer mountain for the last time, the usual early morning stillness had given way to the frenzied activity of excited children, angry mothers and irritated men. There is not a house in the locality where tempers are not breaking and where curses and luggage are not flying. The whole spectrum of human selfishness in on display. For us, the scene was like a beacon shining out in a storm, clearly marking the way before us and we said, almost at the same time, 'That is why we are going to Jerusalem.' Of all the violence and cruelty of the human race, there is nothing that shows up the fundamental weakness of men and women quite like packing for a family holiday. Jesus has packed nothing: no bag, no food, no money, no extra tunic. But then, he is not going to Jerusalem for a holiday.

That night

We travelled with the other villagers until lunchtime, collecting the inhabitants of Gennesaret as we passed through. After lunch at Taricheae, as the others continued round the lake towards Tiberias, Jesus and his twelve chosen companions climbed up and away from the lake on the road to Nazareth, retracing the track they had travelled to Mount Tabor only a week before.

We *have* opted for the short cut through Samaria. With us is Michael and a small troop of specially picked Angels. My Boss approved this modest security force to protect our primary objective from any unfortunate accident on the way. Michael won this request when he pointed out that the Opposition have already installed all their resources in Jerusalem and so are not going to trouble us before we reach the city.

Jesus' mood is lighter than it has been for days. It appears he is much happier to be doing something. He is also relieved to be away from the Galilean crowds. There are still those who would like to see him crowned King of Israel. I noticed that a good many swords have been slipped into the Passover luggage, just in case Jesus should declare war on the Roman Empire.

Lunchtime, the next day

We spent last night in the shadow of Mount Tabor. Jesus was careful to avoid the village of Exaloth. This morning we headed south towards the Samaritan border and arrived in the Samaritan village of Ginae in time for a midday rest. Jesus stayed in a fig orchard, sending Matthew and Judas to buy food. They returned with bad news. The village is closed to all Jews travelling to Jerusalem. Only those intending to worship in Samaria are welcome. This is a blow. We now have no option but to loop eastward and rejoin the Galileans as they walk down the Jordan Valley. Michael, as well as John and James, offered to demolish Ginae with fire from heaven. Jesus told the young brothers not to be so stupid and I passed the message on to Michael. None the less, this is a terrible disappointment. Jesus will now have to enter Jerusalem in the middle of the crowd of Galilean pilgrims and at the height of their nationalistic fervour. (It is usual for Jews arriving at Passover to make a symbolic protest against the Roman occupation.) Those who want to crown Jesus as King of the Jews will be delighted. This is precisely what we had hoped to avoid.

Night time

This morning Jesus was walking fast and with purpose. This afternoon his progress was depressingly slow. There is no chance of crossing the River Jordan before the Galileans and so no chance of reaching Jerusalem before them. James suggested that we slip past them during the night. Jesus said nothing. Peter explained what everyone knew to be true, 'Someone is bound to see us, and if they see the Teacher travelling at night they will all break camp and follow us.' Andrew finished off, 'And if the Romans hear of large numbers of Jews travelling through the night, they will drop on us like hail on winter wheat.'

Everyone is dispirited. Jesus is anxious. I tried to divert his mind by reminding him of his own instruction, 'Do not be anxious . . .' He flatly pointed out, 'I said, "Do not be anxious about your *life*." It is not about my *life* that I am concerned . . .' He was shushed to silence by an equally anxious Archangel Michael.

Next morning

Michael, Gabriel and I discussed our options while the humans slept. Maff joined us with the news that Jesus' mother, Mary, is with the Galilean travellers and is hoping to see her son during the feast. Maff believes her to be unaware that the time has come for our main event. That is comforting for us because her thoughts and fears could easily leave clues for the Opposition.

This morning, before the sun was up, Jesus joined us. I think he was pleased to have our company – his human friends are too frightened to be much comfort at present. He asked after his mother and quizzed Maff about the mood of the Galileans. He was disturbed to hear Maff's reply. They are very excited and there is much talk of heroic victory against Rome, followed by lower taxes under King Jesus.

Gabriel had an interesting idea.

'They need to be distracted into more appropriate thoughts,' he announced. 'I suggest that the Son catches up with them as soon as possible and starts teaching again.' He then spoke directly to Jesus. 'Remind them of the true nature of your Kingdom.'

'You don't understand the human mind,' the Son replied. 'Once a group of men set their mind on a particular goal, it's very hard to divert them from it.'

'Then don't just talk to them,' Gabriel suggested. 'Give them something to do. Send them into the villages of Perea to heal sick people. That should keep their minds off battles and budget forecasts.'

'It probably won't work,' Jesus observed, 'but it's worth a try. The more people who enter Jerusalem with healing on their minds the better.'

'May I make a suggestion?' Maff interrupted, rather self-conscious at being an ordinary Angel in the company of three Archangels and the Son. We all looked at him.

'The Galileans will be crossing the River Jordan this morning and so they will be gathered on the west bank, waiting for their turn to wade across. Once they are over, they will spread out along the road. If you want to talk with them, Sir, you need to get down into the valley as soon as humanly possible.'

'Let's go,' Jesus said and leapt up to wake his companions.

'I thought we wanted to avoid the crowd!' observed a half-asleep Peter.

'There's been a change of plan,' Jesus replied. 'And we need to get to the Jordan crossing as soon as possible. We'll eat breakfast as we go.'

Mid morning

The path down into the Jordan Valley was easy going for human legs. I was interested to share Jesus' feeling of relief when he entered the sheltered orchards of the fertile plain, escaping the rays of the small yellow star that illuminates Earth's day.

The Galileans had already started crossing the river when we arrived, but there were still many hundreds of them waiting for their village name to be called. The reappearance of Jesus caused great excitement and they were delighted to listen to his teaching as they waited.

Jesus asked for volunteers – men and women free from family commitments and not needed for carrying heavy packs. As he had predicted to me earlier, it was the hotheads with swords in their bags who were first to offer their services. He quickly assembled nearly a hundred keen helpers and he is briefing them as I write.

'Go into the towns and villages ahead of us,' he has instructed them. 'When you enter a village, heal all those who are sick and tell them that God's Kingdom is near. Don't take any bag or purse with you, but accept whatever is offered as you go. Those who listen to you, are listening to me; those who reject you, are rejecting me, and the One who sent me.'

Now they are heading for the river, seventy-two of them in all. They have left behind their swords in their bags and are off on a mission of healing and peace. This could just work.

Nightfall

Jesus' new band of missionaries and the horde of travellers are all sleeping off the excitement and exhaustion of the day. As we passed each town, village and hamlet along the way, we were met by young men and women overjoyed to find that sick people really did get better at the name of Jesus of Nazareth.

One pair reported, 'Even the evil spirits submit to us in your name.'

Jesus gathered to himself as many of the young missionaries as were available and spoke to them earnestly.

'Don't rejoice that the spirits submit to you,' he said. 'Rejoice that your names are written in Heaven.'

They looked somewhat startled as their minds were directed away from Earthly matters and towards Heaven. For the moment, at least, their swords and daggers are forgotten.

I was with Jesus as he lay down tonight, his head resting on a pile of earth. For the first time in weeks I could feel a real joy in his spirit.

'Father,' he prayed, 'I thank you that you have hidden these things from the powerful and the educated and have revealed them to the young. It is a delight to see.'

Then he said to his twelve closest friends, huddled under their coats, 'I tell you, many kings and prophets longed to see what you are seeing – but didn't see it. How God has blessed your eyes!'

Next evening

Today followed the pattern the Son established yesterday. We made steady progress through the rich farmlands of the Jordan Valley. Jesus' seventy-two messengers raced ahead of us into farmsteads and hamlets, talking about Jesus and healing anyone who was sick. At the end of the day, after the camp was set up and food eaten, many of the Galilean people gathered round to hear Jesus teach.

Yesterday he taught them about prayer. Today he moved onto the subject of money, prompted, I think, by the jealous comments of Galilean hill farmers as they passed through the fertile plains of the Jordan. Jesus' story concerned a rich farmer who had stored up more grain than he could either eat or sell, but God visited him in the night and said, 'You fool! Your life ends tonight but what have you got to show for it?'

One more day

Another day, travelling on foot. Jesus walked at the very back of the Galileans with his twelve companions. His mood has been calm since we crossed the Jordan. Somehow he has felt safe on the far side of the river from Jerusalem and among his own people. The Twelve, on the other hand, have become more worried with every passing day. They have heard Jesus talking about arrest and death and, though they do not fully understand, they know they are walking into trouble.

'Don't worry,' he told them.

Picking a lily flower, he showed it to them. 'See how beautiful this is? It doesn't weave cloth or sow but my Dad clothes it, and it is better dressed even than King Solomon. If this is how God clothes a flower which blooms today and dries up tomorrow, don't you think he will look after you?'

I am amazed at the Son's lightness of spirit. I wondered if I was no longer linked into his emotions and expected that Jesus would still be struggling, but somewhere in his troubles he has found a deep well of his Father's love and is sharing it with those around him.

'Don't be afraid, little flock,' he told his catch of burly fishermen, 'Your Father is pleased to give you his Kingdom.'

As I write, Jesus is having supper with his family, sitting next to his mother. Angels are inclined to look down on human communication for being rather clumsy, but what a wonder it is to see mother and son side by side, sharing one another's deepest feelings. They have barely exchanged a word all evening and yet the interplay of their love for one another is devastatingly profound. I believe that I am seeing a tiny glimpse of what my Boss so loves in these awkward creatures.

The next day – a Sabbath

Today being the Sabbath, the travellers are staying put. (Jews don't travel on the seventh day of the week.) Those who are in the habit of regular worship descended on the local synagogue, whose leader was more than happy to leave the sermon to 'the renowned rabbi from Nazareth'. Oh, how Mary glowed with pride as her eldest son addressed the packed congregation! Jesus took his theme from the Exodus (when my Boss rescued the entire Jewish nation from slavery in Egypt). I was fascinated to study the different pictures which formed in the minds of the people as Jesus talked to them about that awful last night in Egypt when the first Passover meals were eaten.

The picture in Jesus' mind was of the Passover lamb lying helpless in the hands of its owner as its throat was cut and it bled to death. This was the only part of the story that he mentioned. However, across the synagogue, every mind imagined a different scene. The older men thought of the Israelites escaping captivity through the parted waters of the Red Sea. The young hotheads pictured the whole Egyptian army drowning as the waters returned to their usual position. Both groups looked at Jesus and saw him as the new Moses. The younger women, meanwhile, were drifting into the fantasy of so many Jewish girls, of marrying a man as strong and faithful as Moses. As they did, they considered to themselves that Jesus himself was not married yet and began to plan the reorganisation of his house in Capernaum for when they moved in. As for the older women, unless planning their daughter's marriage to Jesus, they were quickly distracted onto lists of all the things they would have to buy before they could cook their own Passover lamb in Jerusalem. In all that packed synagogue, as far as I could see, there was only one person who really grasped the meaning of Jesus' sermon. It was Mary, sitting in the women's section next to an old and crippled lady from a neighbouring village. As Mary looked in her imagination at that pathetic lamb being prepared for its death, she understood that her son's role in this drama would not be as the new Moses.

Their eyes met across the synagogue and, in that briefest moment of mother and son communication, Jesus realised that his message was too much for these excited peasants he loved so much. If they were to grasp that God's victory lies in the realm of faith and love rather than war and politics, he would have to show them. He stopped his sermon there and then and when all the eyes in the synagogue were on him, he called to the crippled woman seated beside his mother. Even when sitting down, this lady was clearly bent over forwards. When she stood up, the full measure of her disability became apparent because her back remained at a right angle to her legs. She shuffled forwards painfully, leaning on two crude sticks, her face lined with the pain and sadness of the past twenty years. But her eyes told a different story. They sparkled with the light of a faith that had grown with every agonising walk from her home to the synagogue to worship the God she had learned to love even more than she had loved her late husband.

There she stood before Jesus, patient and trusting. Jesus looked down at her and remembered a sermon he had preached nearly three years earlier. 'How blessed are the poor, for God's kingdom is theirs!'

He stepped out from behind the reading desk and stooped to take the lady by her hands. 'My dear woman,' he told her, looking into her encouraging eyes, 'You are set free from your disability.'

He slowly lifted her hands upwards and as he did, her back straightened. Local villagers and visiting Galileans watched, astounded. They had heard plenty of stories of Jesus healing people, but few, apart from those who had been cured themselves, had seen it happen. Jesus had been careful to do such things in private, away from idle eyes and gossiping mouths. On this occasion, though, he wanted people to see. He wanted them to gain some understanding of the real purpose of his mission, to put straight the centuries of twisted truths that have been the fruit of Opposition influence on the Earth.

Just as the congregation were about to break into spontaneous applause at the joy of this wonderful woman, dancing for the first time since her youth, the leader of the synagogue silenced them with an angry assault on the elderly widow.

'Are there not six days in the week for working?' he raged. 'Come and get yourself healed then – and *not* on the Sabbath.'

A wave of shock froze the faces of the startled congregation. Every mind in the synagogue asked the same question. How could he launch such an attack on such a lovely woman after such a wonderful occurrence?

Jesus stood behind the woman, folding his arms around her shoulders. His reply to the synagogue leader was the first airing of his most recent thoughts about how to handle the Jewish leaders in Jerusalem.

'You hypocrite!' he declared sternly.

The congregation held its breath at such strong language.

'Do you give your donkey water on the Sabbath day?'

Not a word was said; the answer was obvious. Livestock has to be fed every day of the week, Sabbath or not.

'Then should not this woman, a daughter of Abraham, whom Satan has kept bound for many long years, be set free on the Sabbath day?'

The leader sat down, red-faced and defeated. Jesus returned to his sermon. Now every ear in the building was listening as he likened the expansion of his Father's kingdom to the steady growth of a tiny mustard seed into a large bush.

When the service ended, the villagers swarmed around the diminutive widow Jesus had cured and the Galileans followed Jesus back to their camp rather as sheep follow their shepherd over the mountains. The synagogue leader sat alone, humiliated, considering in his mind all the things he had heard about the irreverent rabble rouser from Nazareth. I stayed with him as he picked up the pieces of his shattered pride and I knew that news of Jesus' activities would soon get to Jerusalem.

That afternoon

After a traditional Sabbath lunch of stale bread and leftover vegetables, Jesus found himself in the middle of a large crowd of Galileans, augmented by a few dozen locals. All of them wanted to hear more from the man who could heal a sick woman and silence a mean-minded rabbi. He spoke to them in stories and images, urging them to commit their lives and their love to his Father and warning them to avoid being shut out of the Kingdom. It was like earlier days on the shore of Galilee except that there was an urgency in Jesus' spirit.

At one point in the afternoon the son of the synagogue ruler, himself one of the Pharisees (a group of Jews who take their religious observance extremely seriously) came to Jesus to warn him that arrest and even death were being planned for him by the Pharisees and other religious leaders in Jerusalem.

'Leave this place,' the young man urged, 'and go somewhere else.'

'I must keep going today and tomorrow and the next day,' Jesus replied. 'For surely, no prophet can die outside Jerusalem!'

The mention of Death caused a stir in the large crowd and Jesus' words were whispered outwards to the edge of the gathering. Each person made their own interpretation of what he meant: some that he was bravely defying the authorities; others that he was giving in; many concluded that he was simply teasing the sombre Pharisee. Beside me, Michael shuddered at the possibility that Jesus might be revealing more information than is safe or sensible. My own feelings, still closely linked to those of the Son, were melancholy acceptance of a sad truth.

Jesus expressed it better than I could have. He stood up and looked towards the Judean mountains that rise sharply from the Jordan Valley towards the setting sun. Then, with his eyes closed, he said, 'O Jerusalem, Jerusalem, you who killed the prophets and stoned those sent to you! How often I have longed to gather your children together, as a hen gathers her chicks under her wings, but you were not willing! Now, look, your house is destroyed.'

He walked through the crowd and off on his own. None of his disciples or family attempted to follow him and neither did I.

Night time

Shortly after the sun disappeared behind the mountains, marking the end of the Sabbath, a servant girl came into the Galilean camp from the village. She asked where Jesus was and was directed towards the river where he sat, motionless, on a large boulder, looking into the patterns on the surface of the water. I followed. She was from the household of the young Pharisee who had visited Jesus in the afternoon. He wished to invite Jesus to join his family for the celebratory end of Sabbath meal. Jesus was unsure whether or not to accept the invitation and looked to me for a second opinion. I conferred with Michael and then, communicating spirit to spirit, said that the young man had been genuine in his desire to help Jesus; I was confident that it was not a trap.

There is a deepening vulnerability in my Master. Darts of fear frequently flash through his mind and I feel each one of them in my own being. His face tightens each time he braces himself against imagined enemies.

'I will go, if you come with me,' he said. As he walked towards the grey darkness of the early evening, following the girl, we were both doubly alert to every movement and sound. In the busy streets of the village, we proceeded as if an ambush lay in wait for us around every corner.

The girl led us into a large, warmly lit home, furnished with carved wood and deep, embroidered cushions. Josephus, the young Pharisee, greeted Jesus with a firm and welcoming handshake and introduced him to his expensively dressed wife and three young children. As we entered the main room, all set for a rich man's feast, four other men, each identifiable as a Pharisee from their style of dress, stood to greet the visitor. They were all nervous about meeting Jesus. I whispered, 'They are more afraid of you than you are of them.'

Joseph, Nicodemus, Ananias and Gamaliel were from Jerusalem and had travelled down to try to meet with Jesus before he set foot in the city. Their minds were open to his message and their fear was not of Jesus himself but of their colleagues discovering that they had met with him. For all this, Jesus did not relax.

'Secret sympathisers are fragile souls,' he informed me. 'Don't leave me, Oriel.'

The food, by all accounts, was excellent, and the children, for the short while before being sent to bed, were a welcome distraction from the intense conversation at the table. Jesus was invited to visit six-year-old Barnabas' bedroom. He was transformed as he escaped from the studious gaze of the Jewish intellectuals. He threw himself playfully onto Barnabas' cushioned bed. The two of them laughed and played together; then, without warning, Barnabas said, 'Daddy says they're going to kill you.'

Jesus was startled at the boy's straightforwardness.

'Yes, they are,' he replied.

The two were quiet for a moment, then Jesus asked, 'What do you think I should do about it?'

The child sat up straight and sucked his finger thoughtfully. 'I think you should go up to Jerusalem and tell them not to be so silly,' he said.

'I think I shall,' Jesus replied.

He prayed with the boy and blessed him before returning to the nervousness of the dinner table.

An awkward silence was shattered by a crash as Ananias dropped his wine cup onto the table. There was a scurry of servants trying to mop up the spill while minimising the embarrassment of the unfortunate guest. Ananias had some kind of physical impediment which caused his body to shake and in the nervous silence since Jesus' return this had grown worse until he spilt his wine.

Jesus posed a question. 'Is it lawful to heal on the Sabbath or not?'

All five Pharisees had been in the synagogue that morning. They said nothing. Jesus reached out his hand and firmly gripped Ananias' shaking arm. Stillness spread through the man's body, like the rising sun warming a frosted garden, until his entire being was filled with a warm restfulness it had not known for many years. I watched Ananias' brittle faith respond to the strength of Jesus' love. His face was the last part of him to be affected. It flushed from pale grey to a healthy pink; he smiled.

The other guests still did not speak. Jesus did.

'If one of you has a donkey that falls into a well on the Sabbath day, will you not immediately pull him out?'

No reply. Each knew that Ananias had been fully healed. They simply could not reconcile their lifelong commitment to religious tradition with the outrageous simplicity of Jesus.

Then he told them a story about a rich man who held a banquet for many guests – but the guests made excuses and did not come. So the man sent his servant into the streets to bring in the poor and the crippled and the blind instead.

I looked into their thoughts as they sucked on sweet, juice-laden fruits from the table. They understood that the kingdom which Jesus proclaimed was very different from the one they govern from the council chamber in Jerusalem, but they were afraid to step down from the pedestals of wealth, privilege and status upon which they stood.

The silent struggle was disturbed by the sound of voices entering Josephus' courtyard. Everyone looked nervously around, not least Jesus. He sent me out to see what was happening. I found a small group of richly dressed and rather drunk tax collectors. The bright colours of their imported clothes were a sharp contrast to the black wool worn by the Pharisees. At the head of this merry bunch was Jesus' friend, Matthew, who had spent a rowdy evening telling his former colleagues all about his new life as a follower of the famous Teacher from Nazareth. They had decided to come and meet him for themselves and so had arrived, uninvited, at the home of one of their most entrenched critics.

The man of the house tried hard to keep the irreverent visitors out, lest the entire building become ritually unclean from their presence. It was not long before traditional insults began to fly in both directions. When I informed Jesus that it was Matthew with a few friends, he picked up the wine jug from the table, placed it on a tray with some cups and carried the tray into the courtyard. In the moment of calm which greeted his arrival, he said, 'Let's talk out here, it's a lovely evening.'

Jesus then suggested to his host, 'Bring your guests out to join us so we can all talk together.' He looked into the jug and added, 'There's plenty here for everyone.' They did not come.

Jesus delighted Matthew's friends with his stories: of a lost sheep whose owner holds a party to celebrate its return; of a young man who leaves home and squanders his father's money on parties, only to be welcomed with open arms when he walks home, penniless and humiliated. These men, who had made their fortunes by overtaxing their fellow countrymen, were entranced to learn that although they had earned the hatred of their neighbours, they were still loved and valued by God.

For the sake of his other audience, listening from behind the dining room curtains, Jesus added to this last story a part about a jealous elder brother who resented the celebrations in honour of his extravagant sibling. 'You are always with me,' the father told his indignant elder son. 'Everything I have is yours, but we had to celebrate tonight because your brother was lost – and now he is found.'

Everyone has now retired to their beds, each with much to think about. Jesus returned to the camp calmer than he had left it, thanks to Matthew and his band of honest (spiritually at least) men.

Sunday morning

The Galilean camp erupted into a fury of activity at first light. There was extra packing to be done after the weekend stop; older travellers were anxious about climbing the long and hazardous Jericho road; and the young ones were excited at the prospect of entering the Holy City of Jerusalem by the end of the day. Jesus, having almost nothing to pack, acquired a small audience of young children who had escaped from their stressed parents. He was well into a dramatised retelling of the story of Jonah – the part where the escaping prophet sinks 'deeper and deeper and deeper and deeper into the angry ocean' (I remember that day only too well and it didn't feel very entertaining at the time!), when Thomas and Simon arrived with a delegation of irate parents and tried to shoo the children away.

Above parental cries of, 'So that's where you've been, you little jackal!' Thomas took control of the situation and announced, 'Children, the Teacher has very important things on his mind and he could do without you pestering him. Now please leave him in peace.'

Jesus was indignant.

'Wait, wait, wait, wait, wait,' he called, trying to stop the parents from dragging their offspring back into the family arguments. 'Please let the children stay with me and don't take them away. My Father's Kingdom belongs to children like these.'

The parents were, in fact, only too happy to leave their little ones in Jesus' impromptu crèche while they returned to adult concerns. Thomas and Simon remained rather sheepishly at the back.

'The fact is,' Jesus continued, looking at his two followers,

135

'unless you welcome my Father's Kingdom like a child does, you will never enter it.'

The two men carefully sat themselves, cross-legged, on the ground. The children watched disinterestedly and then turned back to Jesus who slowly raised both his arms high in the air and suddenly flung them downwards, saying a very loud, *'Splash!'* The whale had arrived.

As Jesus' story reached its conclusion, his audience had grown in both size and average age. The account of how those ancient enemies of the Jews, the people of Ninevah, had turned to God in prayer and humility, gave the travellers a faint hope that even the cruel might of the Roman Empire could be broken by the words of a great prophet. Almost without exception the adults looked at Jesus, seated in a ring of enthralled children, and wondered if just such a miracle might take place, this year, in Jerusalem.

A voice came from the back of the crowd – a clear, young, cultured voice.

'Good Teacher, what must I to do to gain eternal life?'

Heads turned to identify the questioner. It was Josephus, Jesus' host from last night. He glowed with enthusiasm as he stood upright, awaiting a reply. To see one of the law-bound Pharisees so openly associating himself with Jesus was an interesting development. The significance was not lost on the cynical Galileans. I, too, wondered whether this might lead to a change in our plan.

'Perhaps,' I thought, 'if Josephus and his four friends were to throw in their lot with Jesus, our journey to Jerusalem might have a different end to the one expected.' With my Boss, stories often take unexpected turns.

Jesus showed himself to be his Father's Son with an unexpected reply.

'Why do you call me *good?*' he asked. 'Surely, only God is utterly good?'

My bubble of anticipation popped. I looked into Jesus' mind and saw there the image of a great fruit tree bearing one solitary blossom. I understood his thought: the blooming of one flower comes a long time before the celebrations of a safely gathered harvest. Josephus did not answer Jesus' question; he was startled that his modestly flattering term of address should be treated so harshly. Jesus reminded him of the Ten Commandments and Josephus replied, as any self-respecting Pharisee would, that he had kept them all his life.

The children fiddled with pebbles in the dirt and the adults watched the wealthy Pharisee cautiously while Jesus measured his reply.

'There is just one thing that you lack.' He spoke clearly and with authority. We waited to hear what it might be that this wealthy and well educated man might still need.

'Go home, sell everything you own, give all the money to the poor, and then come with me.'

Josephus stood as if frozen. He thought of his bright children and beautiful wife, and the adrenaline which had flooded his veins froze too. But still, in his heart, there was warm faith.

Jesus spoke again to that lingering glow.

'You will have great treasure in Heaven.'

Icy fear prevailed. Josephus couldn't do it. Too many things held him to his present life. He knew very well what was awaiting Jesus at the end of this day's walk, in Jerusalem. He could not risk being part of it. He turned round and walked home. The Galileans returned to their packing and Jesus watched the proud young Pharisee disappear into the tangled weeds of wealth and privilege. He knew that they would never meet again, ever, and that knowledge made him very sad.

Later in the morning

When everyone was ready to leave, Jesus strode out ahead with his twelve loyal followers. Many of the travellers saw in him the marks of a leader and imagined the day when he might lead a Jewish militia to victory against Rome. Archangel Michael, on the other hand, saw danger. The Jericho to Jerusalem road is notorious bandit country. The steep and twisting track gives ample opportunity for thieves to attack cash-laden travellers heading for the city. By striding out ahead, Jesus would be making himself an easy target, once he reached the hills. Michael asked me for permission to clear the road of any dangers. I considered the possibilities and allowed him to neutralise any common thieves – but only common thieves.

'If the religious leaders or the Opposition have laid any kind of a trap or ambush, you must let it be,' I insisted.

'What about leopards or mountain lions?' Michael enquired.

I smiled and said nothing. Michael took his small force away and I joined Jesus, who asked, 'Oriel, how should I enter Jerusalem? I am not sure.'

'Aren't you going to walk?' I asked, not entirely understanding the question.

'Human minds judge a great many things by how they look,' he observed. 'The way they see me enter their city will have a considerable influence on what they do next.'

'How would the ordinary people like you to do it?' I probed.

'You know that better than me. You hear their thoughts and see their spirits.'

'The Galileans want you to ride on a war-horse with a spear in your hand,' I replied.

Jesus was thoughtful. 'The Jewish and Roman leaders want me to arrive anonymously in the crowd, and to remain so.'

He walked silently, replaying the two images in his mind.

'Well, that is two possibilities ruled out,' he concluded.

'Can you not do what you are doing now?' I asked. 'Walk on ahead with your disciples. It would show you to be independent and in the lead, strong but not looking for a battle.'

'It would also make it very easy for them to arrest me there and then. I am not ready for that.'

Then Jesus simply closed his mind to the issue. He looked down at his feet and thought only of walking and of the road, focusing on the sensation of each bump and dip in the well worn track. I withdrew and joined the Twelve. They, too, were discussing what impression Jesus would make on the people of Jerusalem.

As the lowland town of Jericho came into view, Jesus stopped and waited for his companions. They could see he had something to tell them.

'When we get to Jerusalem,' he began, 'everything written about the Son in the scriptures will be fulfilled. He will be handed over to the Romans, they will laugh at him, insult him, attack him and eventually they will kill him.'

The group walked on in silence for some distance. The disciples did not know who Jesus meant by 'the Son' and Jesus did not attempt to explain.

'And on the third day, he will rise again.'

The disciples still walked on, wondering what their leader was trying to tell them. I too was wondering, wondering what the leader of the Opposition would make of such an announcement.

He has been plotting Jesus' death for so long; how would he react to hear the Son predict his own demise so plainly?

The midday rest

The morning's walk had been fast and flat, a straight road through the fertile fields of the Jordan plain. The travellers made their last pause before the sheer hard work of their annual climb up, up and up into the Judean mountains. Somewhere up there, Michael and his team were searching the caves and crevices for potential danger. Meanwhile, down here, the morning ended with the feel of a carnival.

The Jerusalem road runs through the middle of Jericho, a prosperous town that has grown rich on the passing trade. The people of Jericho, who pride themselves on being quite different from the inhabitants of Jerusalem, were pleased to crowd into the street and welcome Jesus. Any Jew distrusted by Jerusalem is a friend in Jericho and they knew well enough that the authorities in the capital were looking to arrest the Galilean teacher.

As the long line of pilgrims approached the city, it became clear that Jesus' arrival was anticipated. Workers in the fields left their tools and crossed to the road to shake his hand and wish him well. The nearer they came to the town, the more often this happened, and we saw several people sprint ahead to tell of his coming. Jesus calmly paused to take a drink and allow others to go on ahead. He then melted into the middle of the procession.

At the town gate, in his usual place, sat a blind man called Bartimaeus. He was begging for enough food to see him and his family through another day. He had sensed the excitement in Jericho but, as usual, nobody thought to tell him what was happening. When a third pair of hurrying sandled feet slapped past him, he asked what was going on and was told, 'Jesus of Nazareth is passing through.'

Bartimaeus could not conceal his excitement. He had heard plenty of stories about this Jesus and how he made blind people see. He waited impatiently for the famous healer to come, confident that his days of blindness, humiliation and poverty were at an end.

Those at the front of the Galilean travellers, meanwhile, were

139

swelling with pride as they realised the fame and popularity of their rabbi. They were usually considered with suspicion by wary southerners but today, with Jesus in their number, they were welcomed like a homecoming and victorious army. This was a moment to be savoured and remembered.

As they approached the town gates, the cry of a blind beggar shouting, 'Jesus, Son of David, have mercy on me!' was not what they wanted to hear. As each group passed, they shushed at the man whose voice was raised over the murmured conversations of the people. But the more Bartimaeus was told to be quiet, the louder he shouted until his voice carried down the road to Jesus. The Son stopped and asked for the caller to be brought to him. Those at the gate soon received the message and said to Bartimaeus, 'Cheer up! He's calling for you.'

Bartimaeus was on his feet in a moment. Flinging off his coat he plunged through the crowd, guided by a forest of arms that passed him from person to person until he was halted by two firm hands which grasped his shoulders. A voice asked, 'What do you want me to do for you?'

Bartimaeus did not need to ask who it was. It felt to him as if all the prayers he had ever prayed had been gathered into a large bucket and were now being poured over him like a shower of clear water. He smiled like a child and announced in a voice reinforced with honest faith, 'Rabbi, I want to see.'

I looked around the crowd. It was as if every face was a mirror which reflected Bartimaeus' radiant smile, and none more clearly than Jesus himself.

'Go,' the Son said, his face pink with joy, 'Your faith has healed you.'

Immediately, Bartimaeus' darkness cleared and his first sight in many years was the smiling face of Jesus. The two embraced, the people cheered and the procession into Jericho continued.

News of Bartimaeus' healing raced ahead of Jesus, fanning the flames of excitement. What might have been polite applause for Jerusalem's enemy and Jericho's friend flared into cheers and shouts as the town celebrated the miracle performed at its gate. The Galileans loved it – Jesus was their hero – and I found myself being caught up in their enthusiasm. For every human on that road there was a guardian Angel and every Angel rejoiced to see their Creator and Master so energetically fêted by these people. The inhabitants of Jericho have never been renowned for their spirituality; their lives are mostly devoted to the accumulation of money. To Angel eyes such people are faint and colourless, but the arrival of Jesus brought new colour to their souls. This was the greatest act of worship these dispirited Angels had ever witnessed in this greedy town and they were delighted.

We passed through the town square and on into a shaded avenue, lined with large, painted houses. As we entered the avenue I spotted the steady glow of a man, perched in the branches of a tree. I have seen the type before, the cool light of one who prays secretly, someone who has faith they dare not show. Among all the merchants and traders of Jericho this one man stood out to my gaze and I pointed him out to the Son. Jesus walked up to the tree and stopped, looking up into the foliage. Matthew pushed his way to Jesus' side and whispered into his ear, 'His name is Zacchaeus, he's the head tax collector here. He's extremely rich, utterly ruthless and thoroughly hated.' Jesus smiled.

'Zacchaeus!' Jesus called. 'Come down from there.'

A short, fat man puffed his way towards the ground, helped by Peter's strong arms. He nodded to Matthew and looked up at the much taller figure of Jesus.

'My friends and I,' Jesus continued, 'would like to have lunch at your house today.'

'It would be a pleasure,' said the breathless tax collector, leading the way through a gate in the high wall that lined the road. When the gate clicked shut, pandemonium broke out in the street. The Galileans were confused because they usually stopped for lunch just outside the town owing to the fact that the locals neither trusted nor liked the coarse northern crowd. The people of Jericho were enraged that Jesus should spurn their welcome and visit the house of the most despised and notorious inhabitant of the town. Nobody knew what to do and so they all did nothing. They simply stayed where they were and waited to see what would happen next.

Inside the wall, Jesus and the Twelve were seated in the cool of Zacchaeus' fabulous, marble pillared villa. As I write, they are drinking imported wine and eating cured meats – food only Matthew has ever experienced before. A welcome change from the usual traveller's fare of dried fruit and stale bread.

Late afternoon

The lunch break, though sumptuous, was brief. The pilgrims had the hardest stage of their journey before them and could not waste time. Zacchaeus spent precious minutes in deep conversation with the Son and when the time came to leave he called out the manager of his household and led his guests back to the small door in his great wall. The Galileans and Jerichites were immediately alert when they heard the door open. But before they could speak a word, Zacchaeus addressed them.

'In the past,' he declared, 'I have cheated many of you in many ways. But today I have resolved to donate half of all my possessions to the poorest people of this town, beginning with the beggars who sit at our gates.'

A murmur of shock and disbelief spread across the crowd.

'In addition,' Zacchaeus continued, 'all those of you I have cheated can make an appointment with my assistant here, and he will repay you four times the amount I owe you.'

A great roar of appreciation broke out and Zacchaeus stood, calmly watching the effect he was having on the people who used to hate him so vigorously. I watched the tax collector. Here was a man who had explored the emptiness of wealth to its very depths; a man who acquired so much and knew it all to be worthless. Jesus had opened the door to the elegant prison that Zacchaeus had built around his own life, and now he spoke quietly into the tax collector's ear while the crowd's eruption continued. Zacchaeus smiled boyishly, embraced his dumbfounded employee and then followed Jesus onto the road. Jesus had invited Zacchaeus to accompany him on the journey to Jerusalem.

Once again, Jesus walked on ahead. The meeting with Zacchaeus had brought him great joy, but now his mind turned again to his arrival in the city. Remembering that we had a question still to answer, I joined him.

'Oriel,' he said, as soon as he noticed my presence, 'Human wealth and worldly power are such powerful poisons; I must enter Jerusalem in a way that denies them both.'

As he walked, Jesus scanned his mind across the heavy scrolls of Jewish scripture that he had studied all his life, looking among them for a suitable precedent.

'Am I right in thinking,' he asked suddenly, 'that when we

visited Mary, Martha and Lazarus a few months ago, one of their donkeys was pregnant?'

'I'm sorry but I don't take much interest in such things.'

'Yes, I'm sure it was.' He thought for a moment, then said, 'That's what I'll do. I will ride into Jerusalem on a young donkey.'

The pilgrims climbed quietly, their minds busied with the simple effort of raising their fragile bodies upwards with each step, drawn onwards by the promise of their holy city with all its history and tradition. As the afternoon proceeded, the line of pilgrims spread out, Jesus always at the front. The effort of the climb combined with the notorious danger of the road's bandits kept the people in subdued mood.

Near the end of the journey, as we approached the village of Bethany, Jesus once again stopped to let his loyal followers catch him up. He spoke to the first two that joined him, Bartholomew and Judas.

'Go into the village, and in the vineyard next to the large house there, you should find a young donkey. Could you please fetch the animal for me?'

'Master,' asked an anxious Bartholomew, 'Wouldn't that be stealing? What should we say if someone asks what we are doing?'

Jesus smiled at the man's honesty. 'The colt belongs to my good friend Lazarus. If anyone asks you, say, "My Master needs it and will bring it back this evening".'

The two trotted into the village and Jesus returned to the road, accompanied by young John who was content to share his Master's silence. Behind them, from among the Galileans, began the traditional Songs of Ascent, sung every year as the pilgrims approach Jerusalem for Passover. Not far along the road we came to the place where travellers wait for one another. The moment that the Jews reach the top of the Mount of Olives and look across Kidron Valley to the Temple is a very emotional one. It is a moment that families like to share together, and so everyone slows, waiting for others to catch up.

Late Sunday evening

Gradually the number of assembled Galilean pilgrims grew as the travellers completed the hardest part of their week-long journey.

One of the last to arrive was an elderly woman, quite beautiful in her faith and her courage. She was utterly determined to complete this, her last Passover pilgrimage, on her own. As she approached the scattered forms of her younger co-travellers, she was greeted with warm applause and shouts of congratulation. In reply, she called out, 'Come on you lot, no time to sit around, we're not there yet.' To a chorus of groans, stiff and tired limbs were pressed into action once more and as they did, Bartholomew and Judas arrived, pulling Lazarus' young donkey.

The people looked on, intrigued, as the nervous creature was brought to Jesus. For a moment I wished that I had called for Hagogue, our donkey expert. This creature had not yet been ridden or put to work and looked like she might bolt at any moment, leaving Jesus covered with cuts and bruises. That is definitely not part of my Boss's plan.

Judas removed his coat and placed it on the donkey's back. He then helped Jesus to mount the animal. Seeing this, the other Galileans quickly understood that Jesus intended to make some kind of public statement by his entry into Jerusalem. They, too, began to remove their coats and placed them on the road, making a many-coloured carpet for the inexperienced donkey to follow. Before long the aching walkers had forgotten their tiredness and were caught up in the excitement of the moment. They began to sing again, and this time they sang a song about a victorious king, returning in triumph to the City of Jerusalem. The identity of their King was quite clear in the rather ridiculous sight of the tall man riding a small donkey. The animal played its part with composure and dignity, carrying its load along the road into Jerusalem.

In just a few minutes they reached the brow of the hill overlooking the city. Grouped in families, the Galileans stood in silent awe, looking down on the place where, according to their traditions, my Boss – their God – chooses to live. Jesus, surrounded by his followers, looked beyond the grand stonework of the Temple to the muddled streets of the city. He looked towards the hostility and suspicion that he knew was waiting for him in those houses, and tears welled up in his eyes.

'O Jerusalem,' he said quietly, under his breath, 'If only you knew, today, what would bring you peace. But your eyes are blind.'

As they surveyed this scene, Michael joined me. He and I saw what Jesus' human eyes could not, though I believe he could feel it in his spirit: the streets of Jerusalem were crowded with Opposition spirits, like bees in a hive. I was shocked to see that the queen bee – the leader of the Opposition, my former colleague, Lucifer – had set up his rebel court in the great courtyard of the Temple itself. The Court of the Gentiles, built as a place for people of all nations to meet their Creator, had become the headquarters of humanity's most dangerous enemy.

I said to Michael, 'If the Son follows the pattern of his previous visits to this city, that Temple is exactly where he'll go first.'

'I know,' he replied.

'You must leave your troops here,' I instructed him. 'To take them into the heart of that,' I pointed at the Temple, 'would bring disaster. Say nothing and do nothing. Tonight we will meet with our Boss.' Michael went to speak to his militia.

The pilgrims began to make their way down the hill, again singing their victory song. Jesus rode in the middle of the crowd, deep in thought. Some Pharisees pushed their way towards him through the crowd and complained at the people's choice of song. Jesus looked at them wearily, comparing their petty legalism with the faithful enthusiasm of the ordinary Galileans.

'If they keep quiet,' he replied, 'the stones along this road will take up their song.'

The men looked at Jesus impatiently, as if he had gone quite mad, and turned away. But I reflected that these ancient mountains, formed so long before the birth of humanity, would indeed sing praise to their Creator if they could understand his purpose as he rode slowly past.

At the bottom of the valley the road climbs briefly until it reaches the eastern gate of the Temple. Word had reached the crowds inside that the renowned preacher, Jesus of Nazareth, was riding into the city, and hundreds of pilgrims poured out to greet him. They tore palm branches from the trees which lined the route; some waved them, others laid them on the road. All joined the triumphal song that the Galileans had begun.

Jesus, I think, barely noticed the effect his arrival was having. His mind was fixed on the road ahead, on what waited for him inside the Temple gate. The Court of the Gentiles was indeed a hive of activity. The Feast of Passover is peak season for the Jerusalem tourist industry and there are vast amounts of money to be made, exchanging currency and selling animals for use in the week's religious rituals. Such greed is fertile soil for the seeds that the Opposition sow in people's souls, the seeds of choking weeds that strangle faith and love, and ultimately rob human beings of life, destroying their God-given spirits.

Jesus dismounted the donkey and asked Bartholomew to tie it up somewhere safe. He entered the Temple on foot. The leading priests had emerged from their offices to watch him. They were smug with the rich takings of the Passover season, but also afraid of what Jesus might do to their carefully developed business. They were right to be afraid. Jesus picked up a rope from the floor and walked around the vast courtyard, tying knots in the rope as he went. (He has learned something from his three years in the company of fishermen.) When he had finished knotting the rope, he made his way through the crowd to the tables where the priestly staff exchanged foreign currencies for the official coinage of the Temple. He joined the queue and waited, watched by the anxious priests. The leader of the Opposition stayed back, confident that he had the Son utterly outnumbered and impatient to see what he intended to do.

Jesus reached the front of the queue and the cashier looked up, waiting for him to produce some money. The high priest and his staff floated in their black robes towards the scene, watching intently. Jesus looked at them.

'It is said,' he began quietly, *'this Temple is a house of prayer for all nations* – but you have made it into a convention for thieves!'

With that, Jesus took hold of the cash-laden table and threw it on its side. Money of all denominations flew and rolled across the stone floor, causing cashiers, priests and visitors to dive in, grabbing what they could. The leader of the Opposition boomed with laughter at this sudden display of greed and violence. Jesus had not finished. He moved to a table of caged doves and did the same thing. While the people were still on their knees fighting for money, hundreds of white doves escaped their doom on the Temple altars and flew back and forth above the commotion. Next came the pens filled with 'unblemished' sheep, especially bred for the Passover meals at the end of the week. Now Jesus employed the rope which he had carefully knotted into a whip. Within seconds, flocks of liberated sheep were skipping and jumping their way round the courtyard in search of pasture. The other stall holders were hurriedly packing up their goods as Jesus strode purposefully around the market. No table was left unturned, sacks full of coins were grabbed and flung into the mob. Opposition spirits raced among the people, stirring them to greater heights of selfishness, stimulating arguments and squabbles.

The religious leaders observed the chaos, numbed by the colossal financial losses they faced. The leader of the Opposition watched it all from the top of the great gatehouse, amused and entertained. Jesus himself was calm and determined, as his bewildered disciples trotted along behind him. This was no act of sudden fury. He had been planning this moment for years, ever since he first came to Passover as a boy. If the Jewish leaders would not listen to his teaching, he would show them what his Father's Kingdom was about and it was not about returning a profit from people's prayers.

When every table had been turned on its side and every sacrificial animal released, Jesus calmly said, 'It's time to go.' The donkey was where Bartholomew had left it, tied to a palm tree near the Temple gate, rubbing its side against the coarse trunk. Jesus untied it and led the animal back up the road to Bethany where he had arranged to stay with his friends, Lazarus, Mary and Martha.

Late that evening

Tired from their journey, Jesus and his friends were soon asleep after the meal Martha had prepared. It interests me that despite all the danger that surrounds the Son and presses on his mind, the weariness of his body has a greater influence. I would have expected him to lie awake, considering all the possible crises and confrontations of the coming days. But instead, he was asleep within moments – a deep and carefree release brought on by the considerable struggle of bringing his body up from the Jordan Valley into the Judean Hills.

I must now leave him to his dreamless sleep. I have a meeting with my Boss in the Temple. As Jesus' mother is also staying in Bethany with Lazarus, I have invited Maff to come with me. His insight will be useful in the days ahead.

Early the next morning

The Holy of Holies is the innermost sanctuary of the Temple. It is the actual place, according to Jewish tradition, where my Boss lives. The truth is that the Chief Priests have long since abandoned their devotion to their God, and live for wealth and power; my Boss rarely considers it to be a place where he is made to feel 'at home'. It is a bare, empty space, separated from the Court of Priests by a vast curtain.

'Is this curtain here to protect the people from seeing our Boss?' Maff asked. 'Or is it here to protect our Boss from seeing the abominable corruption of the priests?'

'It is there to keep me at a safe distance, so that I do not touch their lives more deeply than they can bear,' replied the voice whose song is the entire created Universe. 'But its days are numbered.'

This was to be a Great Council. With my Boss and the Director were the three other Archangels: Gabriel, Raphael and Michael. Michael was anxious about Lucifer being so close, in his temporary headquarters, in the outer court of the Temple.

'He may be close in the human measure of distance,' our Boss declared, 'But he is separated from us by the prayers of centuries of faithful Jews. In here, were you to bellow at your very loudest, the Lost One would not hear so much as a whisper.'

Each of us reported what we had learned. Michael has been assessing the strength and strategic positioning of the Opposition. Gabriel's task has been to stir up the prayers of all faithful people who are awaiting the fulfilment of our Boss's plan. Raphael, to my surprise, has been listening to the Opposition, quietly and patiently gathering intelligence about their intentions.

It is neither possible nor wise to record for you here the detail of our conference. Angelic minds and spiritual intercourse exist on so many different levels that human words cannot not begin to express. Needless to say, our minds were focussed on our Boss's great plan for humanity and every step of the way we considered the counter-plans of the Opposition. More than that I cannot say – but for one essential detail: at every turn of the road, my Boss has left any final decision to his Son, and that is not in deference to his divine parentage but for the very opposite reason. Jesus is in ultimate command because he is *human*. In all of our earlier campaigns involving members of the human species, planning and decision-making has been the province of the Angels.

Humans are too narrow in their understanding and too weak in their wills to be able to direct the purposes of Heaven. Now, however, our Boss is doing something new; he is entrusting the power of eternity into the fragile hands and brief lives of men and women. Jesus, the son of Mary, is the firstfruit of this new harvest.

For us Angels, our instruction is the same as it has been throughout: we must watch, we must listen, we must keep one another informed. But we must not intervene, no matter how dreadful a turn events might take. The destiny of humanity has been placed into the hands of humanity. So, as I sit and write by Jesus' bedside, I cannot but ponder the shift in my responsibility. I am not here to protect him or advise him or defend him from the Opposition. My task is only to support him and encourage him.

Monday afternoon

The travellers slept late and had a leisurely breakfast before a brief visit to Jerusalem to pray in the Temple. The outer court-yard had been restored to its former status as a sheep market and international bank. Jesus' arrival prompted a flurry of activity on behalf of the Temple Guard who followed closely behind him wherever he went. Their eagerness was unnecessary as Jesus has no intention of repeating the chaos of yesterday. He has come to teach. He sat in a shaded corner with his twelve followers and talked with them about the future. He spoke of a new era in his Father's relations with humanity: of a time when he will work in the lives of ordinary people; a time when everyone will be called upon to account for their own life. As always, he taught them using stories: stories of bridesmaids whose lamps run out of oil before the wedding begins; stories of parties which the invited guests fail to join; stories of shepherds dividing and sorting their flocks.

His audience grew rapidly, from twelve to twenty, to fifty, to hundreds. People from across the Roman world and from Africa delighted in such simple teaching. Jesus was not detailing ever more laws to burden their lives, as is the way of the teachers of the Pharisees; he spoke of a God who loves his people and is prepar-ing for them a new and better life.

The high priest and his political allies watched anxiously, constrained by Jesus' popularity. They are used to the festival of Passover being their time, a time when the people need and value the services of their priests, but Jesus has muscled in on the moment and now the priests hate him all the more.

I have watched them with fascination while Jesus moved effortlessly from one story to another. They had made their decision to have Jesus killed before he even set foot in Jerusalem. Lucifer had whispered into their jealous minds over many months. Now Jesus is seated inside their own headquarters and their hatred is stronger than ever but they can do nothing because the crowds are on Jesus' side. To say even a harsh word to him might cause a riot.

Jesus will not stay for long. Tonight there is to be a dinner in his honour in Bethany.

Monday evening

As I expected, Jesus left Jerusalem after only a few hours and returned to Lazarus' home in Bethany. Jesus and his friends are spread around the various homes of Lazarus' family. Tonight's dinner is at the home of Lazarus' elder sister Martha, whose husband Simon was cured of leprosy by Jesus some while ago. That was the start of a long and fruitful friendship which reached a dramatic climax when Lazarus became seriously ill and died. As soon as Jesus heard about the illness, he asked me to ensure that when his friend died, his spirit was kept near its old body. When Jesus arrived in Bethany four days after Lazarus' funeral, he asked for the tomb to be opened. 'Come out, Lazarus,' he shouted and Lazarus did, alive and well!

Tonight's dinner is a celebration and thanksgiving for Lazarus' renewed life. Everyone is getting ready, not least Jesus, who has been supplied with some uncharacteristically expensive clothes for the event by Lazarus' younger sister, Mary.

Lazarus' sister Mary is a fascinating woman. I can begin to understand how the other Mary (Jesus' mother) has such a deep understanding of her son's intentions; but how Lazarus' sister can have grasped so firmly what even Peter and John fail to understand, is a mystery.

She was late for tonight's dinner. When she finally arrived at her sister's house, she was carrying a beautifully carved alabaster jar of ointment – ointment which, from the reaction of the diners, was of quite exceptional value (and, no doubt, cost). She squeezed her way onto the cushion between Jesus and her brother and when people's attention passed to other things she began to apply the lotion to Jesus' head and feet. As soon as the guests realised what she was up to, all conversation stopped. When the room reached complete silence, Mary proceeded to wipe the excess ointment from Jesus' feet – using her hair.

I have mentioned before that I've found myself to be intimately linked with the Son's human emotions. He responded to Mary's attentions with pure delight. He basked in the profound expression of her love and in her acceptance of what he was resolved to do this week. Though nothing was said between them, he knew that she understood, and in this outrageous act (even by Mary's standards) she was offering her full support. Jesus was in a state of bliss such as he has not experienced since sleeping at his mother's breast. A dart of anxiety flashed across my mind, making me look into their minds for any hint of sexual motivation for this sensation. There was none – only love and faith and bright hope.

This can only have lasted for a few moments, then Judas erupted with indignation. Hot with embarrassment he railed at Jesus for allowing such criminal waste. Most people in the room agreed with his suggestion that the money would have been better spent on supporting people in poverty, not washing feet. Jesus had to drag himself back into the present realities of doubt and cynicism.

'There will always be poor people,' he informed Judas, 'But you will not always have me. Mary has done a beautiful thing. This ointment was intended for my burial and tonight she has prepared me for it.'

The moment passed. Martha distracted her guests with the offer of more food. Jesus did not eat, but talked intimately with Lazarus and Mary, sharing his fears for the coming days. Before long, Jesus thanked his hosts and departed, walking the short distance to Lazarus' home with only me for company. Mary's actions had worked like an anaesthetic on his troubled mind. For the second night in succession he is sleeping peacefully.

Early Tuesday morning

While Jesus slept, I spent the night in conversation with Maff. We talked about the strangeness of our position. Here we are, facing the greatest spiritual battle ever. We should be arming ourselves for a gruelling confrontation between immortal enemies, but instead we are sworn to inaction. It appears that the Son is resolved to go into single combat against the entire assembled force of the Opposition. We can only watch and hope.

Later on Tuesday

This morning Jesus was up early, helped himself to some fruit and walked to Jerusalem alone.

'It's time for action,' he said as I moved beside him, 'And time for action requires time to pray. Nicodemus is on early duty in the Temple. He will be solid company until the hyenas arrive.'

As Jesus strode in through the Temple gate, the leader of the Opposition was waiting with a smug smile. He said nothing; he didn't need to. I could see into his fallen Angel mind. He was gloating and saying, 'Welcome to my lair.' I wondered what he was able to read in my mind.

In the Court of Jewish Men, Nicodemus welcomed Jesus more warmly. There was about him a small measure of the loving acceptance that Mary had expressed last night, but it was mixed with fear – fear that one of his colleagues might see him in such controversial company. Lucifer, by name 'The Carrier of Light', who had passed on the flames of stars from galaxy to galaxy at the beginning of this creation, blew into the embers of that fear, causing it to grow.

Lucifer noticed that I did nothing to stop him and sneered. Frustrated by my own inaction, I spoke to him.

'What small fires you are kindling now, my former friend!'

Nicodemus opened the scroll of the prophet Zechariah and Lucifer left.

'I can't bear all this stuff,' he muttered. What he cannot bear is the love Nicodemus has for my Boss.

As Jesus prayed, his Father drew close to him, holding him in an embrace that spoke reassurance without words.

After Morning Prayer Jesus returned to the outer courtyard and sat on the same bench as yesterday. The first visitors were arriving and he soon had a small group around him, eager to hear him teach. He told a story about a king who entrusted his wealth to servants, expecting them to make good use of the money in their care. While he continued to urge the people to put their faith into action, the Temple filled, his congregation grew and his twelve disciples arrived. Again, Jesus was awarded the attentions of the Temple Guard, who occupied themselves by clearing a greater space as more people gathered.

Then the Chief Priests appeared. They loudly admonished their guards for encouraging Jesus' activities. Caiaphas, the leader of the priests, fired an angry question at Jesus.

'Who has given you authority to do the things that you are doing?' The heads that had turned to the black-robed high priest returned quickly to Jesus.

'I will ask *you* a question,' Jesus replied. 'If you answer it, I will tell you by what authority I am doing these things.'

Blown along by their arrogance, the priests nodded acceptance to the deal.

'John the Dipper,' Jesus said, 'his dunking – was it from God or not? Tell me.'

Three hundred heads spun round again to the back of the crowd and watched as the priests spoke quietly among themselves. Listening to their thoughts, I could see how they have misunderstood Jesus' teaching. They were not at all concerned with the truth or the evidence of John's life; their only interest was in winning the verbal battle with Jesus. 'If we say, "from God,"' they conferred, 'then he will ask us why we took no notice of John. But if we say, "from men," this whole crowd will turn against us.'

For a while they stood, looking at each other with anxious faces. Then Caiaphas spoke up in reply to Jesus, 'We don't know.'

Jesus said, 'Then neither will I tell you by what authority I am doing these things.'

He returned to his teaching, with a story of a landowner who let out a vineyard to tenants who assaulted his servants whenever they came to collect the rent. Eventually the man sent his only son, thinking that the tenants would show him some respect, but they killed him. The priests knew well enough that Jesus considered them to be the corrupt tenants. They retired to their rooms to reconsider their plans.

Before long, just one priest returned and interrupted Jesus with a question about paying Roman taxes. Again Jesus replied with a counter question and again the priest left defeated. More priests came, this time from a different group in the ruling council. Another question was put to Jesus, another question carefully planned to catch him out whichever way he answered.

'You are wrong,' he replied, 'because you do not know either the scriptures or the power of God.'

He dispatched them as sharply as he had the others. More priests came, more questions were put, and each time Jesus perceived the catch and sent them back empty handed. The crowd thrilled at the sheer entertainment of the contest but, even more, they were astonished at the clarity of Jesus' teaching – so simple, so honest, so obviously true.

After a string of such interruptions, Jesus went on the offensive. From the moment he had woken this morning he was resolved to speak plainly, and that he did.

'Woe to you, teachers of the law and Pharisees, you hypocrites!' he declared loudly. 'You shut the Kingdom of Heaven in men's faces and you, yourselves, do not enter. Woe to you, you hypocrites! You travel land and sea to win a single convert and then you make him twice as much a son of hell as you are.'

In this fashion he continued for some while, his final salvo beginning, 'You snakes! You brood of vipers! How will you escape being condemned to hell?'

The leader of the Opposition watched, amazed. The Son had wrestled the initiative from his grasp and then played it straight back into his hands. If there were any doubts in the minds of the priests that Jesus must die, there will be none now. All they have to do is arrange it.

Midday Wednesday

This morning, when Jesus returned to the outer courtyard after early morning prayers, there was a small crowd waiting for him. Word had spread through the inns of the city that a young, fresh-thinking rabbi was teaching in the Temple. There were in the group Jews from across the Roman world and the north African kingdoms. Their mood was of excited interest rather than com-

mitted faith and Jesus responded to it. He dismissed any speculation that he might be planning to overthrow the Roman occupation by predicting that the Romans would, in fact, destroy
Jerusalem. He echoed the sentiments of the great prophets of
earlier ages who had expressed his Father's frustration at the
unbelief of the Jewish people.

'When you see Jerusalem surrounded by armies,' Jesus told
them, 'you will know that its desolation is near. Its people will be
taken as prisoners to all the nations.'

A good many of the people walked out after that. They had
come with hopes of a Messiah. They did not want to listen to a
Jeremiah.

Jesus was seated a short distance from the great clay jars that
are used to collect the financial contributions of the people. At
one point the crowd was distracted from his teaching by the
sound of large amounts of money being poured into these vessels.
Jesus waited and watched as the people gossiped among themselves about the generous donors. Looking into the minds of
those present I saw an irresistible fascination with people who
have so much gold that they can give that grandly. In Jesus' mind,
however, there was sad resignation that, after all his work, the
people are more interested in discs of yellow metal than they are
in his Father's sombre judgement on their nation.

Then, after that group of wealthy Alexandrian merchants had
moved on, there came an elderly woman in the black dress of a
widow. She dropped in two small copper coins that hardly made
a sound as they landed on the mound of soft gold. The crowd
turned back to Jesus; their entertainment was over.

'I tell you the truth,' Jesus said, 'This poor widow has put in
more than all the others combined.'

His audience rippled with polite laughter at the outrageous
suggestion, but his face remained sincere.

'Those people gave only a small part of their great wealth; this
woman has put in the only money she had to live on.' The crowd
thinned a little further.

As the morning passed, the Son called across to me in a
moment of prayer. 'Have you noticed something missing?'

'What?' I replied.

'We have not been visited by the Chief Priests today,' he
observed. 'Oriel, go into their private rooms and see what they are
up to.'

I headed into the labyrinth of passages that makes up the living quarters and administrative offices of the Jewish priesthood. There I found Raphael, seated inside one of the thick stone pillars that hold up the roof. Having been in the continuous company of humans for so much time, the sight of an Archangel suspended in the middle of a solid stone column surprised me.

'What on Earth are you doing in there?' I asked.

'Watching and listening,' my friend replied. 'From here I can see and hear just about everything that happens in this den of iniquity, and the Opposition spirits are too Earthbound to think of looking in such places. Are you looking for Judas?'

'No,' I responded. 'Why?'

'He's in there,' Raphael informed me, pointing through a wall.

Looking through the wall, across an empty hallway and through a second wall I could see a richly furnished office. The people in it were difficult to identify; they were almost as soulless as the walls themselves. But I recognised Judas, one of Jesus' Twelve, and the high priest. I was shocked to see how faint Judas' faith had grown. The Chief Priests were smiling like spoiled children and they handed Judas a purse of silver coins, which he quickly concealed under his clothes.

'What's happening?' I asked Raphael.

'The priests have spent the entire . . . whatever do they call that part of the day when they move towards the light of the sun . . . ?'

'The morning.'

'Thank you. They have spent the entire morning discussing how they might fix Jesus' trial to ensure that he is found to be guilty and deserving Death. Once that was arranged they turned to the apparently more complex task of working out how they can arrest him without creating a riot.'

'But what is Judas doing in there?' I interrupted, knowing that Raphael could easily make his story last several months.

'Oh, he simply walked in and offered to arrange a time and place for them to speak privately with the Son. The priests were so delighted by the idea that they offered to make a contribution towards Jesus' funds.'

I looked carefully at Judas as he slipped guiltily out of Caiaphas' office. Raphael has very little understanding of human affairs even though he can remember and recall them in painful detail. I noticed that an Opposition spirit had attached itself to Judas so I pushed Raphael for more detail.

'Has that spirit been with him all along?'

'Oh, I don't know, my dear. They swim through these corridors like shoals of ugly fish.'

I left Raphael in his pillar and followed Judas back to Jesus. The enemy spirit had definitely attached itself to him. The creature smirked at me conceitedly and scurried off to report to its master while Judas slipped into the back of Jesus' dwindling congregation unnoticed. I will have to wait for a suitable opportunity to inform Jesus of the situation.

Wednesday afternoon

As the day has progressed, I have noticed a distinct change in the make up of the crowd around Jesus. This morning, many had come in search of entertainment; they were hoping for more confrontations or even another bout of money scattering. Most of these have left, bored and rather disappointed. Those who remain are people genuinely interested in Jesus' message and there are a surprising number of priests and council members among them.

When Jesus returned from lunch at a nearby inn, Andrew and Philip (two of the Twelve) introduced him to a group of Greek tourists. These were educated men who had abandoned the ludicrous gods of their upbringing and travelled to Jerusalem to learn about the One who created the Universe (among other things). Jesus talked to them with interest and a fresh hope rose in his spirit. If, as these men suggested, there are a great many people in the Roman world who are looking for a new faith, one that is genuine and true, one that is compassionate and relevant to everyday life, then there will be much fertile soil where the seeds of his teaching can be planted and bear fruit. A sudden lightness of spirit thrilled through my being as it did through his.

When this private conversation with the Greeks drew to a close, Jesus suddenly spoke out to the eagerly listening ears around him.

'The time has come for the Son to be glorified,' he announced, causing a rumour of excitement to spread through the small crowd.

Then he spoke more quietly and with an intense focus on the thought before him.

'Unless an ear of wheat falls to the ground and dies, it remains only a single seed. But if it dies, it produces many seeds.'

The people pondered this simple yet profound image, sobered by the arrival of 'Death' into Jesus' teaching. Jesus didn't move at all during the silence. It was as though his eyes were staring at something only a short distance from his face.

'The person who loves their life will lose it,' he continued, 'while the person who hates their life in this world will keep it for eternal life.'

I could feel a resonance among the people. Jesus was drawing their thoughts beyond the brief existence of human life and directing them towards the timeless life of Angels.

Without warning his concentration broke. He shuddered and became distracted. Jesus' speech became less clear – indeed, he almost began to mumble.

'Now my heart is troubled, and what shall I say? Father, save me from this hour?'

Again he paused and again he stared at the invisible point before him. The people waited sympathetically, somehow understanding that a storm was raging in Jesus' mind. The leader of the Opposition floated down to ground level watching Jesus intently, trying to probe into his troubled mind.

Slowly, Jesus stilled his inner tempest and spoke again.

'No, it was for this very reason that I have come to this hour.'

Lucifer turn away thoughtfully. He had not managed to read the Son's mind. All he knew, as he returned to his vantage point on the Temple roof, was that there was something that he didn't know, a divine purpose that he could neither perceive nor understand.

The men and women around Jesus sat quietly. Eventually he moved for a second time and his demeanour showed a man who had regained control of himself after a fight. Looking upwards in the way that Jews often do when they pray, he said, 'Father, glorify your name!'

Then, as has happened so many times, his Father replied, 'I have glorified it, and I will glorify it again.'

What surprised me was that the people around Jesus clearly heard the voice too. They suddenly looked up and started to chatter among themselves, asking, 'What on earth was that?'

A woman seated close to me said, 'It was the voice of an Angel.'

'If only!' I interjected, but she couldn't hear me.

'The voice was for your benefit, not mine,' Jesus said. 'The time has come for this world to be judged; the prince of this world will be driven out.'

I looked round to see if the leader of the Opposition was listening but he was reeling from the pain caused to him by the sound of my Boss's voice. Jesus, I think, must have known this, because he continued to speak of his mission with a frankness that would have sent Michael into a force ten panic.

'When I am lifted up from the earth,' Jesus continued, 'I will draw everyone to myself.'

He proceeded to discuss these matters for some minutes and I watched Lucifer carefully so I could warn Jesus when he had recovered his composure. It was wonderful to hear Jesus opening out the great plan of his Father's love and to see that men and women were responding to the message with hope and faith.

I signalled to him when he needed to stop and he did. He stood up, gathered his closest followers and left the Temple. On his way up the Mount of Olives Jesus turned off the road into an olive grove called Gethsemane, where he drank from a well. Then, as he had the day before, he rested in the cool of the garden before returning into the hot sun and up the steep hill towards Bethany and supper with Lazarus and Mary.

Thursday – the Day of Preparation

Today began for the Twelve with panic. Jesus was missing! A brief investigation showed that he was not in his bed and no one in the household had seen him since he went to bed last night. Nearly an hour later it was with great relief that the shout went up, 'We've found him!'

Jesus was seated against a stone wall, near the donkey which had carried him into Jerusalem. Sitting beside the Son was his closest human friend, John, who always appreciated his Master's need for solitude.

While the rest of the household were sleeping, Jesus had walked: around Lazarus' small garden, down the lane towards the Jerusalem road and back across two vineyards, before joining the unfussy company of the young donkey. Some while before

Jesus' other companions were awake, John poked his head over the wall and saw Jesus. They exchanged no words, barely even acknowledging one another's presence, but no words were needed.

The sombre peace was invaded by Peter, a man for whom breathing and speaking are like conjoined twins. Having commented on the breakfast and urged Jesus to try it for himself, he turned to the other important business of the day – supper. Or more specifically, the Passover feast.

'Where are we eating tonight?' he wanted to know.

Jesus looked into Peter's eyes for what seemed, even to me, a long time. He spoke in short, broken phrases as if the very act of talking was painful.

'Go down into the city . . . and when you get to the gate . . . a man carrying a jar of water will meet you. Go with him. He will lead you to an inn. When you get there . . . speak to the landlord. Ask him to show you the upstairs function room. I have booked it. Make the Passover preparations there. I will join you after sunset.'

Peter, apparently oblivious to Jesus' mood, leapt to his feet. 'Come on, John lad. If we don't hurry up we'll be queuing in the Temple all afternoon.'

'I'll stay with the Teacher,' the young man replied.

'No, go with Peter,' Jesus responded. 'You know how I want things done.' Then he added quietly, 'Keep it simple, won't you?'

To the impatient Peter he added, solemnly, 'Peter, it's very important that no one knows where we are meeting – not even the other ten. I will tell them later.'

The two friends walked around the vineyard towards the road and Jesus called after them, 'Don't invite any surprise guests. It must be just the thirteen of us.'

John, picking up the anxiety in Jesus' voice, replied, 'It's alright, I understand.'

He added a conspiratorial nod to supplement his message and disappeared from Jesus' view. I continued to watch them through the vines and observed their conversation.

'What's his problem?' Peter enquired unsympathetically.

John considered a heap of different answers and rejected them all. 'Let's just do what he said,' he snapped.

A little later

Jesus met the ten remaining followers at the breakfast table. They fell silent when he walked into the room, all sensing that their circumstances had changed.

'You must not enter Jerusalem at all today,' he told them. 'If you have to leave the house, go in twos or threes. Do not go in large groups and do not go alone. I will meet you here an hour before sunset. Peter and John are preparing the Passover for us.'

At the last sentence, I felt a wave of shock cross the room from young Mary. She looked up suddenly, her face drained of blood. She had assumed that Jesus would celebrate Passover with her and her family. As she pondered her disappointment that Jesus would not be at her supper table, something in her mind told her that she had lost him for more than one evening.

Meanwhile, Jesus' instructions had caused an emotional landslide in the older Mary's mind. 'So the time has come,' she said softly to herself.

Late afternoon

When Jesus left the house he walked alone through fields and up deserted lanes towards the uncultivated hilltops. I joined him, but he asked me to let him be alone. I moved upwards into the sky and watched from a distance. He looked so small and insignificant, wandering across the skin of those ancient mountains. I marvelled that so much should rest on something so small, so delicate and so fleeting, as a man.

When I was sure that Jesus was alone and safe from both political and spiritual dangers, I left him and sought Maff's company. Maff was watching Jesus' mother, as she patiently prepared vegetables for the evening's feast. Over these months on Earth, I have become adept at reading human faces as well as their minds. Mary looked serene as her hands worked methodically on the herbs that will remind the diners of the bitterness of slavery and oppression.

'She is afraid,' Maff told me, reflectively.

'So am I,' I replied.

'Me too,' he added.

We said nothing else all afternoon.

Thursday evening

Jesus and his twelve chosen companions are busy finishing off the last scraps of the roast lamb and wafer bread that make up the annual Passover meal.

Earlier, when Jesus was returning from his day's wandering, I went to meet him, for I still needed to tell him about Judas' disappearance in the Temple yesterday morning. The balance of Jesus' mind is so precarious at present that I had resolved to choose my moment for delivering such devastating news with great care.

His response surprised me.

'I thought it might be Thomas or Matthew,' he said. 'Thomas is so riddled with doubts and Matthew misses the comforts of his former life.' Then he stood still, considering what I had told him and said, 'I'm glad it's not Peter.'

'Were you expecting it?' I enquired.

'It was bound to happen. Lucifer has probed the weaknesses of us all in these past months.'

'But Michael has been watching him, he hasn't come near any of you.' The prospect that I had failed in one of my primary tasks was a heavy blow.

'His methods are not so blunt,' Jesus assured me. 'He works his way down the pathways of the human mind, sowing fears and fantasies. Then he opens untimely coincidences and opportunities which catch us off-guard. He doesn't need to come close or to speak to us in person. Every human mind teeters on the cliff-edge of destruction at certain times and it takes only the slightest nudge to send us plummeting to destruction.'

I looked at my eternal Lord – his flimsy flesh pale, his watery eyes dark from uncertainty – aware that there is so much to human life that I still do not understand.

Jesus walked into Lazarus' garden where nine of the Twelve were waiting, talking to one another in hushed voices. Jesus explained the plans for their Passover meal, telling them to enter Jerusalem in pairs and to be careful not to attract any attention.

While he was repeating these instructions, Judas slipped into the garden. I hardly noticed him; the light of his spirit has become so dim.

An hour later, Jesus was seated in the upper room where Peter and John had prepared the Passover. The room was lit by numerous simple clay lamps and the table loaded with breads and sauces. Jesus sat at the head of the table, waiting for his disciples to arrive. He had walked into Jerusalem with Judas, recounting to him the many things that they have done together over three years of friendship. All the time Jesus was searching for something that might fan the faltering flame of Judas' spirit. Jesus made no mention of his companion's clandestine visit to the priests.

As we waited for the rest of the Twelve to appear, I considered the human obsession with meals and food. By the time the life has dripped out of a lamb or chicken there is, to Angel eyes, just about nothing left of it, only a pile of assorted atoms, rather common ones at that. And yet, you humans have to consume this lifeless mass every day. Even after all this time living alongside humans, I struggle to understand how you keep yourselves alive by eating things that you have killed and then further destroyed with fire. The fact that you take such delight in the act and use it as a form of celebration is a total mystery to me.

As the rest of the Twelve slipped up the stairs and squeezed nervously though the narrow doorway, Jesus watched them greet one another and exchange stories about their journey. He allowed them time to relax and then, when the room fell quiet, he spoke.

'I was eager to share this Passover supper with you before I suffer, for I tell you, I will not take part in another one until its promise is fulfilled in my Father's Kingdom.'

He picked up the crisp Passover bread and held it before them. Carefully and deliberately he positioned his fingers across the surface of the flat, brittle loaf, watched by twelve pairs of curious eyes. Jesus prayed his usual prayer of thanksgiving for the meal. Then, with all eyes still fixed on the bread, his thick, carpenter's fingers poised for action. Suddenly, with a flick of his wrists, Jesus snapped the bread and it fell in shattered pieces onto the table.

The disciples were startled by the violence of his action but I was transfixed by something far more remarkable. The fragmented loaf had come to life, not with the pale life of an earthly plant but with the bright spiritual life of Heaven. It was the kind of brightness that shines from the lives of people who love my

Boss and live their lives for him. And as I gazed at these living shards of bread, I suddenly recognised the life that I was seeing. Just as a human mother might recognise the unique smell of her child, some inner part of me recognised the spiritual light of that bread: it was the life of the Son himself; the life of my Boss; the light that, to my eyes, continually shines from the human body of Jesus.

He spoke and his words confirmed what I had just seen. 'This is my body.'

The disciples looked surprised that he should use such words to describe a few jagged pieces of bread, which was all that they could see. Jesus looked around the table into their confused but devoted eyes and said, 'Eat this to remember me.' Then he gathered up the broken bread and handed a fragment to each of his companions.

When everyone had eaten their piece, Jesus clapped his hands energetically and said, 'Come on, let's eat.'

The Twelve quickly dived into the familiar and reassuring routine of chewing and swallowing the half burnt lamb carcass which Peter and John had spent all day preparing.

As the men ate I drew close to Jesus and studied one of the glowing crumbs on the table. I let out an exclamation which, in human terms, would have been something like 'Wow!'

Jesus said to me, 'This is a new beginning, Oriel. Something totally new.'

I picked up a crumb and held it. It had all the physical features of a tiny scrap of bread and, as well as shining with the unmistakable light of my Boss, it had the weight and beauty of one of Heaven's most valuable treasures.

While I wondered at the coming together of Creator and creation in the humble form of bread, Jesus filled his wine cup with a purposeful manner that made me take note. The disciples too, by whatever subtlety of human communication, stopped their chatter and looked at their troubled leader.

'This is my blood,' he said, holding out the cup.

Twelve faces contorted at such a macabre suggestion, but the room was flooded with the same bright spiritual light. It was as if a new star had been created within the clay wall of the cup.

'Drink this, all of you,' Jesus instructed. The pure light reflected from his disciples' faces but those faces told only of utter disgust at the idea of drinking their leader's blood.

John, sitting beside Jesus, took the cup cautiously and I sensed his relief when the contents first looked and then tasted like ordinary wine. As the rest of the disciples followed John's example, Jesus continued to speak.

'This wine is the blood that guarantees my Father's new promise, to you and to many, to forgive your selfishness.'

The Twelve, startled and confused by Jesus' actions and words, have now returned to the simple comfort of food, emptying their minds as they fill their bellies. Jesus is watching them. He is feeling terrible loneliness – a painful emotion, the like of which I have never experienced before. How strange that he can be in the company of so many good friends and yet be alone. I wish I could help him in some way, but the path down which he is to travel is one that no Angel, no matter how brave, can follow. And so, as the disciples are distracting themselves with food, I have diverted my own fears by writing this diary.

Late Thursday evening

We are in the olive grove again. I am with Jesus, a small distance from his human companions and, once again, I am trying to contain my thoughts by writing them down.

Before leaving Jerusalem, Jesus informed the Twelve that one of their number would betray him. He did not mention Judas by name and that flung them into panic because they each asked, 'You don't mean me, do you?' I think that Jesus did tell John and Peter who it would be, but there was such a confusion of fear and guilt around the room that I found it hard to focus on the particular words being said.

I could not miss, however, an impassioned conversation between Jesus and Peter in which the outspoken fisherman promised to follow his Master all the way to prison and to Death.

'Let me tell you the truth, Peter,' Jesus replied, his voice burdened by the weight of his emotions. 'Tonight – this very night – you will deny that you even know me. And you will do it three times.'

As Jesus said these words the room fell silent and barely a word has been spoken since. I knew that Jesus was not speaking from any intelligence information supplied by Michael. (I would have been informed.) He had looked into the deep workings of Peter's mind and pinpointed the weakest aspect of the big fisherman's character. At that moment every man in the room knew that he was equally well known and that there was nothing to gain from the manly bravado that so often flavours their conversations. Nobody dared speak.

The silent group then passed, unnoticed, out of the city and plodded with numb hearts up the Mount of Olives. I observed how the intensity of Jesus' feelings were imposing themselves on his body. He looked like an old or sick man as he forced his weary limbs up the hill; his face was pale, his head and shoulders drooped and both arms hung limp at his side as his feet shuffled past one another in short, springless steps.

Half way up the Mount of Olives, Jesus turned off the road into the same garden that he has visited each evening this week. He left most of his companions at the gateway, asking them to keep watch. He then took John, Peter and James and walked in deeper amongst the trees. He pleaded with them to keep him company.

'My spirit is overwhelmed with sadness,' he told them, 'right to the point of Death.'

What astounding words!

For the last few weeks I have shared many of the Son's feelings but now, without a doubt, his emotions have reached a level that I am simply unable to experience. John, Peter and James have been his devoted helpers for nearly three years. I have been a loyal servant through many creations. The four of us gazed at him helplessly. We all knew that there was nothing we could do other than watch our friend go forward on his path, alone.

Jesus headed further still into the garden and before he had taken more than ten strides, he collapsed, exhausted, to the ground. The three men, paralysed by fear, did nothing. Perhaps they thought that he had already died. As I looked on, the light of his spirit was so clouded by terror that I too might have mistaken him for dead. But Death could not come so lightly to my Boss's Son. I left John, Peter and James and settled beside him.

For a long while I watched as his emotions battled against his spirit. The weapons for this assault were supplied by Jesus' own imagination and the battlefield was his exhausted body. In time I began to see the images that were causing such terror in his mind. Within the theatre of his thoughts, Jesus imagined his body being hurled, repeatedly, against the stone wall at the bottom of his mother's garden in Nazareth. However, throughout this violent scene, it was not the prospect of dying that frightened him. At each crunching collision his fear was focussed beyond the wall on that which waited for him when the familiar barrier had finally been destroyed by his battered body. I remembered a conversation we had shared two years ago and suddenly I realised the identity of his terror. It was not Death itself that he feared, nor pain, nor humiliation, not even being rejected by the people who had followed him for the last three years. All these things Jesus has accepted as part of his mission. The prospect that has caused the blood to drain from his face and that has left his body in a heap on the ground, is the prospect of *meeting his Father*, my Boss – God.

I was shocked.

My expectation of that meeting had been of a glorious reunion between Creator and eternal Son. But the Son is now human. He shares the guilt of humanity's awful failure to live by his Father's love.

Jesus knows, all too well, his Father's terrible anger at the self-centredness of humanity and he also knows that his Father's anger is about to be directed at him.

So there he lay on the orchard floor in immeasurable despair, murmuring the same hopeless prayer again and again, 'Take it away from me. Please take it away from me.'

I didn't know what to do or say. Watching his trembling body and hearing his feeble cries, I was reminded once again of the nights when he was a small child; he would cry in his sleep and his mother Mary would sit by his bed, gently stroking his head while she sang a simple song.

I made a rash decision. I had to do something for my Lord. I could not undo that which most terrified his human spirit but I could do this one thing. So there in the Garden of Gethsemane I slowed and thinned my Angelic body until it was as faint as Jesus' physical body. Then I carefully smoothed a pale hand through his knotted hair. As closely as I could, I imitated the movements of his mother. I reduced my voice to so gentle a pitch that it moved the air around me and enabled the long-forgotten song to hum in Jesus' ears.

I turned to look at the three companions. Peter and John were asleep. James was looking directly at me in wide-eyed amazement. He could see me but I didn't care. I could not let my Lord suffer so deeply and do nothing.

I turned my attention again to the images flashing through Jesus' mind. The terrible crashing of body against imagined stone had ended and he now pictured himself standing before his Father. My Boss was grim faced. In his hand he held a large cup of foul smelling poison which he was presenting to Jesus. Jesus, knowing what was in the cup, looked directly into his Father's eyes.

This one image remained clear in his mind for a long time. All the while I stroked his hair and sang. Eventually I heard Jesus' voice as he lay in the dried leaves and dust of the garden. 'Father, if this cup cannot be taken away unless I drink it, your will be done.' With that he slept.

The early hours of Friday morning

Archangel Michael came flying into the garden accompanied by a squadron of his finest soldiers.

'They're coming!' he exclaimed urgently. I reached down and gently shook the still form of Jesus.

'It's time,' I said.

Jesus looked refreshed. His eyes were clear, the lines on his face less deep. In his spirit there was a sense of purpose. The image I saw as I looked into his thoughts was of an arrow which had just left its bowstring, speeding directly towards its target.

Jesus, in turn, shook his three companions awake, urging them to pray. Before he had finished talking, the quiet of the garden was invaded. Lucifer, the leader of the Opposition, led the way. Behind him came a band of demonic thugs who positioned themselves directly in front of Michael and his force. Lucifer momentarily turned to me with a look that said, 'This is my operation – don't you dare interfere.' Behind him walked Judas, leading a small crowd of priests and Temple guards.

Judas walked straight past his startled friends and headed for Jesus. He walked towards us with his head held high, his arms out-stretched and a smile on his face.

'Hello, Teacher!' he said and threw his arms around Jesus, kissing him on the cheek.

'Judas, are you betraying me with a kiss?' Jesus asked. But Judas had no chance to reply. Rough hands threw him aside. The same hands grabbed Jesus and pushed him to the ground, passing ropes around his arms while a sword was held threateningly in his face. Peter leapt into the fray, brandishing a dagger and shouting incoherently. In a blind rage he managed to cut one of Jesus' captors on the side of his head.

Jesus shouted, 'Enough of this!'

He stood up in the centre of the muddled heap of men and everyone looked at him, surprised that their intended victim should take control.

First, Jesus spoke to Peter. 'Put your weapon away. Don't you know that I could call up twelve armies of Angels to defend me?' Lucifer glanced round at me anxiously, the smile vanished from his face. I ignored him.

Next, Jesus turned to the leaders among the priests. 'Am I a terrorist that you have come to get me with soldiers and weapons? Every day I have been with you in the Temple!'

Lastly he turned to his former assistant, now his deadly enemy. 'Lucifer, this is your hour,' Jesus said, 'when darkness rules.' I could feel Michael beside me, itching to capture his stunned adversary but I did not give the order. Once again the leader of the Opposition tried to fathom the mind of his Creator but failed. Instead, frustrated, he pushed one of the officers of the guard and he, in turn, shoved the backs of his men. They did the same to Jesus and the whole sorry band began its journey out of the garden and down the steep hill towards Jerusalem.

I followed at a distance with Peter, who was feeling utterly alone. He had no idea that he was accompanied by the most powerful military escort that Heaven could provide. Instead, when he turned around, all he could see was that the rest of the Twelve – Judas included – had run away. Peter repeated to himself the promise he had made to Jesus at supper, 'I will go with you all the way to prison and even to Death.'

As we made our way, the road was fenced with Opposition forces. Long lines of rebellious spirits looked on in silent amazement as their leader brought the Son into Jerusalem under arrest. When they saw two Archangels bringing up the rear with the troops against whom they had fought for so long, they assumed that we too had been captured. They jeered and snorted at us as we passed.

I no longer needed to share the Son's emotions, I could feel the naked indignity of defeat for myself. This was, most certainly 'their hour'.

169

Michael had never experienced anything to match this. He spat into my ear, 'I have to get out of here somehow and raise our forces.'

I looked ahead to Jesus, still walking upright and confidently. There was no hint of the captured prisoner about him and I suspected that if the Temple guard and Opposition spirits were taken away, he would still be marching into Jerusalem to face his enemies. I muttered to Michael indifferently, 'You can do what you like.' Then I added more urgently, 'But *you must not interfere!*' The next time I looked around, he was gone.

The arrest party made for a small door in the city wall, beside the Temple. Through the doorway and down a narrow, private alley, we entered the courtyard of the high priest's house. Jesus was chained to two guards. Someone lit a fire. Gradually the people settled down. As they waited for something to happen, they gathered round the heat and light of the fire, chattering among themselves.

I looked into the thoughts of the different people present, discovering that very few of them were interested in Jesus at all. They did not hate him, all this was simply something to alleviate the routine boredom of their lives. There was much speculation about what would happen to him but most of the gathered guards and hangers-on didn't really care. There was, however, one person in the small crowd who did care; Peter had found himself a spot where he could sit in the shadows and watch Jesus.

A servant girl was distributing wine supplied by the high priest to mark the night's Passover celebrations. When she came to Peter, she recognised him and declared to anyone who was listening, 'This man was one of his followers.'

'What do you mean?' Peter retorted crossly. 'I don't even know him.' He buried his face in his wine cup.

I looked across to Jesus who had recognised Peter's voice and was trying to locate his friend in the flickering firelight.

After a while, boredom set in. One of the guards stood up. 'I've got an idea,' he announced. 'This Jesus character is supposed to be a prophet. Let's see if he's any good at it. Has anyone got a blindfold?'

A cotton scarf was produced, which the guard tied around Jesus' eyes. He then tiptoed to one of his colleagues, whispered in his ear and instructed Jesus to stand up. The second guard walked up to the blindfolded Jesus, slapped him hard on the cheek and returned to his place. The first guard pulled away the scarf from Jesus' face and said, playfully, 'Go on then, tell us who hit you.'

Everyone laughed and the guard, pleased at his success, repeated the process again and again and again. Each time, Jesus said nothing. And each time, emboldened by his silence, the aggressor hit or kicked him harder than before.

At one point the guard invited Peter to take a turn. Peter declined and the man said, 'Are you one of them?'

'No, I'm not.' Peter replied gruffly. Someone else volunteered and the game continued.

When the officer in charge of the guard became concerned at the amount of blood on Jesus' clothes and the extent of the swelling on his face, he called a halt to the game. So the guard changed the rules from physical blows to verbal insults and the sport continued.

All the while, the cramped courtyard echoed with laughter. For me, this second game was worse. To sit and listen to living creatures idly mocking the One who had so lovingly formed them and sustained their life, was dreadful torture. Part of me would happily have crushed their feeble bodies there and then, but I reminded myself of the reason I was there.

I looked closely at Jesus, his face a mosaic of bruises, his clothes smeared with dirt and blood. He was tired but he was standing firm. Inside his mind that arrow was still flying towards its mark. He was mostly ignoring the continual downpour of verbal abuse except that he prayed, momentarily, for each person as they spoke. The majority of his thoughts were devoted to focusing on his Father's love, the last part of this mind given in repeated prayers for Peter. At one point, when the proceedings were interrupted by the arrival of more wine, I went right up to Jesus.

'I just wanted to tell you I'm here,' I whispered. 'I'll do anything you ask me.'

I hoped he might instruct me to rescue him from this awful theatre of blasphemy but he only said, 'Thank you.'

As the night wore on and the fire died down, the people and their game grew tired. Jesus and his guards sat down, the blindfold was left on. Every time the game ground to a halt, someone came up with a fresh insult, but they rarely produced much laughter and the guards had long since given up trying to get a reaction from Jesus.

Gradually the darkness gave way to the colourless light of early dawn and when one of the guards pulled off Jesus' bloodied blindfold to wipe his own nose, nobody seemed to notice. People were simply talking among themselves, wondering when they would get home to their families and whether they would be paid extra for their night's work.

All of a sudden, one angry voice rose above all the others, its broad Galilean accent unmistakable.

'Man, I don't know what you're talking about! I don't know the man.'

It was Peter and while he was denying any knowledge of Jesus, a cockerel announced the arrival of daytime, strutting importantly into the courtyard as it crowed. Jesus turned towards Peter and, for the first time since the Garden of Gethsemane, their eyes met. Inside Peter's mind the massive tower of pride and self-belief which dominated his personality crashed into dust. He stumbled clumsily away from Jesus' gaze, his eyes pouring tears as he went. I turned to Jesus. In his thoughts he was talking to the now absent Peter. 'Peter, I always knew you might do that. I do not love you any the less now that I have heard what I understood for so long.'

An hour after dawn

Not long after the cockerel had emerged from the high priest's house, it was followed by its owner. I was struck by the similarity between the two creatures: both were small with an exaggerated air of self-importance; both looked overdressed; both loud; both hampered by a small brain.

Caiaphas strutted past Jesus and squawked, 'Bring him with me.' With that he disappeared through a private doorway into the Temple complex.

Jesus walked awkwardly, his limbs stiff from the injuries of the night. I followed him down dark, stone corridors, empty of people but teeming with Opposition spirits, all preoccupied with different errands. It seemed that the Opposition had taken over the priests' quarters. The high priest Caiaphas was escorted by two senior Opposition agents in much the same way that Jesus was by his guards. Both men were captives.

As we approached the council chamber I saw a crowd of aggravated guardian Angels who had been refused entry when their charges went inside. They flocked to me, demanding an explana-tion. 'How can the Jewish Council expect to achieve anything without us?' one asked. I directed their attention to their Boss's Son as he walked past. No other reply was necessary.

At the entrance to the chamber I met Jeshaphael, an Angel I'd known very well before he betrayed our Boss and was banished from Heaven.

'You can't go in,' he told me bluntly.

'If I do not follow the Son through that door,' I said, 'I shall go to fetch Michael and his entire army.'

Jeshaphael was trapped in indecision. Clearly he had not been given authority to decide for himself but, equally clearly, he believed that he should have. Freedom and independence are lux-uries that the leader of the Opposition does not allow. He hovered with indecision. I made as if to leave and quickly he told me to wait. Evidently, my presence was one eventuality Lucifer had failed to plan for. I was encouraged and pushed my advantage.

'Maybe I should go and speak to your leader?' I suggested.

'No need for that,' Jeshaphael replied. 'Go in. You won't be able to do anything.'

He was probably right but I was relieved to be with the Son again. I was also pleased at having forced a small crack in the enemy's ranks. Through that crack shone a faint ray of hope.

Inside the council chamber there was no waiting. As soon as Jesus arrived, the proceedings began. Lucifer swept into the chamber, prompting the hundreds of spirits in the room to focus their attentions slavishly on his single purpose. When I looked around the room, those Jewish councillors still loyal to my Boss stood out from the rest. Their spines were tingling at the strong presence of evil around them. Behind the leader of the Opposition came Caiaphas, the high priest, black robes billowing as he walked. He took his seat in the centre of the council chamber and called for Jesus' trial to begin.

There were some brief formalities to confirm that the prisoner was indeed Jesus from Nazareth, itinerant teacher and healer. Jesus remained silent and refused to co-operate with this interro-gation. I was surprised. I studied him closely to find out why. Again I sensed that arrow hurtling towards its mark. His mind was focussed on what lay ahead; he knew that the Council of the Sanhedrin had already made up their mind. They did not need his help.

Caiaphas was irritated by Jesus' silence. He felt that his authority was being bruised. Before long he lost patience and fired off the question that most concerned him.

'If you are the Messiah, the Saviour of the Jewish people, tell us.'

Jesus looked directly into his eyes. The council chamber is not a large room and the two men were close to one another. Jesus has become an expert at reading the subtle messages published in every human face. In the high priest's face he saw a cocktail of anxiety and doubt: anxiety about losing the power and wealth he has fought so hard to achieve; doubt at the faint prospect (in his judgement) that this country carpenter might just be sent by God. In his mind he remembered that, over a thousand years before, his God had used another insignificant man from an obscure village, a man called Gideon.

If I could have taken that fragment of honest doubt in the high priest's mind, and inflated it to useful proportions, I would have done. But as he returned Jesus' gaze, Caiaphas' determination froze and became as hard as ice.

'If I were to tell you,' Jesus replied, 'you would not believe me. If I were to ask you what you believe, you would not give me an honest answer. But this much I will tell you: from now on, the Son of Man will be seated at the right hand of Almighty God.'

This reply delivered a hammer blow to Caiaphas' frozen will. Where there was already weakness, cracks emerged. Before the question, 'What if he really is the Messiah?' could emerge to the surface of the high priest's mind, the leader of the Opposition whispered into his thoughts a different, more dangerous question. Lucifer stood back and grinned with satisfaction. Caiaphas leant forward, weighed down by the gravity of his next enquiry.

'Are you,' he asked solemnly, 'the Son of the Most High God?'

A gasp of shock emerged from almost every human mouth in the room. The high priest had said the unspeakable and put into words an idea that self-respecting Jews dare not even think. To pose so blunt a question, whatever rumours may have spread about Jesus, was shocking.

Again Jesus looked at his accuser, searching for remnants of faith and hope. Lucifer's smile faltered. His plan could still be scuppered if the faint embers of spiritual light in the priest's soul could be rekindled.

My attention flicked from the priest to the former Archangel, to my Boss's Son. Everything hung, at that moment, in the balance of Caiaphas' mind. What did he care for most? His God or himself? Lucifer was not willing to risk his entire plan on the decision of the high priest. Without any noticeable signal, his lackeys forced the same simple question from the lips of anyone present who they could manipulate. Before long, the room was infected by a rising murmur of enquiry.

'Are you the Son of God?'

Individual voices rose above the noise.

'Answer him then!' and 'Are you or aren't you?'

At a signal from the leader of the Opposition the voices were hushed and the council chamber fell silent.

'You are right,' Jesus suddenly announced. 'I am.'

The room erupted. Caiaphas' mind snapped shut and he ripped apart the fabric of his official robes. Jesus had declared the ultimate blasphemy and the men of the Sanhedrin wanted to stone him to death immediately. As I struggled to take in the angry chaos that surrounded me, I could see the faint lights of those who did believe Jesus to be my Boss's Son, but those lights were rapidly smothered by Opposition spirits who surrounded them and bombarded them with fear – fear of their own death should they reveal their support for the blasphemer.

Caiaphas took control of his council. He had prepared a schedule for the day and now it was time to act.

'Brothers!' he shouted, calling the room to order. 'We do not have the authority to put a man to death. We must take this prisoner to the Roman Governor.' His suggestion did not win the hearts of those baying for blood. The Romans were their immediate enemy and the Roman ban on Jewish executions rarely stopped them. Nonetheless, Caiaphas was right and there was something in his manner that compelled them to wait. The high priest's inner group of advisers stood and followed their leader to the door, the rest of the council were close behind. Only a few, those who secretly admired Jesus, slipped quietly away, back to their homes.

Jesus was escorted out of the Temple buildings, through a back gate and across the Governor's courtyard to the Praetorium.

And here we are waiting. Pilate, the Roman Governor, seems to be in no hurry to satisfy the bloodlust of the Jewish Council. The council members are milling around, gossiping excitedly. Lucifer has gathered his entourage to brief them. I am alone.

Jesus is calm and his mind focussed. I wish the same were true of me. I have summoned Michael and a significant force of Angels so that we can match the Opposition presence. I am still committed to my Boss's plan and intend to see it through, but there are so many things that could go wrong; I dare not leave us totally unprotected.

Mid morning

Pontius Pilate, the Roman Governor, kept the priests waiting for a considerable time. He finally emerged muttering about being busy but his thoughts betrayed him. He was bored by the high priest and his petty schemes and wanted to put the Jewish leader in his place.

I had never taken much notice of the man before. He is small in stature, his mind is dominated by bitterness and resentment. He made little effort to conceal his dislike of the Jews.

'What is it this week, Caiaphas?'

The high priest's reply had been carefully prepared.

'We found this man unsettling our nation. He opposes payment of Roman taxes and claims to be a king.'

The Governor looked at Jesus, taking in his simple clothes, his tired posture, and judged him to be a common peasant. He laughed and walked up to Jesus.

'Are you really the *King* of the Jews?' he asked mockingly.

Jesus looked into his eyes as he had done with Caiaphas. He saw what I could also see: Pilate simply didn't care. But the Roman urged him to reply and Jesus did.

'Yes, it is as you say.'

The Governor smiled with self-satisfaction and wheeled around to face the priests.

'I find no basis for a charge against this man,' he said casually. He then walked straight past them, ordering, 'Release him.'

Caiaphas was not ready to give up.

'He has been stirring up people all over Judea with his teaching. He started in Galilee and spread his poison right down to Jerusalem.'

At the word 'Galilee', Pilate stopped and returned from his doorway.

'If he is from Galilee,' the Governor said deliberately, 'then he is the responsibility of Herod. And as 'Prince' Herod is in Jerusalem this week, you can take your complaint directly to him.'

He smiled again and walked swiftly back into his palace followed by the clanking armour of his private guard.

I reassessed the situation. The leader of the Opposition seemed content; Caiaphas had been humiliated and consequently was all the more resolved to dispense with Jesus. The high priest looked at Jesus, his thoughts like thunder clouds.

'To Herod!' he ordered and strode off, taking with him a small delegation of his closest advisers.

Herod, one of the nominal Jewish princes set in place by the Romans, has a palace on the north side of the city. The small troop of Temple guards escorting a prisoner though the narrow streets attracted little interest. Caiaphas kept the party moving at a swift pace out of fear that Jesus might be recognised and people come to his defence. One of the priests ran ahead to announce their arrival and, at Herod's palace, the gates swung open in welcome.

Prince Herod was waiting in his entrance hall and instructed his own guards to take Jesus into a private chamber. The priests clamoured for his attention but Herod dismissed them with a wave of his arm and disappeared from view. He wanted Jesus to himself.

Herod had long wanted to meet Jesus. He had arrested Jesus' cousin, John the Dipper, and kept him in prison for many months before killing him. John had fascinated Herod and there were many who claimed that Jesus was John returned from Death. More than anything, Herod wanted to see one of the miracles he had heard so much about.

Jesus didn't even look at the man. Eventually, desperate to provoke a reaction from Jesus, Herod sent for one of his household slaves, who was sick, and begged for her to be healed. Jesus looked at the terrified woman, offering her his compassion, but a physical restoration would have been impossible in such an environment of mockery and fear. The sick woman herself saw Jesus as nothing other than the cause of this latest humiliation. Before long, Herod gave up. He pushed and bullied Jesus to the door, telling him that he was a great disappointment. When the door was opened, Herod kicked him out into the hall beyond. The huddle of anxious priests looked up as their prisoner crashed to the floor in front of them.

Caiaphas attempted to take control of the situation, but controlling Herod was difficult; he has neither the legal discipline of the Romans nor the religious fervour of the Jews. He is a pampered pet of the occupying Roman government, kept with the specific intention of undermining the power of the Jewish Council.

The priests produced a string of accusations against Jesus but Herod was not interested. The only charge that interested him at all was the one Caiaphas had used in front of Pilate, that Jesus claimed to be a king. Herod saw it as an opportunity for some entertainment and called for one of his royal robes to be brought for Jesus. Herod himself draped the garment over Jesus' shoulders. His soldiers saluted Jesus and, between bouts of giggling, shouted, 'Hail King Jesus, Emperor to the fishermen!'

Caiaphas watched anxiously. This was getting him nowhere. He would have to return to Pilate and present a more urgent case against Jesus.

Lucifer, on the other hand, was still relaxed, confident that Caiaphas would despatch Jesus personally if he had to. Lucifer was also buoyed up by my inaction. Again and again he looked across to Michael and me, trying to work out why we were doing nothing. Although he could not read our thoughts, the longer we were silent, the more his confidence grew.

To his credit, Michael has been unusually calm today, more so than he has been throughout the Son's life down on this watery planet.

Caiaphas ordered Jesus to be returned to Pilate. We all processed back across the city to the Praetorium, where, once again, we have been made to wait.

Late Friday morning

By the time the Roman Governor had emerged again from his fine stone palace, most of the Jewish Council had arrived back from the Temple precincts. Pilate marched across his courtyard towards the large herd of priests. His mood was one of utter frustration that the petty-minded Jews were bothering him once again. However, halfway across the neatly paved yard, his eye was caught by the sight of Jesus, dressed in Herod's expensive cloak, several sizes too big for him. Pilate immediately appreciated the prince's joke. Summoning a guard, he sent the man to Herod with a message, 'Ask him if we can borrow the cloak for a while. It looks rather good on the carpenter.'

That done, Pilate's scowl returned and he completed his journey towards the waiting priests.

'I was hoping not to see you again today, Caiaphas.'

Caiaphas cast a carefully prepared line in the direction of his adversary.

'Herod is not interested in maintaining peace in this city, but you and I know that we cannot afford trouble when Jerusalem is packed with pilgrims for the Passover.'

The hook caught. Keeping the peace at Passover time was always a concern for Pilate, but he did not want to be manipulated by Caiaphas.

The Governor replied, 'You brought this man to me, claiming that he was stirring up rebellion. I examined him in your presence and found no basis for a charge against him, neither has Herod – evidently.'

The two men looked at one another with cool aggression.

'Therefore I will have him whipped and then . . .' A sardonic glint sparkled in his eyes. 'And then – in honour of your Passover Feast – I will release him!'

Caiaphas' blood pressure rose instantly and something similar happened within the leader of the Opposition. Lucifer glared at me, assuming that I had used Pilate to outwit him. Caiaphas and his colleagues exploded with anger. They surrounded the Governor like hyenas round an injured antelope. Waving arms in exasperation and pointing fingers, they bayed for Jesus' blood.

'He must be killed,' they insisted, repeating their message with rising hysteria.

Pilate's guards approached anxiously, watching for any sign of physical violence.

One voice in the mob rose above the others.

'If you want to give us a Passover present, we will have *Barabbas*.'

This brought a great roar of approval, followed by numerous shouts of, 'Give us Barabbas!' Meanwhile the Governor tried to make himself heard over the clamour but the priests joined their voices and began to chant, 'Crucify him! Crucify him! Crucify him!'

The Roman politician conceded, lowered his arms, and slipped out of the fray, taking sanctuary in the heavily armed company of his personal bodyguard. Lucifer took control of the situation – Pilate was clearly shaken, Caiaphas was wild with rage – he had to act. He dragged the high priest away from the pack and stood him, straight and proud, directly in front of Pilate. Lucifer spoke firmly to his black-clad puppet, 'Stick your chest out and say nothing.'

Pilate was clearly intimidated by the high priest's bold manoeuvre. Caiaphas' veiled threat of violence on the streets of Jerusalem had focussed his mind but he did not intend to concede without a fight.

'Why?' he bellowed.

The Governor allowed his question to echo around the enclosed courtyard and waited for silence. When all that could be heard was the distant clamour of crowded streets, he spoke again, this time quietly.

'What crime has this man committed?' He did not wait for an answer. 'I have found no grounds for the death penalty. I will have him punished and will then release him.'

Lucifer was right next to Caiaphas and barked at him, 'Do not move a muscle and say nothing.'

The chant of 'Crucify him' began again and this time the voices of the priests were joined by those of a thousand Opposition spirits. I do not suppose that Pilate's ears could hear their cold voices but I have no doubt that his spirit was shaken by them. Briefly, the Governor consulted with the chief of his guard, who nodded his head. Pilate indicated to Caiaphas that he wished to speak and the high priest held up his arm for quiet.

'Very well,' the Roman said in a matter-of-fact way. 'Let's crucify him.'

There was silence. Nobody moved or spoke. All eyes were on the Roman Governor, waiting for him to do or say something further. But he stood firm, his hands clasped behind his back. He was waiting, but what for? Pilate exchanged brief conversations with his chief guard. People whispered to their neighbours, trying to understand what Pilate was planning. It was clear from his face that he was pleased to have regained control of the situation. After a while he dispatched one of his staff on an errand. When the man returned there was a brief conversation, confirming whatever they anticipated, and the wait continued.

I looked around again. Caiaphas was bemused but had resolved to be patient. Pilate had agreed to execute Jesus and he did not wish to change his mind. Lucifer could see into the Governor's mind and was also content to wait, relishing his victory.

Last of all I looked to Jesus – the subject of all these murderous plots – standing in the middle of the courtyard, removed from everyone else apart from two Temple guards, one at either shoulder. In a moment of internal horror I realised that neither I nor anyone else had paid any attention to the Son since Pilate's arrival. The keystone of all creation had become an insignificant pawn in a power struggle between the rival rulers of Jerusalem.

I drew close to him and tried to perceive his thoughts and feelings. Jesus had just been condemned to die. Death is something that is completely outside the experience of spiritual creatures such as Angels, let alone our Creator, but the Son had accepted mortality and was standing on the edge of that perpetual meaninglessness.

I studied my Lord deeply. His entire being was focussed on the narrow path before him and on the few people who stood with him on that track: two indifferent guards, the high priest and the Governor. Jesus was praying for them, praying for their families, for their futures, for their faith.

The leader of the Opposition was watching me. He longed to know what his former Master intended to do but I do not believe that he can see love. He is at home with the brutal ambition of the politicians but the contents of Jesus' mind would have made little sense to him.

I returned to Michael, who seemed calm.

'Aren't you worried?' I asked him.

'Look at it this way,' he whispered back. 'We know precisely what Lucifer intends to do but he would give half his army for a small insight into why we are here and doing nothing.'

'Shh! He's listening.'

'I know,' Michael returned.

I could not share Michael's optimism. I watched Jesus last night, racked with sheer agonies of despair. The part that he most fears has not even begun. The closer we come to the epicentre of our Boss's plan the clearer I can see how terrifyingly fragile it is.

Still we wait.

Shortly after noon, Friday

As the assembled swarm of priests waited, they began to relax with the growing realisation that the Galilean carpenter, who had undermined their authority for the past three years, was about to die. Meanwhile, Caiaphas sent several of his aides scurrying off with errands and messages. The Temple guards who were minding Jesus sat down, inviting him to join them. That made Pilate anxious. He worried that he might lose the control he had struggled to achieve.

He shouted over to Jesus, 'Stand up man! You are my prisoner. You do nothing unless I tell you.'

Jesus' intense concentration on the task before him had not wavered at any stage through the morning and it did not change then as he stood again, followed by his embarrassed guards. Pilate was clearly pleased to have everyone in the courtyard looking at him and resolved to exploit this advantage.

'Centurion!' he ordered. 'Take this carpenter-king and give him thirty-nine lashes.'

The centurion and three others marched swiftly away from Pilate and relieved the Jewish guards of their charge. Jesus was swept purposefully around the Praetorium wall and out of human sight.

'Stay here and keep an eye on the Opposition,' I instructed Michael.

I quickly caught up with Jesus. For the first time since the Garden of Gethsemane, he was struggling to keep his mind focussed. Fears were taking over; he felt alone and his faith in his Father's plan was clinging like a small crab clings to a rock in the face of advancing waves.

'This is only pain,' he reminded himself. 'This is only physical pain. I have experienced pain hundreds of times: every time I nicked my hand with a saw; every time I hit my finger with a mallet. This will be no different.' And he prayed. 'My dear Father, help me through this flogging. Help me to love these soldiers. You love them. You love their families. Help me.'

With similar thoughts repeating their messages around his mind he tried to prepare himself as the soldiers routinely stripped off his clothes and secured his tired body to a wooden flogging post.

Human pain is something I have never experienced but as the

first lash of the studded whip fell on Jesus' bare back, a surge of anger and panic blasted through my mind. Clearly, I was still experiencing Jesus' human feelings. While the soldier raised his arm in preparation for the next stroke, Jesus battled to sweep away his fear and find something to love in the man who was assaulting him, but the blows came too fast. He had no time to prepare himself for them. Before long his back was a sodden mess of blood and torn flesh and the state of his mind was little different.

As the centurion counted the lashes, Jesus became calmer. It seemed that he was now barely feeling the repeated blows; his pain had reached some kind of limit. He was able to concentrate on his prayers again and began to sing a psalm within his mind, singing in rhythm with the regular splat of the blood-soaked whip.

At thirty-nine the Centurion called a halt and gave instructions for Jesus to be untied. I gasped as he simply slid to the floor, his mind blank. Only his body was alive. A soldier strutted across the yard carrying something.

'I gather he claims to be a king,' he announced. 'I've made him a crown.'

The man walked up to Jesus. In his hand was a thorn branch that he had plaited into a hoop. The soldier crouched down beside Jesus' motionless body and paused.

'He's out cold, sir!'

The centurion calmly gave an order. 'Pour some water over him.'

This was done by a second soldier and Jesus groaned. The two soldiers pulled him up and leant him against the flogging post. The first forced the barbed crown onto Jesus' head, then bent down with his face close to Jesus' and said, 'Now you're a real king.' I watched the man's mind. There was no hatred in his thoughts. Jesus looked into his eyes and saw an ordinary man who was trying to make a horrible job bearable. He just managed to say, 'Thank you,' before the other soldier struck him on the head with the water jug; thorns dug into his scalp and his head fell back against the post.

Jesus was barely conscious as the whole company of Pilate's private guard assembled in the courtyard to laugh at the prisoner. Herod's robe was draped over his shoulders and the centurion watched his men as they relaxed and enjoyed themselves for a few minutes. Then he gave an order for Jesus to be returned to the Governor.

Quickly and efficiently, the soldiers removed the cloak, poured more water over Jesus, hitting him one last time with the wooden jug. They pulled his clothes back over that tattered back.

As the Son was half escorted, half dragged out of the stable yard, the weaver of the thorn crown called, 'Ey! You've forgotten this!' He ran forward and placed Herod's cloak over Jesus' shoulders to a cheer from the assembled soldiers.

That was the sight which interrupted the excited conversations of the Jewish priests as they waited in the Praetorium courtyard. Pilate was standing in the same place, hands still clasped behind his back. Everyone looked at the blood-drenched prisoner, dressed in a royal robe and wearing a crown made out of thorns, unable to stand without the support of two young Roman soldiers.

Governor Pilate was amused by his soldiers' work and taunted the Jewish Council members, proclaiming, 'Here is your king!'

'Take him away and crucify him,' came the high priest's swift reply.

Pilate laughed. 'Do you want me to execute your king?'

Michael drew my attention to the Opposition leader, who was looking anxious. Lucifer could see, as we could, that the Governor was making one final attempt to release Jesus. 'The man is innocent and has suffered enough,' he was thinking.

Lucifer gave a single command and the Opposition spirits moved among the priests, stirring up their jealousy and fear. The priests shouted venomously, 'Take him away' and 'We have no king.' Then they returned to their chant of 'Crucify, crucify, crucify!' This time their faces were twisted with rage.

I heard an Angelic voice behind me shout, 'Shall we stop them?' I turned and saw an entire battalion of Angels – numerous ranks of Heavenly warriors, poised, waiting for a command to engage with their age-old enemy and save their Lord. Michael and I exchanged a momentary glance and I addressed our army.

'No one must take any action whatsoever without my express permission. Do you understand?'

I returned my attention to the angry mass of chanting clerics to discover that the entire force of Opposition spirits was staring at me in disbelief. None of them looked more confused than their leader. It lasted only a moment because the priests' chant quickly faded when they saw an execution party march into view from behind the Governor's palace. There were three condemned men – each carrying his own cross – surrounded by a heavily armed troop of soldiers. They headed straight for Pontius Pilate.

When they reached the Governor, they stopped. Pilate remained where he was and spoke quietly to the soldier in charge of the prisoners. I listened carefully.

'Which is the one called Barabbas?' Pilate asked.

'The one in the middle, sir.'

'Release him.

'Sorry, sir?'

'Release him, you idiot.'

'Yes, sir.'

The man looked across to the centurion who nodded his agreement with the unusual command. He walked over to the second prisoner in the line, lifted the heavy wooden cross from his shoulder and told him to leave. The undernourished terrorist moved from his place in the execution party and a great cheer went up from the priests. At last they were sure that they had won the day. The leader of the Opposition, on the other hand, was still anxiously surveying the army of Angels behind me.

Jesus was escorted to the vacant cross and it was lifted onto his shoulder. He struggled to take its weight. Lucifer's entire following closed in around their prize and, as the executioners continued on their way, Lucifer himself went to the front, taking his place beside the centurion.

Michael and I, accompanied by our own battalion, brought up the rear with the priests. Governor Pilate did not even wait for the procession to reach his gate. He returned swiftly to the palatial comfort of his home.

Outside the Roman army compound, the street was packed with people who had come to see the spectacle. Clearly, Caiaphas' many messengers had been spreading the news of Jesus' doom. I scanned the faces in the crowd. There were a few scarred with hatred for Jesus and a few distressed by his demise. Most of those gathered in the narrow street were there simply because they had nothing better to do and were attracted to the prospect of a celebrity execution.

My studies of the human minds around me were interrupted. Jesus had collapsed under the weight of his cross and soldiers were swarming around him.

'He's not going to make it, sir,' one was saying, and another added, 'You'll have to commandeer someone to carry it for him.'

It was the centurion's turn to survey the crowd. I remembered one particularly bright face that I had noticed, a young man who was full of hope. I directed the centurion's gaze towards him. The centurion responded surprisingly easily to my guidance and ordered the man to step forward.

'Name?'

'Simon.'

'Where are you from?'

'Cyrene.'

'Where on Earth is that?'

'North Africa.'

'Are you a citizen of Rome?'

Simon smiled at the absurdity of such a question being put of an African. 'No.'

'Good.'

The centurion had been following the official protocol for forcing someone to carry a load.

'Pick up that man's cross and follow us. It's less than a mile.'

Simon was ushered to Jesus' side and the splintered cross was hoisted onto his shoulder. The crucifixion party moved on again and I felt better for having done something to help. For hours I had been watching helplessly but at least I had arranged for Jesus a sympathetic companion on his last Earthly journey.

As he staggered towards the place of his execution, Jesus' mind focussed on the faces that lined his route. Deep in this thoughts he was saying to each individual, 'For you. And for you. For you.' His eye especially picked out those who were screaming abuse at him and to each his thought was the same, 'For you.'

Then without warning Jesus stopped, causing considerable confusion among the soldiers. He stepped to the side of the road to speak to a group of widows, dressed in their customary black. The centurion signalled to his men to leave Jesus for a moment while they helped themselves, and Simon, to a drink. The widows were professional mourners, women who attend funerals to lead the required wailing on behalf of the deceased's family in return for a good meal. They had been lending their rehearsed grief to the noise of the crowd.

'Don't mourn for me,' Jesus told them. 'Weep for yourselves and your children.'

The centurion called for the death march to resume and Jesus returned to his place. For the first time, he looked at Simon. Simon knew at once that he was not looking into the face of a common criminal. Jesus looked into young eyes that were bright with sturdy reliance on his Father's love.

'Thank you,' he said weakly.

Simon was jabbed in the back by the blunt end of a spear and moved on.

We made our way towards the city wall. Jesus still fixed his attention on the people who lined his path. He seemed to draw strength from them. Not only did they provide a focus for his mind but they became the focus of his entire purpose.

The procession squeezed itself through one of Jerusalem's lesser gates and out into the midday sun. A short way beyond the city's fly-ridden refuse heap stood a small, bare hillock. At its rock-strewn summit, Simon was relieved of his burden and dismissed. Jesus stood and watched as experienced soldiers laid out the tools required for a crucifixion: hammers, nails, ropes. Items that would have been at home in a carpenter's workshop. Jesus surveyed them with the eye of an expert, noting the weight of the hammer, the length of nails. For a moment these familiar objects filled his troubled thoughts, until they were picked up and put to their dreadful purpose on the prisoner who had been walking in front of him.

The air was awash with curses and blasphemies as the man struggled, kicking and biting, until overpowered by the might of Rome. The bones in his wrist crunched as a large nail was driven through them and into the wood below. Hollow screams echoed through my spirit as this man, who had lived for his own pleasure, suffered the kind of agony that he had inflicted on others.

My attention was distracted from the grisly scene by Michael, who directed my gaze at the Son. The leader of the Opposition had moved right up to him and was gloating at him. What he was saying could not be reported in human language. Jesus ignored him, choosing instead to watch as the first prisoner's cross was hoisted upright and allowed to drop a considerable distance into a hole cut out for it in the rock. The man's body pulled at the nails which secured him and then crashed against the rough wood. He opened his mouth to scream but no sound came out. I imagine that the shock and pain were beyond expression. Large timber wedges were driven into the hole to secure the cross, sending shock-waves through the agonised body. When the hammer blows ended, the man unleashed a torrent of abuse against God, the Romans and anyone else his eye noticed. The soldiers did not stop to listen. They gathered up their tools and moved on to Jesus.

Jesus was shaken by the sight he had just witnessed. He had seen men crucified before but not from such close quarters, nor with the knowledge that his own body was about to be subjected to the same catalogue of agonies. He did not resist as the soldiers removed all his clothes and laid his tattered back along the splintered wood. As ropes were secured around his chest and shoulders, Jesus looked into the faces of the hard working Romans.

'Father,' he prayed, 'Forgive them. They do not know what they are doing.' He smiled weakly at his executioners.

Four nails were passed across. Jesus prepared himself for a burst of pain as the point of the first nail was positioned at the base of his hand. I looked into his mind, deliberately ignoring the physical events around me. Jesus watched the nail, waiting, anticipating, then, *crash*. His mind lost all focus for a moment, spinning in dark terror; then I heard the voice of Lucifer talking smoothly into Jesus' thoughts.

'Curse God, go on. Everyone does, it's only natural.'

Jesus turned his mind to the second nail, avoiding Lucifer's whispers. Another crash. This time he knew what to expect. The third and forth nails were driven through his ankles. With these new pains added to the trauma of his earlier flogging, Jesus' brain began to drift at the edge of consciousness. When he was raised up above the square hole in the ground the centurion stepped forward.

'Gently lads, gently.'

The cross was lowered rather than dropped.

'I'll secure it, you do number three,' the centurion instructed.

His men moved on to the third prisoner and he pushed the wedges in with his feet, avoiding the terrible jarring that would have been caused by the soldiers' hammers. He then stood, considering his unusual victim, still crowned with a wreath of thorns. Meanwhile, the last cross was erected. Its occupant, perhaps, had learned from Jesus' example. He did not resist.

The job done, the Romans packed away their tools and picked over the victims' belongings, looking for anything of value. They selected the hand-woven undergarment that Martha had given

Jesus and decided to play dice for it. The crucifixion had been accomplished with typical Roman efficiency. Now there was nothing to do but wait. Wait for Death.

When the soldiers had finished their work, the crowds soon dispersed. There is little attraction, it seems, in watching three men slowly die. The members of the Jewish Council returned to their families and Caiaphas arranged for a rota of representatives to witness Jesus' end.

'I don't want to take any risks,' he said. 'Send a messenger if anything unusual happens and let me know when he is dead.'

With that he returned across the valley to his wife and children.

When their leader was out of sight, the remaining priests unloaded their frustrations on Jesus. It was a Jewish holiday, the day of Passover, and they were annoyed to be working.

'You saved all kinds of people,' they shouted at their now helpless adversary, 'so they say. If you're our Messiah, chosen by God, why don't you save yourself? Then we can all go home.'

Two of the soldiers joined in. 'You're supposed to be a king,' they jeered, 'so where's your army? Aren't they going to ride in and rescue you?'

I looked around at his army, now numbering many thousands of Angels, crowded around their Master. They could have overcome the Romans and taken Jesus down from that cross as easily as a woman picks fluff off her dress. But they did not. They were waiting, hoping for an order from me and at that moment I was sorely tempted to give it.

A messenger arrived from the Governor's office, carrying the charge notice to hang above Jesus' head. The men either side of Jesus each had their crime suspended over them. 'Murderer' read the sign for the first. 'Terrorist' said the other. The centurion reached up and passed the cord over the top of Jesus' cross. The notice proclaimed, 'This is the King of the Jews'.

One of the priests stepped forward. 'We can't accept that,' he declared.

'Not my responsibility,' returned the centurion with a patient smile. 'It's the Governor who issues the charges.'

A second priest joined in. 'Can't you just rub out *"This is…"* and replace it with *"He claimed to be…"*'

'I'm afraid I can't. Anyway, I don't have any chalk.'

That was, in fact, a lie. Human lies sound hollow to an Angelic ear and I suspect that the small lump of rock that he was fingering in his leather pouch was indeed a piece of chalk. The priests stepped back and one of them hurried off to the city to report to the high priest.

The murderer on Jesus' right read the charge. 'So you are our *saviour*, are you? Well get on with your job and save yourself. And you can save me while you're at it.'

Painfully, Jesus turned to face the man; the spiked crown tore into his scalp. But before he could speak, the terrorist on Jesus' left joined in.

'Do you have no respect for your God?' he shouted at the murderer. 'Or for your fellow sufferer?'

He paused while a flash of pain shot through his body.

'You and I are here because we've got what we deserve but this man has done nothing wrong.'

The murderer simply spat. Jesus slowly turned his head to face the first person to have spoken in his defence all day. He was a Zealot, a member of a fanatical group dedicated to overthrowing Roman occupation and returning the Jewish people to the rule of law given by my Boss. Jesus admired the self-sacrificing commitment of the Zealots, even though he decried their murderous methods. He looked into the earnest eyes of a man prepared to die for his faith.

The man spoke again, the hardness of his zeal tempered by the imminence of death. 'Jesus, remember me when you enter your righteous kingdom.'

Jesus struggled to reply.

'I tell you . . . the truth.' He took several breaths before he could continue. 'You will be . . . with me . . .' (more laboured breaths), 'in Paradise.'

I was startled by Jesus' reply. Could a man of such violence be so quickly welcomed into my Boss's home? I quickly looked across to Lucifer to see how he had responded to Jesus' words. He was scornful, urging his minions to laugh at their enemy's foolishness.

Time passed. The three men, the Source of all love among them, were lost in their private agonies. The soldiers were prepared for a long wait. The two remaining priests were bored. A cold wind was blowing, bringing thick cloud to the Judean mountains.

Three hours later

While I was recording these events, various people came and went. At times entire families made their way out of the city and stood for a while watching and talking; then they returned. I looked around me. All the Opposition spirits had arrived. Among them were many who are familiar to me. I had worked with them before they gave up on love and went their own way. These dark spirits were far outnumbered by the assembled ranks of Heaven. Every single spirit who serves my Boss in this Universe had also made their way to the little hillock of Calvary to be with their Master as the light of his life slowly faded.

Lucifer surveyed the gathered Angels nervously, knowing that he would stand no chance if the fury of Heaven should turn against him. He did not understand that the fury of Heaven was aimed at a different target.

Martha and Mary were there – they had walked down from Bethany at the news of Jesus' execution – and a number of other women who had travelled with Jesus from Galilee. Nearer to the three crosses were John, the brother of James, and Mary from Magdala (who Jesus met at Matthew's party). Behind them I noticed my colleague, Maff, and knew that Jesus' mother could not be far away. Yes, Mary was huddled in a thick shawl as close to her son as the soldiers would allow. The sadness of her soul was so profound that it was painful to observe. To her mind the entire Universe was emptying and on the brink of destruction.

Still we waited. Jesus was fading, his breath shallow; he was only occasionally conscious now. Then my Boss appeared. A wave of terror rippled through the Opposition, matched by a ray of hope in the spirits of Heaven. The thick fog in Jesus' mind cleared and he looked into the eyes of his Father. His thoughts did not match the glimmering hopes of the Angels; they echoed the sheer terror of the Opposition.

This was what Jesus most feared. This is what had reduced him to cold sweat and hot tears in the Garden of Gethsemane. In his Father's face he did not see love but only pure anger, the utter hatred of every rebellious act and every selfish thought amassed by generation after generation of human beings across the world.

'My God!' Jesus begged. 'My God!'

He fought for breath, desperate to cling to the love and mercy that he remembered in his Dad. Then my Boss turned his back on his Son and – to the absolute horror of the hosts of Heaven – he left.

A roar of celebration swept up from the Opposition. Jesus' body slumped, hanging by the nails in his wrists, crying out in his total loneliness, 'Why have you abandoned me?'

Lucifer anticipated that the end was near. He picked a group of close supporters and assembled them at the foot of Jesus' cross. The hosts of Heaven looked on in paralysed silence. John joined Mary and helped her to her feet.

Jesus began to gather breaths, building up his strength for one last cry. He raised his head, looking beyond his enemies, beyond his mother and his closest human friend, beyond the millions of Angels who longed to save him. He looked into the emptiness beyond and shouted as loud as he was able, 'My Father, I leave my spirit in your hands!'

That was his last breath. The light of his life went out and his defeated spirit slid from its body. Lucifer was there to catch it but there was no triumphant shout from the Opposition. I imagine that they, too, were overwhelmed by the enormity of what had just happened. Lucifer held tightly to his prize. His followers closed around their leader as he carried his limp quarry away. They passed in front of Michael and myself and stopped. Whereas all human spirits are bound by the ties of their myriad selfish activities, the Son was ensnared in *every* crime and callousness that has ever been known in all humanity's sorry history. He had been weighed in my Boss's scales and found wanting.

Lucifer said nothing, he simply looked at me. There was no smile on his face, no mockery in his eyes. It was almost as though he was waiting for my permission for him to continue. I stared back, too numb to respond, as the leader of the Opposition carried my Master away to the place where he stores all the human dead – to Death. The whole company of rebel spirits followed.

When they were gone, I could see that the centurion was once again standing by Jesus' cross. He was oblivious to the spiritual drama that had just taken place around him, his gaze fixed on Jesus' disfigured corpse.

'Surely,' he said, turning to Mary and John, 'this man *was* God's Son.'

I couldn't bear to stay any longer and I did not have the courage to turn and face the devastated Angels behind me. I returned to my office, relieved to be away from that dreadful place, my spirit heavier than it has ever been.

I have done what my Boss required of me. I have kept to his every instruction. What he planned has happened. But I do not feel any satisfaction. He risked everything for the sake of humanity. And it seems to me that everything has been lost.

Away from Earth, in timeless Heaven

I sat in my office, lost in thoughtlessness. A stream of solemn Angels drifted past my door. They were making their way to the Gathering Place where our Boss assembles us at moments of great importance. On this occasion, though, there had been no instruction to gather; no word at all from our Boss. It seemed that in such extreme circumstances there was nothing else for the Angels of Heaven to do but to be together, in the home of our Creator and Master. Gabriel slipped silently into my room, his spirit as dull as my own.

'You will have to talk to them,' he commented after a while.

A spark of anger flashed across my mind.

'You do it,' I retaliated. 'You're the *great messenger!*'

He absorbed my aggression without responding. Before long, both Michael and Raphael had joined us. None of us spoke, our spirits empty, there was nothing to say. I found myself being irritated by all three of them. Age-old niggles returned: my jealousy of Gabriel, my impatience with Raphael, my distrust of Michael. The love that used to flow so effortlessly from my Angelic being seemed to have vanished.

At last, Gabriel spoke. He looked directly at me and said, 'It has to be you.'

Together, we made our way to the place where all of Heaven was assembled, but Heaven felt very empty. Millions of Angels looked forlornly to me for some explanation, yet I had little I could tell them. It is not possible to express the subtle themes of Angelic discourse in crude words; it would be better represented in the complex harmonies of your world's great orchestras. But these words will give some flavour of my message: 'My fellow servants, it is true. The One who is the Source of all our music has been carried off to the place of utter silence. His song was sung exactly as he chose. It is not yet completed.'

I walked out. On the way back to my office I passed my Boss's door. I stopped and knocked. There was no reply. I knew that there would be no reply but I knocked again, and again, and again. Soon I was hammering on his door with all my energy, shouting, 'I don't like this. I don't like it at all.'

Raphael found me and guided me gently back to my room where he has stayed with me.

Early Sunday morning

I was not comfortable in Heaven and decided to return to Jerusalem. I avoided Saturday. Nothing much happens on the Jewish Sabbath and I was too full of my own grief to be able to cope with that of Jesus' Earthly companions. I arrived in the city as the Sabbath sun was setting and people were emerging from their homes to resume their business. I toured the city, searching for a familiar face and eventually found Mary of Magdala with some of the other women who had supported Jesus. They were at a market, buying grave clothes and burial spices. I did not know what had happened to Jesus' body after his death. Clearly there had not been enough time to complete the customary burial rituals before sunset and the start of the Sabbath.

I searched Mary's mind for information about Jesus' body. Then I left the market and followed the trail of Mary's memories. I made my way past the place where Jesus was executed. The crosses had been removed. All that remained of Friday's grisly events were three pools of dried blood. I moved on. A little way further on I came to a small hillside garden where there was a tomb carved into the rock. The garden was heavily guarded. There were two very different groups of guards: at the entrance of the garden and beside the tomb itself I found a detachment of Roman soldiers; the other guard was made up of Opposition spirits. The latter noticed my arrival but ignored me. They were confident in their victory and knew that I presented no threat to them. Unseen by the Romans I settled myself down next to the vast circular rock that blocked the way to Jesus' empty corpse.

Through the night, the Roman guard changed at regular intervals and several Opposition spirits passed by to see where Jesus' story had ended.

As the sky brightened and the birds resumed their morning calls, my thoughts were interrupted by the sound of laughter. The laughter was neither human nor demonic, it was the unmistakable laughter of Heaven and it came from inside the tomb. My spirits suddenly soared and the Opposition guards froze. They stared through the rock in disbelief and then fled without a backward glance. I stayed, enchanted by a sound more welcome and more beautiful than the song of any bird. It was a laugh that I instantly recognised – the wholesome mirth of my Boss. I leapt up and listened, excitement flooding my spirit. Beside my Boss's life-restoring delight I could hear a chorus of thousands, even millions of other voices, all joining in the ecstatic cacophony.

Then, without warning, the laughter stopped and a single voice penetrated the solid rock between us. It was a human voice – but richer and fuller than any human voice I had heard before. It was the voice of Jesus.

'Come on, Oriel, let us out. It's rather crowded in here.'

'There's a guard of Roman soldiers,' I replied. 'What shall I do with them?'

'Put them to sleep or something,' he suggested, 'but hurry up, I'm getting squashed.'

I dealt with the soldiers quickly and turned my attention to the stone. Moving rocks around is not something that Archangels do very often, so I studied the rock for a while, heckled by amused voices from within. Lucifer and a detachment of his key henchmen arrived but I ignored them; they presented no threat now. They did not stay for long.

I moved the stone slowly, being careful not to break it. When it was finally out of the way I was astounded by the sight that greeted me. I had expected to see the Son returned to his usual Heavenly form, sharing inseparable unity with my Boss. But there before me stood Jesus the human, although he was far more than human. The hazy form of his physical humanity had been transformed into the full beauty of Heavenly life. I was dazzled by his appearance.

'Out the way, Oriel,' he called exuberantly. 'There's a lot of us in here.'

I stepped aside and out of the tomb came my Boss followed by a long line of bright, shining humans, the first of whom was Jesus.

'Who are all these?' I asked the Son, who stopped beside me.

'All the people who have died who have ever loved me,' he replied.
The Heavenly humans emerged from the tomb in a steady stream, all following my Boss.

'Is there anyone left in Death?' I asked.

'Sadly, yes,' Jesus said. 'There are those who still insist on going their own way, even when offered complete forgiveness and timeless life.'

His thoughts were distracted by the sight of someone entering the garden by the traditional route, through the gate.

'Quick, Oriel!' he said. 'It's Mary! I don't want her to see me yet. You'll have to deal with her.'

'What shall I tell her?' I asked.

He was gone.

As soon as they had rounded the corner of the path, Mary of Magdala and her companions discovered that the tomb was open. I do not think that they could see the continuing stream of redeemed women and men (as all of Death's former prisoners now had Heavenly bodies I suspect they would be hard for human eyes to see).

Mary walked straight past me and, stepping over the sleeping Romans, she stooped to look into the tomb. To her it was dark and empty. She conducted a thorough search of the stone slab where Jesus' old body had been placed on Friday evening. While she was discussing her findings with her friends, Gabriel, Raphael and Michael arrived. The news had reached Heaven.

I quickly explained the situation to them.

'What should I do?' I asked.

'Leave it to me.' Gabriel replied. 'I'll talk to them.'

'Don't frighten them, Gabriel,' I warned. 'They've had a traumatic few days.'

'I have done this before, Oriel,' he retorted.

'I know,' I said. 'That's why I'm going to join you.'

Together we thinned our spiritual beings until our brightness was reduced to the narrow spectrum of light that human eyes can see. The women were terrified and fell flat on their faces. Gabriel gave me a resigned smile.

'They scare easily, these humans,' he said.

I spoke to the women. 'Why are you looking for a living man in this place of Death?'

This seemed a strange thing to be saying, considering the long queue of very much alive humans who were still filing past us.

Gabriel added excitedly, 'Jesus isn't here. He is alive!'

I cast him a slightly impatient look, asking him to leave the talking to me.

'Don't you remember what he told you while you were still in Galilee?' I continued, to the women. 'He told you that he would be arrested and killed and he also said that on the third day he would rise again.'

They nodded their heads as the memory rose sketchily in their minds.

Suddenly something clicked into place in Mary's thoughts.

'Come on girls!' she said to her companions. 'We must run back and tell the others.'

And off they went. One of them, Joanna I think, turned and called out, 'Thank you!' as they disappeared.

Gabriel and I returned to our usual brightness and were joined, almost immediately, by Jesus.

'Where were you?' Gabriel asked.

'Behind that rather large cedar tree,' he replied, pointing with a human arm bright with Heavenly light.

'May we ask why?' Raphael added, tentatively.

'You may,' Jesus responded, but with a familiar gleam in his eyes he said nothing further. There is a playful aspect in my Boss's character which can be found in human children but which tends to get lost as they grow up. It was such a pleasure to see it again in Jesus after weeks of fear and dreadful anticipation.

'Why?' I asked, reasserting Raphael's question.

'I need to speak to Peter first,' the Son said.

'What about John?' I suggested, putting in a bid for the only one of the Twelve who had been with Jesus all the way to Calvary. 'He was *there*, you know?'

'I know,' Jesus smiled. 'That's why I must speak to Peter first.'

Our conversation moved on to details of the Son's incarceration in Death and the story of how he had broken free from its stifling constraints and spoken to all the souls held captive there. He told us how he had offered them the gift of Heavenly freedom, but his story had barely begun when John came sprinting up the hill into the garden, followed, at some distance, by the older and less energetic form of Peter. John stopped at the step down into the tomb, looking in. Peter, when he finally arrived, stumbled straight inside. John followed.

The liberated souls of the dead, who were still streaming out, looked curiously at the two men who stood staring at Jesus' abandoned grave clothes. Watching them, it was quite clear why Jesus wished to speak to Peter first. John was calm. He remembered Jesus' words about rising again and believed that it had indeed happened, even though he couldn't understand exactly what it meant. Peter's mind, on the other hand, was spinning. All manner of irrational thoughts were cascading through his head. He feared that even Jesus' dead body could not bear to be in the company of a man who had denied knowing him three times over.

Jesus whispered to me, 'Oriel, you direct John back to the others, and I will talk to Peter in private.'

I placed in the young man's mind a reminder that there were nine others, waiting anxiously in Jerusalem for a second opinion on Mary's report. He got the message, made his apologies to Peter and ran off. Peter did not want to stay alone in the dark. He staggered out into the garden and turned away from Jerusalem, closely followed by Jesus.

'Wait for me here,' Jesus called as he left.

Sunday evening

I waited in the garden for some hours. Gabriel and Raphael quickly tired of the limitations of time and returned to Heaven. Michael and I stayed, greeting the seemingly endless procession of risen dead. Among them we saw many familiar faces: Abraham, who we once visited along with Gabriel; Abraham's wife Sarah, who cooked a meal for us; Gideon, who I found hiding in a winepress; Balaam, who was so insensitive to Angelic presence that his donkey saw Michael before he did. The list is long. Elisha the prophet, recognised me immediately and was quick to ask after his predecessor and mentor, Elijah.

'He'll be waiting for you, I'm sure,' I told him. 'I saw him only a few weeks ago.'

Jesus finally returned in the middle of the afternoon, by which time Michael had also left me. The grave was still emptying its precious cargo. Jesus was pleased at the outcome of his meeting with Peter. He said, 'Come on, let's go into Jerusalem.'

But we didn't get there.

As we were approaching the city gate, two of Jesus' disciples were walking in the opposite direction, their shoulders drooping, their faces long.

'That's Justus and Cleopas,' Jesus exclaimed. 'Where are they going?'

Justus, though not one of the Twelve, had been a regular companion of Jesus since he first arrived in Capernaum. Cleopas I recognised, but did not know well. The two of them walked straight past us, deep in conversation.

'I'll go and ask them,' Jesus announced, following.

'They won't be able to see you,' I added, helpfully.

'I think I have plenty of experience of being human,' Jesus replied, amused at my advice.

He walked after them down the road, rapidly catching them up. The two disciples heard his footsteps and turned to greet him, but they did not recognise Jesus. (I still don't know whether he intended that or if it was a result of the vast change he had undergone.)

'What are you two talking about so intently?' Jesus asked.

They were both thoroughly miserable. Cleopas replied, as the three men continued to walk, 'Are you the only person in Jerusalem who doesn't know what's been happening in the city these last few days?'

'What things?' Jesus asked innocently.

'About Jesus, the prophet from Nazareth,' Justus replied. 'We had hoped that he would rescue Israel, but the chief priests had him crucified on Friday.'

There was a long, dismal pause. Eventually Cleopas told of Mary's early morning visit to Jesus' tomb and of John's report after he returned. When their story was finished, Jesus smiled warmly.

'How foolish you have been!' he said.

His companions were surprised. Jesus continued, 'Didn't the prophets say that the Messiah would have to suffer in this way and only then enter his glory?'

A small flame of hope returned to the men's spirits and they invited Jesus to explain what he meant. So began a long conversation which lasted for all of their two hour journey. When they arrived at the village of Emmaus, Justus and Cleopas turned off the road and Jesus made to bid them farewell, but Cleopas urged him to stay the night with them, as the sun was beginning to set.

When the three travellers had washed, Cleopas served a simple supper. He invited Jesus, as his guest, to give thanks to God before the meal. Jesus picked up the bread, spoke out a short prayer and broke the loaf, just as he had on countless occasions – and just as he had on Thursday night. Once again, the bread became incandescent with Heavenly light and the two men suddenly realised who their visitor really was.

Immediately, Jesus rose up from his place. 'Come on, Oriel,' he said, as the two men stared, dumbfounded, at an empty seat. 'It's time to leave.'

We went outside and watched as Cleopas and Justus raced out through the door and ran back up the road to Jerusalem.

'We'll wait until those two have had time to share their news with the others,' Jesus said. 'It'll give you a chance to catch up with that diary of yours.'

Back at my office

We returned to Jerusalem to watch the arrival of the two out-of-breath travellers. But first we visited the Temple. Business was continuing much as usual apart from one noticeable difference: the enormous curtain which separated the Holiest Place from the Court of the Priests had been torn in two, right down the middle.

'Look at that!' said Jesus, excitedly. 'That curtain represented the awful separation between me and the human race. Did you rip it down, Oriel?'

'I was far too miserable to do anything so grand,' I replied.

To our great sadness, the curtain was being repaired.

'It will all be destroyed soon, anyway,' Jesus commented as we departed.

We arrived at the home of John Mark and his mother just in time to see Cleopas and Justus clamber, exhausted, up the stairs to their upper room. I went to follow them but Jesus stopped me.

'Give them time to get their breath back and then tell their story,' he said.

We watched and listened from outside while the two men told about their journey to Emmaus and their conversation with Jesus. The disciples then informed them of Peter's meeting with Jesus. When that was done, Jesus said, 'Let's go in.' As soon as we were inside, he dimmed his Heavenly brightness so that his friends could see him.

'Peace be with you,' he said cheerfully.

Their reaction was anything but peaceful. 'It's a ghost!' one of them screamed. The rest stared in terror.

While the disciples looked at their Lord in horrified disbelief, Jesus turned to me with a wry smile.

'I think you're too hard on Gabriel. Humans *do* scare easily.'

Then he turned to his friends and said, 'There's no need to be alarmed. It's me.'

They were still unconvinced.

'Here, take a look at my hands and feet,' Jesus continued. 'You can see the nail wounds.'

He stepped forward, arms outstretched, and the disciples stepped back. There, indeed, were the injuries of his brutal execution, gaping holes in his recreated body just where they had been on Friday. I don't know how I had failed to notice them before.

Some of the disciples began to edge towards Jesus.

'You can touch me if you want,' he added. He continued to cajole them into belief. 'A ghost doesn't have flesh and bones as you can see that I have.'

They were beginning to warm to the idea but I could see that they were afraid of believing too much in case the vision evaporated and they found themselves all alone again.

'What have you got to eat?' Jesus asked, determined to resolve the issue.

After a little clattering in her cooking pot, Martha stepped forward with a plate of fish. Jesus set himself down at the table and tucked in enthusiastically.

'Excellent!' he said. 'I don't think that was cooked by Andrew.'

Andrew laughed and so did the others. At last they relaxed and accepted that Jesus really was alive. He stuffed another large fingerful of the fish into his mouth and spoke through it, saying, 'Martha, your cooking is as wonderful as ever. Is there any bread?'

When his plate was empty and wiped clean, Jesus turned his attention to the confusion of his friends.

'This is what I told you would happen, when I was still with you,' he said. 'Everything that is written about me in the scriptures had to be fulfilled. And this is what was written. Now, repentance and the forgiveness of sins will be proclaimed to every nation.'

'Are you going on a world tour?' Matthew asked, excited at the prospect of Jesus visiting the great cities of the Roman Empire.

'No, I'm not,' Jesus replied. 'You are.'

Matthew's brief excitement gave way to shock. Peter stepped forward. 'We could never do it without you,' he said firmly.

'You are witnesses to everything that's happened,' Jesus told them.

He stood up and walked over to Peter. He leaned over Peter's head and breathed a long breath over the burly fisherman.

'Receive my Spirit,' he said and then moved to Andrew. To Andrew he did and said the same thing. Jesus worked his way around the entire room and as he breathed on each of them, something remarkable happened. The Director – that most indefinable person of my Boss's self – spread from the Son into the lives of the disciples. Each man and woman became noticeably brighter, and that new brightness had the unmistakable character of my Boss's own life. And yet, as I watched in amazement, I could see that in every one of them, that light was different. The Heavenly light coming from each disciple was a unique fusion of their own life and the life of the Director. These human beings were becoming my Boss's children right before my eyes.

When Jesus had finished, he stood in the middle of the room and said, 'If you forgive anyone their selfishness, they are indeed forgiven. On the other hand, if you deny anyone forgiveness, they are not forgiven.'

This confirmed my understanding of what had happened. Jesus had given these human beings an authority that no Angel has ever been allowed, an authority that has, in all creations, been reserved to my Boss – the authority to forgive sin.

Then Jesus said, 'Let's go for a walk.'

Everyone gathered their coats and followed their risen Lord into the night air. He led them out of the city and up the familiar road towards Bethany. I was pleased to see that he was walking with John, the two of them chatting animatedly. I was also pleased when he walked straight past the Garden of Gethsemane. I do not have happy memories of that place.

At the top of the Mount of Olives, Jesus stopped and waited for his followers to join him. When they had all gathered he said to me, 'Oriel, it's time for us to go home.' He began to say a prayer of blessing over his disciples and as he did, he set off for Heaven, returning to his full brightness as he went. We moved slowly until the end of the prayer and then, instead of 'Amen' the Son said, 'Let's go.'

We returned to the timeless brightness of Heaven to find the long line of people who had been rescued from Death being welcomed into Life. Now that we were free from the narrow channel of Earth's time, we could see there were people among them from many ages and centuries. They were all filing into the Gathering Place of Angels which had been set with tables for a sumptuous banquet. At the entrance, my Boss was greeting each one by name and Angels were showing them to their places.

When Jesus arrived, a great cheer went up from both humans and Angels. It was so good to see Father and Son back together as one. I watched them embrace and realised what a great strain their separation had been. The two of them began to dance ecstatically around the vast hall accompanied by the singing of the assembled multitude.

As I looked forwards into my Boss's timeless home, I saw that everyone who ever loved him was already gathered; yet, when I looked back towards Earth, the shining men and women that I had seen this morning were still arriving. Looking down towards Jerusalem, I realised that my Boss's life was still stretched between Heaven and Earth because the Director was now living in the spirits of Jesus' followers, sharing the continuing traumas of human existence.

The Son and his Dad danced their way up to me and stopped, radiant smiles dominating their faces. Angels began to serve food to those seated at the banqueting tables. The Son led me out of the Gathering Place, towards my office. We passed the open door to my Boss's rooms. At my door we stopped.

'Thank you, my friend,' Jesus said, looking deeply into my eyes. I basked in the delight of his company. 'What are you going to do now?'

I thought for a moment and said, 'I think I need a rest.'

He turned back towards the Gathering Place.

'I'm going to a party,' he said. 'Don't you want to join me?'

An extract from ORIEL'S TRAVELS – to be published in Autumn 2003

In my office – free from the unrelenting pressure of time

I've just been called to a meeting with my Boss.

'Oriel,' he said. 'I have a job for you.'

There was something in his tone of voice which warned me that this is not going to be simple and that something prompted me to open up my diary.

Back in my office

'After your excellent work looking after my Son during his human life,' my Boss began, going directly to his point as usual, 'I would like you to take on another human challenge for me.'

His use of the word 'challenge' confirmed my suspicion that the task was not going to be easy.

'I have been looking for a man or woman to travel to the heart of the Roman Empire and tell its citizens the story of my Son's life.'

He paused.

'Who have you chosen?' I asked.

'A man called Saul, from Tarsus in Turkey.'

'You have picked a Turk to tell a Jewish story to the citizens of Rome?'

I knew it unwise to question his judgement but there was nothing to be gained from keeping my thoughts to myself. My Boss always knows them anyway.

'You know me, Oriel,' he replied with a twinkle in his eye that invited me to ask for further information.

'What is it that makes Saul the right man for this job?' I enquired.

'That is for you to discover,' my Creator replied, his eyes still twinkling.

The Son, who was seated beside his Father as usual, joined the conversation.

'Saul is a Jew – he got that from his mother. He is also a Roman citizen – which he inherited from his father. He has spent the last three years studying at the rabbinical university in Jerusalem.'

'I like the man already,' I replied enthusiastically. 'I always said you should choose some followers from the university.'

'You did indeed,' the Son said, and now he was the one with a twinkle in his eyes. 'That is why you are clearly the Angel for this job.'

'Where and when will I find the man?' I asked.

The communication that holds Eternal Father and Son in perfect unity is too deep for any Angel to fathom, but they allowed me to see a ray of playful amusement that passed between them. I recognised it at once, and it set my spirit on guard. It warned me that there is something about this Saul that does not match the picture in my imagination. I shall just have to travel down to Jerusalem and meet the man to find out what.

Just outside Jerusalem – AD 32 (*I always struggle with human dates and calendars*)

Arriving at the narrow, private gate in the city wall that leads directly to the Temple complex, I spotted my man immediately. A small mob of angry priests was dragging a prisoner out into the sunlight from the labyrinth of passages behind the Temple. My Angelic eye was led directly to the shining spirit of the condemned man – he had the indestructible Heavenly life that is my Boss's gift to all his Son's human friends. I quickly scanned the minds of the priests. The source of their anger was obvious: they were jealous of this man's faith. They were dragging him out of the city with one purpose, to dispose of this follower of Jesus in the way that they had wanted to get rid of Jesus himself two Earth years earlier. On this occasion they were not going to waste time pandering to the Roman Governor; they were going to do the job themselves – with stones. The group was led by a small, tight-spirited man whose mind was consumed with determination to exterminate all memory of Jesus' life.

My first task was to rescue my man from his immediate fate

and lead him to safety. The angry mob dragged their victim down into the filthy valley where the city's rubbish is dumped. There they threw him to the ground and prepared to end his life by the crude method of throwing rocks at his head until his brain could take no more and closed down. Before this energetic execution began, the priests removed their coats and handed them to their leader. I grabbed my moment.

Standing between the hounds and their prey, I called for the attention of all twenty-three Angel guardians present.

'Stop the hands of your charges and don't let them throw a single stone,' I ordered, with the authority granted to all Archangels.

'Our Boss has chosen this Saul to tell the story of his Son right in the heart of the Roman Empire. He must not be killed.'

There was an awkward silence. Then a particularly depressed Angel spoke up. I had no doubt that he was the guardian of the condemned man.

'This isn't Saul,' he said.

'But he must be!' I replied.

'This is Stephen,' the Angel informed me. 'He's just been condemned by the council for asserting that our Boss's Son is our Boss's Son.'

I was confused. I was sure that I had come to the right time and place to find the man my Boss had chosen.

'So which one *is* Saul of Tarsus?' I asked the assembled Angels, while the furious priests were gathering large stones to hurl at Stephen's head.

Twenty-three Angelic faces all looked in the same direction. They knew exactly which man was Saul of Tarsus. I turned round, following their gaze, and to my horror they were looking at the young Pharisee whose arms were laden with his companions' coats – the leader of the mob!

The priests were all looking at him too, waiting for the order to kill Stephen. While I was watching, Saul gave a sombre nod and the stones began to fly, crashing into Stephen's skull.

So who is this man?

Twenty-one centuries after he walked the dusty roads of Palestine, Jesus Christ is still famous around the world. Our dating system pivots around the year of his birth. Every day in homes and offices around the globe people quote and misquote him, use his name as a swear word and argue about his significance.

CLOSER TO GOD FOR NEWCOMERS: MEET THE REAL JESUS by Belinda Pollard offers an encounter with Jesus through the Bible. It includes 40 brief excerpts taken from Luke's Gospel (the Bible text on which *Oriel's Diary* is based) and the Book of Acts, with helpful insights. It describes Jesus' life and the effect he had on the people he met. It's straightforward, jargon free and you don't need to know anything about Christianity to read it.

ISBN 1 85999 459 8 £2.65

To order this and/or request a free catalogue of Bible resources from Scripture Union:

- phone SU's mail order line: 01908 856006
- email info@scriptureunion.org.uk
- fax 01908 856020
- log on to www.scriptureunion.org.uk
- write to SU Mail Order, PO Box 5148, Milton Keynes MLO, MK2 2YX

You might also like to **request free samples** from our range of personal Bible reading guides:

CLOSER TO GOD – experiential, relational, radical and dynamic, this publication takes a creative and reflective approach to Bible reading with an emphasis on renewal.

DAILY BREAD – aims to help you enjoy, explore and apply the Bible. Practical comments relate the Bible to everyday life, combined with information and meditation panels to give deeper understanding.

ENCOUNTER WITH GOD – provides a thought-provoking, in-depth approach to Bible reading, relating biblical truth to contemporary issues. The writers are experienced Bible teachers, often well known.

SU also produces Bible reading notes for children, teens and young adults. Do ask for details.

Scripture Union, 207–209 Queensway, Bletchley, MK2 2EB.